CHAPTER I

She heard the distant scream as soon as the elevator doors opened. She almost paused, but instead walked on purposefully towards the exit. It had been a long, hard day since they called her in to the intensive care unit at 5 a.m. that morning, and now it was time to go home. In any case, it wasn't unusual to hear screams coming from the emergency room. It was none of her business. As usual, the corridors were quiet at 9.30 in the evening as the hospital wound down for the night.

Until the next scream came. This time she stopped.

'No ... no ... please, no!'

She sensed that this was not the usual ER scream of pain, or confusion, or cold turkey. This was the sound of something else, a spectator, an onlooker, watching something awful.

She turned and walked towards the doors of the ER.

It was quiet, except in Bay 1, where it was chaos. She moved quickly, taking in the scene. The small child lay still and apparently lifeless on the trolley, her limp body a mottled blue against deathly pallor. The young intern was trying to get an intravenous line into her tiny arm and screaming at the nurses for assistance. Outside the bay, with a full view of the proceedings through the open curtains, stood a young couple. He couldn't have been more than twenty, and he stood with one arm around the girl's waist, gnawing at the knuckles of his other hand as he watched his daughter's life ebbing slowly away. His wife sobbed uncontrollably as she felt the same helplessness and inevitability forcing themselves upon her.

She walked past them into the bay.

'What've you got, Doctor?'

The intern looked round at her as if to say *who the fuck are you?* but the tone of her voice made him pause for a moment.

She didn't wait more than a second for an answer. She

5

moved to the child, snatching the stethoscope from him and nudging him aside.

'I said, what have you got, Doctor?' she repeated loudly, as she looked at the youngster, felt her pulse, checked her pupils.

'Er ... two-year-old child, known asthmatic, brought in with respiratory distress, difficult breathing, collapse. I'm trying to get i.v. access. I've asked the nurses for adrenalin and steroids but they're so slow....'

He stopped talking when he saw she was already listening to the child's chest. Not much point in that, he thought, she's not even breathing any more.

Suddenly she plucked the stethoscope from her ears and yelled so loudly that he jumped.

'She's obstructed. White needle.'

Before he could even think what she meant, one of the nurses had broken the seal, pulled out a white-tipped large calibre needle from its packet and taken off its protective plastic guard.   She held it out for the young woman, who had gently extended the child's neck until its Adam's apple was protruding through the skin.

She took the needle from the nurse, and held it between her middle finger and thumb then traced her index finger down the midline of the child's throat from her chin, over her Adam's apple, pausing just below it.

She transferred the needle to her index finger and thumb, and put the tip gently on to the infant's skin.

Behind her, her mother took in her breath with an audible gasp as she watched the needle poised over her daughter's throat.

She pushed it in gently but firmly, feeling the tough cricothyroid membrane give way as it passed into the windpipe. The child's chest expanded suddenly as she sucked air once more into her starved lungs. As one breath followed another, the mottled blue patches on her skin began to fade. The hissing of the precious air rushing through the needle into the small body seemed to mesmerize them all until the spell was broken once more by her voice.

'Jane, hold the needle.'

The nurse did it without hesitation.

' 'Scope!'

A second nurse slapped it into her hand and she moved

A Serious Affair

By the same author

Serious Misconduct
Serious Intent
Serious Abuse

A
Serious
Affair

PATRICK
RILEY

ROBERT HALE · LONDON

ISBN 0 7090 5903 5

Robert Hale Limited
Clerkenwell House
Clerkenwell Green
London EC1R 0HT

Photoset in North Wales by
Derek Doyle & Associates, Mold, Clwyd.
Printed in Great Britain by
St Edmundsbury Press Ltd, Bury St Edmunds, Suffolk.
Bound by WBC Book Manufacturers Limited,
Bridgend, Mid-Glamorgan.

i

towards the head of the table, again gently bending the child's neck back, opening her mouth and slipping the laryngoscope down her throat, as she peered into the larynx.

'Ah!' she said, quietly, almost to herself, then loudly, 'forceps!'

The same nurse handed her a pair of gleaming curved forceps and watched as she slowly inserted them down the aperture created by the laryngoscope, closed the jaws gently, gave them a small twist then slowly withdrew them and held them up.

Holding a plastic red clown's nose.

The child began to breathe spontaneously in noisy gasps. She threw the forceps on to the trolley and turned, pulling out the needle and holding a linen swab over the puncture site.

Within a few moments, the child's eyes opened and she looked around coughing, and crying with confusion and fear.

She told the ER nurse to bring in the parents, let them stay with her, but admit her under paediatrics for the night for observation. Then she took the intern's arm and walked him with her to the office.

She stood before him, looking up at the young brown eyes, then down at his ID badge.

'First day?'

He nodded.

'Doctor Thompson, you got this one wrong. It happens, but this could have been fatal. Learn some lessons from it. In particular, learn to call for help early when you need it, until you get used to the job. And don't you ever try to shift the blame for your own inexperience or problems on to the nurses who were here before you arrived, and will be here after you leave. They know the ropes down here, Doctor. Learn from them, and you'll learn a lot.'

He looked at her, with a mixture of anger, fear and awe.

She gave a small smile.

'Come and see me tomorrow. I work up in the ICU. We'll talk it through. Now go and tell the parents their daughter's going to be OK.'

Dr Anne Bell left the room and made for the exit, grateful that she'd given in to her curiosity. It was always a bad move to get sick in August. In August, the new interns arrived. July 31 they were medical students. August 1, doctors. *Embryo* doctors.

She walked out into the late summer evening and paused, taking a deep breath and gazing up at the scarlet skies over south Boston before yawning and walking slowly to her car, feeling suddenly pleased with her long day.

Doctor Gary Masters raised himself to his full six-foot-two height and stretched, arching his back. He had been working on the Danish Land-Race pig in the animal house of the University of Miami Hospital Department of Experimental Surgery for four hours and he was getting tired. In a normal day he could do two four-hour operations, make ward rounds, do some administration and then get in a game of racquetball before dinner, but the research usually had to be done out of hours, instead of or *after* all that stuff. Now it was 10.30 and he was on the final specimen in the *National Institute of Health Miami Study into the Use of Pig Membranes for the Correction of Cardiac Defects*.

Which, in plain English, meant using animal tissue to close holes in the heart.

And Gary Masters knew that no one, but no one, in the entire United States, never mind anywhere else, was even close to him in the field. Which was why he had got the grant in the first place. Which was why he expected a much bigger grant when the time came to take the application of the technique into the human clinical field. Which was why he thought he had a better than even chance of getting the post in Boston he was being interviewed for the day after tomorrow.

He had wanted to get back to Boston since the day he had left six years before. He had spent his student days there, and interned at the Massachussetts General before specializing in surgery and getting the cardiac residency then faculty position in Miami. He liked the South and the facilities at Miami were excellent, but he was Boston born and bred, and he had always known there was nowhere else on earth he would consider settling down when the time came. And Miami was becoming more and more dangerous, with the constant influx of poor, homeless and disillusioned refugees from Haiti and Cuba. He leaned forward again over the table. He was dressed in operating greens as if he were in the genuine operating room. This was as sterile a procedure as it would have been in a human, for any infection in the implanted membrane would ruin the results and jeopardize the success of the technique. The anaesthetist had gone for coffee, but he too would be back when the time came to wake the animal up, just like in the regular operating room upstairs. His assistant, a young medical student doing extra work to help pay her way through college, looked up at him from time to time, marvelling at his skill and his dark good looks, loving the way his black hair curled down beneath his operating cap, feeling privileged to be working with one of Miami's best cardiac surgeons. And one of Miami's most desirable men.

He completed the suturing, leaned back again, then called over his shoulder in the direction of the staff room, 'I'm closing, Gus.'

He turned to the pig, strapped on to the surgical table and connected to the anaesthetic machine, and began the chest closure in the usual routine way. He was good, and it didn't take long. He was almost finished when the anaesthetist, an overweight, unfit-looking man, wandered in slowly, his belly protruding between his trousers and top, his mask halfway down his face, as he chewed the remains of the pizza he had been devouring when the call came.

Masters gave an almost imperceptible shake of his head. He could choose his colleagues in the clinical field, but not many guys wanted to put in animal overtime, so he had to take what he could get. Gus Peters had a soon-to-be ex-wife and a disgruntled mistress to support so he needed all the work he could get. Even if it meant putting pigs to sleep.

'But why pigs?'

Masters looked up at his assistant.

'What?'

'Why pigs?'

'For the research?'

'Yes.'

He smiled beneath the mask, only the creases by the side of his eyes betraying the fact.

'Not a lot of people realize that in medical terms, in anatomical terms, in *tissue* terms, the animal which most resembles the human being is the pig. The tissues are similar, the heart is similar, even the kidneys are more like the human kidney than any other animal.'

'Wow!'

He ignored her youthful enthusiasm, having long before recognized the advantages, but also the potential dangers, of his good looks and their possible effects on young girls.

He finished his closure and nodded to the anaesthetist. 'I'm done. Wake her up and see her into recovery.'

Gus nodded, wiping his lips with the back of his hand and turning to his machines.

Masters turned back to the medical student.

'Thanks Elaine. Appreciate your help. Send your claim into the finance department as usual and they'll settle up at the end of the month.'

'Thank you Doctor Masters,' beamed Elaine, feeling like a real surgeon as she peeled off her mask, hoping he might notice her full mouth and perfect teeth and suggest they meet for a drink later.

He didn't. In fact, he was gone before she could even say goodnight.

He took a shower in the changing-room, put on clean OR greens, and went to his office where he almost fell into the chair, plonked his feet on the desk and then let out a noisy cry of triumph.

'Yeeeeeehoooo!'

Suddenly invigorated, he leapt to his feet and jogged around the desk a couple of times, then sat down again, laughing.

It was finished. The best NIH-supported research project he could ever have hoped to complete. Totally original, introducing an entirely new surgical technique into cardiac surgery which would revolutionize standard practice. The pig membrane would effectively close cardiac defects in children and adults, would cover weaknesses in the heart muscle after coronary thromboses, just like a puncture repair kit on a mountain bike tyre. And rejection would not be a problem with modern drugs. They had used pigs' valves for years in humans. He had taken the technique a quantum leap further.

'Yeeeehooooo!' he cried again.

He'd got the licence to operate on the pigs, got the anaesthetists, got the operating time, taken a chunk out of the pigs' heart chambers, then sewn in the patches, trying first bladder muscle, then peritoneum, and finally brain membrane. The brain worked best. The muscles were OK but they lost some of their qualities in transplantation. The peritoneum was too fragile. The tight, silk-like *dura mater* was better, providing strength with elasticity. The twelve brain membrane cases were all alive and well up to ten months after surgery. Most of the others had either died, or needed re-operation to replace the other patch with the membrane, and now *they* were still alive too.

Goddamn! He couldn't wait to do it to a human heart. He *knew* it would work just as well. On kids with holes in their hearts. On adults who had heart attacks which left them with what they were told was a weak area of heart muscle, but what the cardiologists called an aneurysm which, whatever you called it, was likely to burst at any moment in the future causing instant death but which had no current cure other than a transplant.

Until *now!*

He felt the adrenalin surging through his body as the excitement gripped him.

Two interviews to come. One tomorrow with the NIH to present the results of the Phase I study in animals, and to present his application for the Phase II grant extending the work to the clinical human field. The other the day after with the Surgical Division of the Faculty of the University Hospital of Southern Massachusetts. For the Chair in Cardiac Surgery.

He *had* to get that job in Boston. It would be the ultimate achievement. Home again, taking with him a research grant running into millions of dollars, and the high-profile position to introduce a revolutionary technique into clinical practice in one of the Eastern seaboard's most prestigious university hospitals. He gave a sigh, wishing there was someone to share his excitement. He was tired, but Phase I was over. Now it was time to celebrate. Go to a bar with a beautiful girl, have a few beers, go eat, crack a couple of bottles of champagne, then go back to his place, or hers, and make the sort of passionate energetic love that follows a magnificent achievement such as tonight's.

Only there wasn't any beautiful girl in his life at the moment. No time. The work had obsessed him and occupied virtually every waking moment for the past year. Oh sure, there had been a few one-night stands, but they were just to pass the time, keep him from forgetting how to do it, prevent his prick from withering away from disuse. They were the lucky ones.

Pretty, available, energetic, eager. No shortage of available chicks down in Coconut Grove, or South Beach, to keep him happy, though none of them had been invited back into his bed a second time. There was too much to do to get tied down, snared, entrapped by some blonde bombshell or bimbo brunette. They had simply served their purpose, contributed to a great time, then been discarded.

Bye Bye Baby. Don't bother calling. I'm busy. Busy pushing back the frontiers of heart research in the greatest country on earth, before a establishing a department of national, or even international, excellence in beloved Boston, Massachusetts.

He leaned back in the chair, his hands behind his head, enjoying the moment, the feeling of triumph, of achievement, of power. He knew destiny was calling him.

On a deserted beach in Cuba, ninety-five miles from where Gary Masters was dreaming his dreams, another young man paused for a moment, looking up from his work, listening intently in the darkness.

After a few moments he relaxed.

'Tito, you are too cautious,' he said to himself, raising the hammer once more to bang home the nail. It was halfway to its target when he heard the creak of the floorboard above and halted its trajectory in mid-air, kneeling on the damp sand, hammer aloft, frozen in flight.

Their voices were unmistakable now, and the smell of their cigarettes, as their footsteps moved slowly closer and closer above him. He shrank down, his face pressed against the wet sand, beside the damp planks of wood, as the waves lapped around his ankles.

They paused for a few moments on the pier, before he heard them stub out their cigarettes, rotating their boots from side to side on the floorboards above him, like they were squashing cockroaches, or breaking the fingers of young dissidents, before they moved on, laughing coarsely, their rifles rattling against their gunbelts.

He lay still for at least five minutes after he could no longer hear them, then raised himself, brushing the wet sand from his cheeks, shirt and trousers.

Within fifteen minutes he was finished. He looked down at the raft with a mixture of pride and doubt.

It was made from ten, ten-by-one-foot planks, each lashed to the next and all then nailed to three cross planks underneath, one at each end and one in the centre. A vertical plank of the same size provided sides to the rough craft, with extra ballast from pieces of rubber tyres lashed to the four corners.

It might make it.

It *had* to make it.

He stashed his creation under some old driftwood and tarpaulin beneath the pier, then walked out on to the shore. It was a cloudy night with little wind, but he knew that the weather was about to change, that the 5 m.p.h. wind from the east was going to change the next day to a 15 m.p.h. wind from the south, with a medium swell, before the next hurricane headed up from the tropics. It had to be tomorrow. Tomorrow or never. Tomorrow or die.

He took the long route home to his small apartment on the outskirts of Havana. Carmen was waiting for him, a small slim girl with the dark eyes and long black hair of a true Cuban. She threw her arms around his neck and kissed him passionately then put her finger to her lips.

'Shh,' she whispered, 'Maria has just got off to sleep.'

He nodded, kissed her again briefly then tiptoed quietly to the bathroom to wash.

They ate some salad and bread before he told her.

'Carmen,' he said, 'it has to be tomorrow.'

She gasped, and her hand went up to her mouth to stifle the noise.

'Tomorrow?' she whispered. 'Why?'

'The raft is finished, the winds are right. If we miss this time, the hurricanes will come; we might not get another chance.'

She paused. 'I am frightened.'

'I know. Me too. But it has to be. We cannot stay here any longer. And we must get help for Maria, or she will be beyond help.'

She nodded. 'I know. But my parents ... to say goodbye ...?'

He shook his head. 'No time.'

'I cannot go without seeing them, Tito.'

'No!' he said, too loudly. They both looked towards the small bed in the corner of the room, but no sound came.

He rose from the table and knelt before her.

'*Mi cariño*,' he said, quietly, 'we have no choice. Not just the winds, the waves. Jose Madrigo came to me today. Castro's Special Service are rounding up more dissidents this weekend.' He looked directly at her. 'He thinks this time my name is on the list.'

They looked at each other.

He nodded, slowly.

'You know what that means?'

She put her arms around his neck and pulled him to her.

'Then we must go. Tomorrow.'

She got up. 'I will pack.'

He sat at the table, watching her walk quietly to the bedroom. He knew they had no choice. Life in Havana had become too bad to go on. Castro had promised so much in '59. His parents had told him of the glory of the revolution, the joy of overthrowing Batista's regime, the sense of freedom.

The cry of *Socialism or Die.*

Socialism *and* Die, more like.

Things had never got better, except for the elite within Castro's inner circle. And his SS. For the rest, things had stayed tolerable, until the Berlin wall came down, the cold war ended, the Soviet Union split into its component parts, and the Communist subsidies dried up. Then, the gas dried up too, and the food supplies, and the wages. In his job as a doctor, he earned less in a week than a cab driver on a Saturday night in Havana. That was socialism in Cuba. Castro and his fat cats lapped the cream. His hard men got the milk. The people got the water. If they were lucky.

It was time to go. Not just to build a better life in the United States for his family, but now, to survive. He had become a marked man since university, where he had joined a right-wing group and participated in lectures, debates, publications, on an alternative form of government. He had been run in a few times for demonstrating, got an occasional beating from the police.

But, since qualifying, things in the hospital had got worse, and his attitude had got harder. It was one thing to see workers with no work, farmers with no crops, but to watch patients with no medicine, sick children with no therapy, surgical cases with no operating facilities to treat them, was just too much. His conscience kept him working in the hospital more than one hundred hours a week for a pittance, but even that was not recognized, and now, he was just a step away from the door being kicked down in the night, and being hauled out of his bed, naked and helpless, to be beaten senseless then taken to God knows where and probably never be seen again. What then of Carmen and Maria?

He felt a knot of fear in his stomach. But could they reach Florida on the pathetic raft he had put together? Him, his wife, and their three-year-old daughter? Could he put them in the mortal danger of embarking on a ninety mile or more journey on a home-made craft through the wild Florida Straits to find landfall in the USA? If the waves didn't get them, the sharks probably would. But if they could only get there, find land, then the Government of the United States of America would grant them immigration status as they had all Cuban refugees since the revolution in 1958, and they could find a new life there. In freedom. The lure was too much to resist, the alternative too awful to contemplate.

He heard a small cry from the corner of the room. Carmen had Maria in her arms, and was swaying gently from side to side to comfort her. He walked to them and put his arm around his wife's shoulder as they stood there together in the gloom, contemplating their last night in their homeland, and what tomorrow might hold for them.

CHAPTER 2

Idaho is famous for its potatoes.

Or so most people think. After all, go to a Tads in New York, a Butcher Shop in Dallas or Chicago, a Denny's almost anywhere, and what do you get with your 14-oz filet mignon, or your 28-oz T-bone?

Fries or a baked potato.

A baked *Idaho* potato.

After Luther Burbank brought the first seeds from his New England garden in 1872, Joe Marshall, the legendary 'Idaho Potato King', made Idaho the native home of the russet Burbank potato and ever since Idaho has consistently produced them in enough numbers to feed the entire United States, and more.

Some imagine that's the only thing Idaho does, grow potatoes. Which is fine with most Idahoans. Why advertise the wild beauty of the Snake River in the south, or the rugged drama of Silver Mountain in the north, and invite their despoliation? Why ask outsiders to come and hunt the elk, deer, or caribou which roam free through its fertile lands and forests? Forget it. Leave the hunting birds to fly the blue skies. Let the bountiful chinook salmon fill the wild Snake and Salmon Rivers. Let large expanses of the land remain virtually unchanged from the time when only the tribes of the Nez Perce or the Shoshone-Bannock rode its plains. Let the world think all Idaho is good for is growing potatoes. That way, the Idahoans can keep their closely guarded secret and continue to inhabit their private paradise.

Anne Bell smiled as her thoughts drifted back to her childhood. That was what *she* used to think, growing up on her parents' farm on the Snake River plain, twenty miles from the town of Hagerman. Her father was a Mormon, like so many of the settlers in that era, whose hard work and ability led to the damming of the rivers, the development of revolutionary irrigation systems, and the transformation of desert into some of the most fertile land in the West. Her mother was an Irish girl from Coeur d'Alene in the north whom he had met when he ventured, out of curiosity, into a Jesuit Catholic church there while visiting his aunt. It had been love at first sight for the young Mormon farmer and the dark-eyed colleen with the wild black hair so typical of her native Galway.

Against the wishes of both parents they had married and settled down to farm potatoes and run a few head of cattle and sheep west of Twin Falls. They remained childless for twenty years, a plight both sets of parents regarded as a punishment for the mixing of two incompatible faiths until, at the age of forty-two, Kathleen Bell gave birth to a daughter.

And Anne Bell grew up like everyone else thinking all that happened in Idaho was the growing of potatoes to eke out a living. And feeling like she had harvested most of them, as she accompanied her father after school and during vacations throughout her childhood, planting the seed potatoes, nurturing the plants then filling her apron with the russets to sell at market. Until he got the harvesting machinery and they entered the twentieth century.

It was her mother who taught Anne Bell that there was more to life than Idaho and potatoes. She owed a lot to her mother....

'So, ladies and gentlemen, can we get the last candidate in, then break for lunch?'

Jerry Weinberg's voice brought her back to the present. Lunch ... yes, she was hungry. No wonder she was thinking about potatoes!

The committee had interviewed three candidates for the Associate Professor of Cardiac Surgery post since 9 a.m. that morning. One young ambitious senior resident from Chicago, one steadier, older applicant from New York, and an established cardiac surgeon from Norwalk, Connecticut who was seeking an academic appointment. There was only one name left on the short list. She looked down at her notes.

Gary Masters, from the University Hospital of Miami. A Harvard graduate, so he had the Ivy League background. She had learned that in this part of the world, a degree from Brown, Columbia, Cornell, Dartmouth, Harvard, Princeton, Pennsylvania or Yale was like a starting bonus of ten, equating such candidates with a qualification regarded as equivalent to those from the best colleges of Oxford or Cambridge. It often ensured short-listing, and always guaranteed at least a sympathetic start to proceedings when applying for a post in the north-east. Not that she had had that kind of help when she sought her current position. She looked around the table at the interviewing committee, mostly Ivy Leaguers themselves.

Jerry Weinberg sat at the head of the table. Although he was a urologist and not a heart surgeon, he was also director of surgery and, as administrative head of the entire surgical department, he assumed the chair, even for the appointment of a cardiac specialist. A tall, well-built man with blond hair and tanned features, he was one of Anne's favourite surgical colleagues. To his right sat Harvey Bergman, general surgeon and, between Harvey and herself, David Meeson, chief executive officer of the surgical directorate. To Weinberg's left sat Lester Pearson, senior cardiac surgeon, and next to him, Paul Schering, chief of paediatric cardiac surgery. To his left sat Jennifer Kling, a lay member representing the management board.

The door opened and Gary Masters walked in.

He paused for a moment, surveyed the committee waiting in ambush for him, let a small smile play around his mouth then said, 'Good morning, ladies and gentlemen', almost as if he were welcoming them to be interviewed by him.

He stood behind the chair, waiting for the invitation to be seated and for proceedings to commence.

Jennifer Kling smiled up at him as Jerry Weinberg said, 'Good morning, Doctor Masters. Please, sit down and make yourself comfortable.'

Which is just what Gary Masters did, before listening intently to the questions from each interviewer, answering them politely and competently whether they were about surgical technique, his plans for the department, his research fund-raising activities, his management experience. Until he got to Paul Schering, who looked at him intently before asking, 'Your animal research is interesting, Doctor, and I note that you hope to start human studies soon if the NIH approves your grant request. Do you think it might have an application in children as well as adults?'

'Oh yes,' replied Masters, almost too quickly. 'I would see this work as being universally applicable to any heart defects, be they congenital, or acquired.'

'And who would you see doing these techniques?'

'Why, any competent cardiac surgeon trained to do them. But initially, the surgeon with the most experience in the particular technique.'

'Meaning you?'

'Yes, I guess.'

'How much paediatric cardiac surgery have you done, Doctor?'

'One year as part of my residency in Miami.'

'And you think that is enough for this kind of work?'

'I do.'

'And what do you see as the next developments in your technique?'

Masters paused for a moment, smiled then said, 'Laparoscopic heart surgery.'

There was silence around the table until Jennifer Kling spoke. 'Could you explain what you mean by that, Doctor?'

'Of course. I mean, performing the corrective surgery using the membranes I am developing, but through a telescope rather than by open surgery, thus avoiding the need for the traditional huge chest wound and open heart incisions.'

'Can you do that?' asked Bergman.

'Yes. I've already done it in three dogs. So long as the surgical laparoscopic technique is good, it's simply a case of placing reliable sutures in the right places, just like any surgery. We still need to stop and de-function the heart by by-pass of course, and possibly temporarily collapse one lung, but this would certainly be the way to go.'

Jennifer Kling, who had decided many minutes before that there was only one man in her book for the job, and it wasn't any of the previous candidates she'd seen, nodded approvingly, not understanding a thing he had said as the others contemplated what they had heard.

'Any more questions?' asked Weinberg eventually, looking around the table.

'Just one.'

'Yes, Doctor Bell?'

'Setting aside any of the routine clinical duties of the job –

day-to-day surgery, training, teaching, administration of the department – if you were appointed to this post, and your research was approved by the hospital and the ethical committees, can I assume that it would be under the control of a steering committee upon which intensive care would be fully represented?'

'Well, yes ... possibly. I don't like the concept of committees – we all know a camel is a horse designed by a committee, right ...?' He looked around, once more interviewing them. 'But if you mean full consultation and mutual agreement with proper protocols which, in any case, the NIH would demand, then the answer to your question is yes.'

'Including the selection of cases?'

'Well....' Masters shifted his position slightly. He was thinking as fast as he could. He didn't want to promise what he didn't want to deliver, and he didn't want to hand over any control of his own project that he didn't need to. But he could see where this cookie was coming from. She was smart. She was bringing him into the open, making him expose his intentions, getting him off the fence, and at the same time guarding her own interests and making sure she had some say in what ended up on her ICU.

Anne Bell looked straight at him, waiting for his response. Eventually he spoke, meeting her gaze. 'I think the selection of cases for cardiac surgery should be left up to those best qualified to make that selection.'

'No matter the consequences on the ICU of poor or inappropriate selection?'

Now he knew he was right. She was trying to establish if he was a cowboy who would operate on hopeless or unfit cases just to crunch the numbers, producing a successful surgical result in terms of protocol, but a case which might linger on the ICU for days or weeks even, blocking the beds, entailing high dependency care, before getting out to the regular ward again.

He paused a little longer then said, 'I think you can rely on the fact that if I was responsible for those processes, there would be no inappropriate selections and you would have nothing to fear in ICU terms.'

He smiled at her reassuringly, and they continued their optical duel before he broke off and looked around the table again, inviting more questions and wondering if she believed him.

She didn't.

'Well, thank you Doctor Masters,' said Jerry Weinberg. 'As you may know, we are eager to reach a decision today, but there will obviously be some extensive discussion before the committee breaks up. Might I suggest that you get some lunch, and be back in the waiting-room by three o'clock? If the committee has not come to a decision by then, we'll let you all get back to home base and call you later. Thank you for coming.'

Masters stood up and flashed them a final smile.

'Thank you,' he said, then turned and walked out of the room.

The formality of the proceedings left with him, as the members of the committee individually stretched, stood up, removed jackets, shuffled papers, and generally wound down.

'Well,' said Harvey Bergman, draping his jacket over the back of his chair, 'that's the easy part over.'

The door opened and a waitress wheeled in a trolley of sandwiches and coffee. Twenty minutes later, they resumed their places around the table of the oak-panelled boardroom to get down to business.

Jerry Weinberg spoke first.

'Ladies and gentlemen, before we get down to the nitty-gritty, is there anyone whom the committee feels does not qualify, and can be excluded from further discussion at this point? Lester? Paul?'

Lester Pearson thought for a few moments before answering. He was a handsome man in his late fifties with steely-grey hair and pale-blue eyes beneath a wrinkled brow. He had always been slim, but only a few close friends realized his current lack of weight was attributable to a more persistent and progressive cause than long hours and hard work. He had virtually started and built up the cardiac department at UHSM personally and he knew that he was, in effect, bequeathing his achievement to a successor.

'Well, I think the Chicago man' – he picked up his glasses and peered through them at his notes without putting them on – 'Nelson,' he continued, looking up, 'is too junior. This is not a job to jump straight into from senior resident. He doesn't yet have the experience to be a head of department.'

He looked at his surgical colleague on his left.

'I agree,' said Paul Schering, thinking the last thing he needed was for paediatric cardiac surgery to be at the mercy of someone straight out of training.

Weinberg nodded, and looked at the other members of the committee enquiringly.

'Agreed,' said Harvey Bergman.

'He was OK,' said Anne Bell. 'He'll get a good job in a year or two. This one's just a little too soon for him.'

The lay members of the panel nodded acquiescence to the opinions of the professionals without comment.

Weinberg drew a line through the name on the papers before him and pencilled a few comments in the margin.

'Any others?' he enquired.

There was silence.

'I have a problem with Bankowicz from New York.'

The others looked up enquiringly at Anne Bell.

'Well,' she continued, 'he has a good position at Montefiore, has been senior surgeon there for nine years, lives in Westchester County; apart from the fact that he's probably a little past his best innovative work, I can't help feeling his main motive in applying here is to get out of the Bronx.'

'Who can blame him for that?' muttered Harvey Bergman, and they all laughed.

'I agree,' said David Meeson, the administrator. 'And he had little idea of managed care, provider priorities – he was a bit old school.'

Lester Pearson looked across at him with an expression of distaste, before saying, 'He's too light anyway. He had his chance at Montefiore to do great things and just trod water. He made it to the short list, but I don't think he's the best man for the job on clinical grounds.'

Jennifer Kling nodded her agreement.

'Well,' said Weinberg, drawing another line across the paper, 'that leaves us with Bristow from Norwalk, and Masters from Miami.' He looked to his left. 'Lester?'

'Both good men. I liked Bristow. Steady, a good clinician, Cleveland Clinic trained, known to have an excellent pair of hands, satisfactory if unspectacular curriculum vitae. He'd be a safe choice. On the other hand, Masters is undoubtedly impressive. Not as proven as Bristow, younger, less experience, but clearly an innovator, excellent research record, made a strong name for himself in the South. He'd make people sit up around here, that's for sure.'

He said no more, not wanting to cast his vote before hearing comments from the others.

'Paul?'

'Bristow impressed me. He has all the basic requirements. He was conservative without being over cautious. He seemed to want to fit in to the department rather than disrupt it. Masters struck me as a bit of a whizz kid. Undoubtedly talented, but I didn't like the way he felt he could just march in here and start doing paediatric surgery after only one year's experience.'

Yes, thought Anne Bell, I thought he'd trodden on your corns a little, Paul.

'Harvey?'

'Well, they are both eminently appointable and I'll be happy to go with the opinion of the specialists in the field. I'd just say that while Bristow would indeed be safe, as Lester said, Masters has the advantage of being a highly successful fund-raiser; he got the NIH grant for Miami almost single-handed, and there seems little doubt that he'll get another one and a half million for the clinical study, money which will come straight here. He could make this department a very high profile, research-led centre over the next few years, and we all know that that kind of success attracts more and more in the way of rolling funds and support. I can't help thinking that gives Masters the edge.'

Anne Bell smiled to herself. Yes, she thought, and it might just have some spin-offs for your laparoscopic department at the same time, eh Harve?

'I agree,' interjected David Meeson without invitation. 'He struck me as just the sort of productive, high-profile young surgeon we need here at South Boston. What do you think, Jennifer?'

'Masters would have my vote, also,' replied Jennifer Kling, without adding that he could have her body any time he cared. 'He has a certain presence, an image, a vibrancy which impressed me. The other man was, well, a bit grey and ordinary.'

'That's not always a bad thing, ma'am,' said Lester Pearson in a tired voice. 'Ordinary and safe are not necessarily bad attributes in surgery.'

'Yes, but not for a Head of Department in a city as competitive as Boston,' said Meeson, thinking the sooner this old, reactionary surgical goat was pensioned off and out, the better.

'Quite,' added Jennifer Kling, 'we need to be high profile to survive.'

There was silence for a few moments before Weinberg said, without looking up from his papers, 'Dr Bell?'

Anne looked around the table. 'It is fairly clear to me that both men can do the job. They have all the training and experience necessary, so we have to look at other factors. Bristow would bring an unspectacular, solid, conservative style to the post. I am sure he would continue the excellent work of the past, attract good research fellows, be productive, and maintain the characteristic which has given this unit its reputation over the years, that of respect, for if there is one thing this department has throughout the Eastern seaboard, it is the respect of its peer departments.'

She looked around, then continued, 'Masters, on the other hand, would bring some panache, colour, adventure to the department. His animal research is good, very good. That does not mean it will be equally good in humans. It could bomb, wasting the NIH grant, making us look pretty stupid. Or it could be a major contribution, putting us on the national and even international map. We have to decide whether we want to take that chance, that *risk*.'

Lester Pearson looked across the table at her.

'Have you decided, Anne?' he asked.

'Not entirely. I was captivated by his enthusiasm, then alarmed at his response to my questions. I don't want us to saddle ourselves with a self-indulgent, independent, over-ambitious individual who might plough on with no regard to colleagues or other departments in pursuit of his own dreams or goals. Unfortunately, on the basis of a one-hour interview, I find it hard to spot that kind of person and discriminate them from the true innovator who will give the cardiac department the development it wants for the next decade. I'm just not sure which kind of beast Masters is. If he is the latter, we should appoint him. If he is the former, we would have to live with the consequences. In ICU terms, they could be very severe consequences.'

'Well, I guess we have to decide one way or the other,' said Weinberg. 'Speaking as a surgeon, rather than director, I have to say I liked Masters. He's an enthusiast, a pioneer. He would bring a fresh outlook to the place, there's no doubt he would generate a significant amount of research with presentations and publications which would be very good for the whole surgical section; the possibility of an initial one and a half million grant, which would set the scene for further awards, is high attractive. If I have to cast a vote, it would probably go with him.'

Ah, Jerry, Anne thought, you're just seeing yourself ten years ago, only you have the attributes of honesty and integrity. Does Masters have those, that's the question?

They talked on for twenty minutes more before Weinberg realized they were beginning to go round in circles.

'Well, ladies and gentlemen, I sense we're beginning to repeat ourselves – I think it's time we had a vote.'

He looked around, then said, 'I'll move round in turn. Lester?'

'This is my *alma mater*, Jerry. Can I reserve judgement till the end? I'd like the privilege of giving the final vote when I see how my colleagues feel. I'm very close to this, you know.'

Jerry Weinberg smiled at him. 'I understand, Lester,' he said, gently, then looked around at the others and asked, 'Any objections?' in a tone which suggested that there had better not be any.

There weren't.

'Paul?'

'Bristow.' Without hesitation.

'Jennifer?'

'Masters.'

'Harvey?'

'Masters.'

'David?'

'Masters.'

'Anne?'

'Bristow.'

Weinberg looked at Lester Pearson. 'Well, Lester, old buddy, it's Bristow two, Masters three, and it's your call.'

He nodded, then looked around the table and said, 'Some of you may not know, but I won't be around to see the results of our deliberations. I have prostate cancer and, as Jerry here can testify, the bone metastases are taking their toll. What did you say last week, Jerry? Three months, six if I'm lucky? Hell, lucky. It may as well be three weeks. I only wish I could be around to help the new guy, ease him in, give him some help. But I can't, and our decision must be made. I'd rather like to play safe, know things might stay as they are. They're OK, most other units are in worse shape, some better. But no one with ambition, no department, hospital, company with ambition, can stand still and expect to progress. So I have to give my vote to Masters. He has what I once had, a burning ambition to achieve. I sensed it as soon as he walked in the door. He's not cocky, he just knows he's good and wants the chance to prove it. The department can only benefit from such enthusiasm.'

He looked up at Jerry, and said forcefully, 'Masters!'

Anne Bell felt almost ashamed of herself. Oh you dear, sweet old man, I hope to God you're right, she thought, as Jerry said, 'Thank you, Lester, and thank you for making a casting vote unnecessary.' He looked over at the secretary taking the minutes.

'Charlene, would you call Dr Masters in, please?'

She got up and left the room, returning a few moments later with Gary Masters, whom Jerry Weinberg invited to sit down.

'Dr Masters,' he said, 'this committee would like to offer you the post of Associate Professor of Cardiac Surgery here at the University Hospital of Southern Massachusetts. I would like to ask if you wish to accept the post?'

'Oh, yes, sir. I sure do. And I'd like to thank the committee and assure them that they will have no reason to regret their decision.'

I hope not, thought Anne Bell, I sure hope not.

CHAPTER 3

They left their Cojimar apartment at midnight. He held Maria with his left arm, and carried a large suitcase with the other, while Carmen carried the two bin-liners of belongings and food. They took the back streets to the beach, stopping occasionally to rest, and to look furtively behind them for the Special Services, Castro's secret police. Developed since the revolution along the lines of the Russian KGB, the SS were the most feared men in Cuba, with ultimate power of life or death on his streets – or torture and suffering for their personal entertainment in his prisons. A few wispy clouds raced occasionally across the dark-blue sky, crossing the August moon to cast ghostly shadows against the white buildings and dusty streets as they made their way to the shore. The beach was deserted. He led her on to the sand to the pier, put Maria down and pulled out the raft from under its camouflage before standing up to see his wife's reaction. She looked at it, then back at him.

'This is it?' she asked.

'Yes.' He shrugged.

'We can make it ninety miles over the ocean in this?'

'We have to. It's all we have.'

'It's all we have....'

Her shoulders drooped and she looked at him, the husband she loved, the doctor she admired, the father of her child, as she wondered how any country could drive such a good man to commit his life and that of his family to the ocean on a few planks and rubber tyres.

She walked to him.

'If it has to be, we must do it,' she whispered, and she held him to her in a hug he knew was meant to convey that it might be the last they ever had.

He felt his eyes sting with unwilling tears, held her tight, then gently took her shoulders and faced her.

'It has to be, Carmen,' he said quietly. 'There is nothing here but starvation, misery, or death. It can only get worse. We must earn our freedom, and return again when Cuba also is free.'

She took her daughter's hand, took a deep breath, and said, 'What do you want us to do?'

He looked at her, wishing things were different, determined that they would be some day.

'I'll pull the raft out to the shore. You bring the bags. We'll put them on, push the raft into the water, then you and Maria climb on. I'll push us out into the deeper water and jump. Then we're on our way. To the USA.'

He laughed suddenly.

'On ... our ... way ... to ... the ... U ... S ... A,' he chanted.

She smiled, suddenly feeling that it might be all right after all.

Within an hour the lights of Cojimar village had disappeared behind them, and, as the waves buffeted their tiny raft in the darkness, she shivered and began once more to doubt the wisdom of their decision.

Anne Bell was just about to leave her office on the intensive care unit when she heard the knock on the door.

'Come in,' she called, as she filled her briefcase with papers to take home. Her day seldom ended when she left the hospital. She looked up as the good-looking young man walked in, closing the door behind him then turning to face her. It took a few moments before she recognized him as the emergency room intern. 'So you found your way up here?' she asked.

He cleared his throat.

'Er ... yes, sure. I ... er ... I just wanted to say thanks for the other day. That kid was virtually dead and I didn't know what to do to save her. I guess I panicked a little ... a *lot!*'

'Sit down,' she said, closing her briefcase, and drawing up a chair to face him. She watched the young doctor, remembering her own fears and faults when she was fresh out of medical school.

'You know, we all do it,' she said.

He looked at her. 'What?'

'Get the letters after the name, take the leap from student to doctor, then think we're the greatest thing since sliced bread and expect everyone else to think the same. Like they'd all been waiting for it to happen. *"Wow! Here he is at last, the guy we've all been waiting for."* When in fact, most of them have been doing the job for years, and suddenly this fresh-faced kid wet behind the ears appears and starts ordering them around as if he's the local expert.'

He nodded, glumly, recognizing the scenario. 'It's all round the hospital, you know.'

'There's no better bush telegraph than a hospital.' And no better way to bring someone down to earth she thought. Then, sympathetically, she said, 'Look ... by the way, I don't even know your name....'

'Oh, it's Andrew Thompson.'

He held out his hand, and she shook it.

'Andrew? Andy?'

'Andy.'

'Well, look at it this way, Andy. You've made your mistake, and it's over. You've learned from it. All the other interns will make their own mistakes, just as bad, maybe worse. They're to come. Tell them you bombed, then remind them they've got it to come. Everyone does, believe me – it's part of the learning curve.'

'Yes, maybe....'

'Definitely. How are they treating you in ER?'

'They're really good, the nurses. They're helping me a lot. But the residents are keeping a real close eye on me, stopping me doing things, taking over without telling me why.'

Sure, she thought, covering themselves, protecting instead of training. She might have a word with Jim Taylor, the ER chief of staff, get them to lighten up, help him along....

'And how's the child?'

'Oh, fine,' he said, 'went home yesterday.'

'Well look, Andy, I want to thank you for coming up to see me. I think it shows you've got the makings of a good doctor, if you can recognize your mistakes and learn from them. If things don't improve down there, come and see me again, or give me a call. I've got a little pull in ER. And let me know if there's anything else I can do to help you.'

He stood up.

'Thanks Doctor Bell, I really appreciate it.'

'Sure.'

She opened the door and watched him go, glad that she wasn't still at that stage of her career. Not that it hadn't been fun at times. But better to be in control....

Twenty minutes later, she sat in a corner seat on the 'T' – Boston's rapid transit system subway – and leaned her head against the window, succumbing to the drowsiness of a long day and several disturbed nights. She slipped gently back into Idaho 1977.

Her mother was calling her.

'Anne, Anne, come down here, quickly.'

She left the small wooden desk in her room and ran down the carpetless stairs, her bare feet banging on the floorboards.

'What is it?'

'The letter, it's here.'

Her mother stood there, at sixty as beautiful as she had ever been to Anne, with her now greying, long, black Spanish hair and blue Galway eyes. She held a brown envelope aloft in her hand. Anne stopped in front of her, making no effort to take the letter.

'Where's Dad?'

'Where do you think? Out in the south meadow.'

'We've got to wait till he's here – we can't open it without him.'

'We can. He's never missed a day's work since we got married, and I don't think he'll interrupt one now, even for this. I don't want to wait till tonight to find out. I *can't* wait. Can you?'

Anne paused, then said, 'Hold on to it, and wait.'

She dashed out of the front door in her bare feet, the door and the mosquito guard banging shut behind her.

Twenty minutes later she was back, leading her bemused father through the door behind her by the hand. He looked at his wife and shrugged his shoulders, taking off the stetson and wiping his brow with a large bandanna.

'Well, I'll be ...' started her mother. 'How'd you ...?'

'Never mind,' said Anne, impatiently, 'He's here. Now where's the letter?'

She made her father sit on the sofa, as he shook his head and looked at his daughter from eyes set deep in the weatherbeaten face of a farmer used to working in the unforgiving climate of the Rockies. She took her mother's hand and made her sit beside him as she took the envelope from her.

She looked at them both, tore open the envelope, and looked at the letter.

They watched her, Kathleen Bell slipping her hand into William's and squeezing it in anticipation.

Anne looked up. Serious at first, then with a tiny smile, before she leapt in the air with a whoop of joy and ran to them as they stood up, throwing an arm around their necks and hugging them to her.

'We did it, we did it!'

Her mother extricated herself from her grasp and stood back.

'You're in?' she asked, 'You're in Boise College?'

'Yes, yes!' she replied. 'I'm going to be a nurse!'

Her mother took her hands and they danced round the floor, before turning to her father as he sat there, watching them.

'Does this mean I can get back to my potatoes now, Anne?'

There was silence for a minute before his grin widened, and he took each of them by the hand and led them round and round in another dance of joy, like a twenty year old at a barn dance. They broke up and he looked at his daughter, then his wife, then his daughter again, before hugging Anne in a long, warm, affectionate embrace.

'My little girl, going to be a nurse,' he said. 'Well done, darling, well done. How I'll get the crops in without you Heaven only knows.'

She stood facing him, looking into the dark eyes, and said, 'You'll manage.' Then, more seriously, 'Thanks Dad, thanks for everything. It's all down to you and Mom.'

She looked at her mother.

'Thanks, Mom.'

They all hugged again, this time with a warmth and feeling that only comes from deep, shared love, before Anne said quietly, without moving, 'That's the first time I ever danced with you, Dad; thought it was against your religion.'

Her father grinned. 'I'm not a Catholic, Anne – I don't have to confess it.'

Anne and her mother snorted with laughter as he turned and walked towards the door.

He pulled it open and looked back at them, tall and

handsome still at sixty-two, in his denims and plaid shirt.

'I knew it would be hard when I married you, Kathleen, I never knew you'd give me a daughter twice as bad.'

They saw the twinkle in his eye as he put on his stetston, turned and left. They heard him whistling as he walked away from the house.

Her mother turned to her. 'Well, Anne, you'll be leaving for the big city, then.'

'Looks like it Mom. Come September.'

She began to think about it. First time away from home. First time on her own.

'It's not that far,' she said, not sure if she was reassuring herself or her mother.

'Sure, it's no distance at all. Oh, well done, my little darlin',' she said, and hugged her only and very precious daughter once more.

Anne woke with a start as the 'T' went over an uneven track and pulled into the station.

Copley.

One more stop to go. She sighed, remembering the dream, wondering where it had come from, relieved that she had woken up one stop before her destination rather than three or four after. She got out at Arlington and walked across the common and the park to her apartment. She leased the top floor of one of the grander houses in one of Boston's finest streets, a legacy of the senator's daughter she had brought back to life on the ICU. A severe pneumonia case, brought in in respiratory failure, she had been on a ventilator for six days, close to death, needing constant attention from Anne and her team until she gradually began to respond to treatment and finally recovered completely, leaving Anne Bell in a state of total exhaustion. Until that time she had lived in a first-floor apartment over an art shop on Newberry Street. The senator and his wife wanted to give her something special in return for the life she had given their daughter, and he offered her a long-term rental of the top floor of his family home, emphasizing that it had always been separate from the rest of the house, being his parents-in-law's apartment; after their deaths, with only the three of them in the rest of the house, it had just been closed up. Wasted space. So the rent, ridiculously small, was agreed, and she fell in love with the place – a distinguished, old, four-storey brownstone in a cobbled yard with trees and flowerbeds behind a large wrought-iron gate. A side-entrance led into a hallway and staircase to the top floor. Her apartment comprised a large living-room, a smaller dining area adjacent to a kitchen, a large bedroom with en-suite shower and toilet, a smaller bedroom and a large bathroom. More than enough for a single girl. From the living-room window, she could see part of Boston Common, and from her bedroom, a glimpse of the John Hancock tower rising over her adopted city.

She showered, changed into jeans and a Patriots T-shirt, and fixed a meal for herself from the freezer, before settling on the sofa with her briefcase and working through her papers. After a short while, she rested her head on the sofa back, and closed her eyes, thinking of the appointments committee and wondering if the confident, handsome, young heart specialist was going to deliver all he seemed to promise. Or drop them all in it. When she woke, it was 9.45 p.m. She made coffee and brought it back to the living-room flicking on the TV for News at Ten, dividing her attention between her work and the news reports. By 10.30, she had had enough, and began putting her papers back into the briefcase, only half listening to the weather man:

'... *while down in the south-east, hurricane Chris has turned west away from the mainland and has been downgraded to a tropical storm, so is no longer a threat to Miami or the eastern seaboard. But don't get complacent, folks, Debbie is just filling out about one hundred miles south of Key West, and looks like she may cause some trouble in that area, and Ernesto won't be far behind her. Watch this space, you Florideans.'*

She flicked the switch off, and went to bed.

She had more to worry about than hurricanes in Florida.

CHAPTER 4·

She was a screamer.

He didn't mind the screaming, it turned him on a little, but she was a scratcher too, and the scratching got deeper and deeper each time so he started yelling and wriggling too until the scratching stopped and she went back to just screaming. He rolled her over once so she couldn't get at his back but she didn't seem to like being on top, even though it felt great for him. She carried on for a few minutes, but just when he was really beginning to enjoy it she did the same thing to him, flipping him over so that he was on top of her again, and the screaming resumed. She sure knew what she wanted. And how to get it.

Just like him.

He'd left the interview and finished the formalities at UHSM, picked up his bags and headed for the airport for the late flight back to Miami, celebrating by upgrading himself to business class and arriving slightly drunk at 9 p.m. He'd toyed with the idea of hitting the town to celebrate some more, but he felt suddenly drained by the adrenalin-powered high of the day and the inevitable low of the evening aftermath. When he got to his apartment, he had flopped into a chair fully dressed, and had fallen asleep. He woke at 2 a.m. feeling drowsy and irritated at giving in to fatigue and wasting the evening but, at the same time, relieved to be able to undress and crawl into bed.

The next morning the alarm woke him at 6 a.m. as usual. He leaned over, switched off the clock, then remembered what day it was. The first day of the rest of his life.

He jumped out of bed and almost ran to the bathroom.

He had an excellent day at work. The research was finished; he'd got the job he wanted; there was time now to see to the hundreds of things he'd deferred and postponed for weeks – make calls, work on some papers for the journals, send off a few abstracts to meetings, tell a few people he'd got the professor's job in Boston.

Wind down.

Later, after he finished for the day, like the loner he was, he wound down by himself at the Green Street Café in Coconut Grove, south of the city, choosing a sidewalk table, and enjoying the warm Miami dusk and the relaxed atmosphere of the area. He drank a couple of Bud Ice beers, and ordered pepperoni pizza with house salad and a half carafe of Cabernet. He'd only taken one bite when he saw her approaching, a confident, relaxed but electrifying swing of the hips signifying that this was one chick who knew what she was doing. Tall, dark Mediterranean looks, good figure fitting snugly into a tight black dress, black heels clicking on the sidewalk. She was almost gone before he realized she'd spoken.

'Is it good?'

Then she was past him. He turned his head to watch her go, a slice of pizza halfway to his mouth, and she turned with a half smile. He smiled back and held the pizza slice up, offering it to her with his eyebrows raised. She walked on. He hadn't really thought she was the pepperoni type.

He was wrong.

Within three minutes she was back, heading straight for his table like they had a date, sitting down opposite him without pausing, and helping herself to a slice.

'Mmmmm. Not bad,' she said.

The waiter appeared and she ordered a glass of Chardonnay.

'Kathryn Skiathos,' she said, looking into his eyes with a confident direct stare. 'Who are you?'

He smiled back. Some women sure have balls, he thought to himself. Within an hour they were in bed at her place.

He'd participated in sexual olympics before, but this was different. What started as a hasty demanding sprint, slowly progressed to medium distance, before developing into a pentathlon and maturing into a marathon.

But for Gary, it was no problem.

If she wanted to screw quickly or slowly in nineteen different positions, then start again in reverse order, she'd come to the right guy. He'd played ball, pumped iron, jogged for years, kept himself in condition. He'd done his own stress electrocardiograms, pushing himself beyond what any patient could ever tolerate just to see how good his heart was. It was very good, and his racing pulse always got back to normal rate in less than forty seconds. Oh, yes, this heart surgeon had a better heart than most and, combined with his fitness and the adrenalin of his success the day before, he could give this chick a night she would never forget.

But she was hungry, and experienced, and after two hours, he was beginning to think she was as fit as he was. When his erection finally showed signs of not being able to manage double figures, he went down on her again. This time, when she climaxed, he kept it going, holding her down in spite of her efforts to stop him, and stimulating her more and more, holding on to the orgasm until it hurt and she begged him to stop.

When he moved up on top of her and kissed her, it was with a sense of triumph; she held him tight, kissed him with her full wet mouth, then turned her head away, exhausted, as if to say, *nice one, buddy, you win.*

He wasn't going to argue.

He slept till 10 a.m. When he woke, he didn't know where he was for a moment, until an ache in his groin reminded him of the previous night. He turned his head, but he was alone in the queen-sized bed. He stretched, and dozed off again.

He woke to the sensation of her wet tongue brushing his sleeping lips before it moved slowly down the side of his neck to his right nipple, then his left, then slowly down his stomach. He opened his eyes and saw her dark head go down before feeling the initial pain of a further assault on an already abused appendage give way to the warm pleasure of a truly expert blow. It went on and on, until the pleasure began to give way to an unaccustomed ache, followed by increasing discomfort as his body trembled with unsatisfied anticipation. And still she held the climax away, increasing the pressure until he thought he might burst, keeping him just on the edge of ecstasy without letting it happen. Just when he thought it might, he felt her pause, and she raised her head and looked him straight in the eyes.

He stared down at her, feeling helpless and desperate, wondering if he should throw respect and dignity to the wind and finish the job off himself, before she gave a small, triumphant smile and went back down.

He groaned then shouted with pleasure and relief before she left him, drained and gasping like a helpless animal.

He knew she had exacted her revenge.

She returned a few minutes later with coffee and croissants. He sat up and took the plate and cup she offered him.

'You always this lively?' he asked, after a while.

'Only when my husband's away,' she replied, taking a large bite of the pastry.

'You didn't say you were married.'

'Would it have made any difference?'

He looked at her without replying. She knew the answer anyway. 'What does he do?'

'Import-Export, electrical equipment and chemicals. Travels around the States and South America. He's in Rio this week.'

He looked around the bedroom. It was a sumptuous apartment, beautifully furnished in an upmarket area of Coconut Grove. He must be doing OK.

'When's he back?'

'Friday.'

There was silence.

He wondered if she expected him to see her again, and if he really wanted to, but his pelvis was aching and the thought of another night like the last was, at that moment, not the uppermost thing on his mind. He hurt all over. But he suspected he might feel different later in the day. She was some lay. He drank the coffee and lay back. She followed suit and snuggled up to him.

'I've got an appointment at noon,' she said.

'I'll leave before then.'

'Stay as long as you like.'

'No, I've got things to do.'

'Surgery?'

'No, just office work.'

A few minutes later she spoke again. 'I'd like to see you again.'

He liked her. She was direct, and honest. She wasn't overawed by the fact he was a big-time surgeon, didn't want to get complicated.

She just wanted to fuck him.

He turned his head and looked at her. 'Me too,' he said. 'How about Thursday?'

'Fine. Come here, anytime after five.'

'You sure he won't be back?'

'I'm sure.'

They dozed for a few minutes before he glanced at his watch, slipped his arm from under her and went to the bathroom. He let himself out.

He drove home in an elated mood, pleased with the night and his celebrations. He parked the car and made his way to his apartment. He took a shower and changed clothes, intending to start the tedious process of sorting things out in preparation for packing, but delaying the task on the excuse that a caffeine fix was needed first. He sat down with his steaming mug of Folgers, turned on the TV and flicked through the channels. What a novelty! He was *never* home this time of day. But he was disappointed with day-time TV. Apart from a couple of cartoons, and an old Audie Murphy western, it was chat shows all the way. *Donahue, Regis and Kathy Lee, Ricki Lake, Geraldo, Oprah.* Different anchors, same audiences. He smiled to himself. Maybe they *were* the same, hired out by Rent-a-Chat-Show-Audience Inc. He continued his flicking. *Jerry Springer, Maury Povich. Jenny.* Christ, the whole fucking country was just one gigantic chat show. And the topics – *unwanted childhood pregnancies, artificial insemination and adoption for lesbian couples, benefits for single HIV positive ethnic minority parents* ... he wouldn't have been surprised to hear them discussing *geriatric venereal diseases in men over seventy with inflatable penile implants,* and eventually concluded that even packing was preferable to daytime TV.

He looked around the room, wondering where to begin.

He started with the journals. Five years of back numbers of the *Journal of Cardiac Surgery, American Heart Journal, American Journal of Cardiology, Journal of the American Medical Association.* Did he really need all these? The library had everything he might require. How many times had he consulted these volumes in the past year? He decided to keep the previous and current years' issues, and ditch the remainder.

He put them into two neat piles and stuck a Post-It label on each. He wondered if that was enough for one day, knew it wasn't, and turned to the books. He kept most of his scientific books at the hospital. This was his leisure reading. The complete paperback works of Ed McBain, Dean Koontz, John Sandford, nine biographies of Kennedy, Collins English Dictionary, six Fodor's travel guides, the American Heart Association Membership Roster, various bits and pieces he'd picked up on the spur of the moment and never read....

He kept them all.

He looked round the living-room, which was beginning to seem bare already. As it should, he thought. After all, this was the end of an era, the beginning of a new one. He felt excited again at the prospect of the move to Boston. He sat down at his pine bureau to sort out the contents. Suddenly a vision of Kathryn Skiathos passed through his brain and he paused, staring into infinity, remembering the night. He had never known anyone like her. She was ... almost his female counterpart ... confident, arrogant, aggressive, demanding ... it was not what he was used to. He'd given her his best and she'd returned it with interest. There was nothing he didn't like about this woman. Apart from one thing: she was married.

And the last thing he needed right now was a relationship with a married woman.

Even so, he almost wished he was seeing her tonight, then realized a little rest for his equipment might not be a bad thing if Thursday was going to be a repeat of Tuesday. He turned to clearing out the desk, but his thoughts kept returning to her, going over the evening from the moment she passed him at the café and said *is it good?*

Oh yes, it was good. Very good indeed.

He got up and went to the kitchen, returning with another mug of coffee. He'd get back to the packing later, he thought, sitting down and flicking the TV on again.

Montel Williams ... Bertice Berry ... Rolanda ... pregnancy rates amongst teenage prostitutes....

He drained the cup, flicked to CNN, and laid his head back on the sofa, shutting his eyes and drifting off into a doze, as the screen showed a group of half-naked Cuban refugees being picked up off a makeshift raft in the choppy seas of the Florida Straits by the US Coast Guard Cutter *Chandeleur*.

'Where are we?'

Tito didn't answer for a moment, then he looked over at her

and said, 'I don't know.'

It was their second day at sea. He had estimated that with 15 m.p.h. winds, the makeshift sail of sheets and broom handles, and some rowing, they might cover the ninety miles between Cuba and the mainland in a day and a half, two days tops. The old compass he'd brought had reassured him that they were heading roughly north-north-west, but still there was no sign of land. The wind had shifted then dropped during the first afternoon, and he was afraid they might have drifted away from the American coast. He didn't want to admit it to her, but they could be anywhere.

The first day had been worse than they had expected. When the wind dropped, the sun became unbearably hot and they had no shelter. They had had to cover Maria to protect her, but that just made her too hot and she was already blistered where the sun had got at exposed parts of her arms and legs when she tossed the sheet off. They weren't much better. They had to ration the water, and they were parched and dehydrated. They had seen two sharks circle the raft and had sat huddled together in fear until they lost interest, Tito gripping a makeshift spear in one hand, and a baseball bat in the other, in case he had to fight them off. Once, they had seen a ship on the horizon heading in what looked like their direction and Tito had jumped up and down waving the white sheet to attract attention, rocking the raft so much that they thought they might all tumble off, but to no avail.

'I'm frightened, Tito. What if we are drifting away from land? We have little food and water. We cannot last more than another day or two.'

'I know, I know,' he replied, not for the first time questioning the wisdom of his decision to leave. 'But we cannot be far now. I've kept an eye on the compass and rowed only in a north-north-west direction. We *must* be right. The sun has told me we are going towards America. And the stars. I have kept watch, Carmen. I am sure.'

He was not as sure as he sounded. After thirty-six hours of watching, rowing, tending the sail, with only an occasional doze, he was exhausted. He knew his judgement must be suspect. But they had no choice. He put the paddle down and moved carefully over to sit with her, putting his arm around his young daughter's shoulders.

'We will be all right. As we get nearer the coast there will be more traffic. Liners, yachts, Coast Guard vessels. They will help us. And once we get to Florida, once we set foot on land, then we are free. Legal immigrants. Like all those who have gone before us since the revolution. We know that there is automatic freedom in America for us.' He leaned over and kissed her. 'And we will soon be there.'

All they had to do was reach the American coast.

Or so he thought.

What he didn't know was that the day he picked to leave his homeland, 500 other Cubans had had the same idea, and had taken route-one across the Florida Straits where they had made headline news on arrival on the shores around Key West, and caused Governor Chiles to return from vacation to face an unexpected immigration crisis. The following day, 2000 more took to rafts, boats, inner tubes, bathtubs – anything that would float, starring on every news station in the nation as a mass flotilla of exiles followed the example of the first few and decided to leave the poverty and misery of Cuba behind for the safe haven of the USA. The Florida Straits became an exodus of maritime escapees until, to stem the threatened flow of thousands more, Chiles declared a state of emergency and the US Administration abruptly changed the rules, and halted its twenty-eight-year policy of granting automatic asylum to Cubans who made it to America or were rescued at sea. From that moment, those picked up at sea were to be returned to the American Base of Guantanamo Bay on the southernmost tip of Cuba. Those who made it to Florida were to be taken to a detention centre at Krome to await further developments, repatriation in some other friendly country, or return to Cuba.

Return to Cuba.

As he gazed at the horizon, praying for a glimpse of land, Tito Pereira knew none of this, and believed that when they set foot on US soil, they would be free.

He gripped his wife's hand, stood up and reached for the paddle again. Before he could grab it, the boat shuddered and pitched and he fell down beside her.

'What happened?' she asked.

'I don't know.'

They looked around, wondering if they had hit something. They knew it must be the other way round. Something had hit them. She put her arm around Maria, and hugged her close. The next blow was worse, and left Tito in no doubt, even before he saw the dark shadow glide away on the other side of the raft. He felt a griping pang of anxiety in his gut, and he knew a few more attacks like that could shake the planks apart, break up the raft, and leave them all to the sea. And the shark. He crawled to the edge of the raft, peering over the side.

'Be careful,' she said in a whisper, as if the shark might hear.

He saw it make its next pass, saw the fin approaching, watched it dive, held on and rode the impact as it came up under the boat. He heard his wife and child scream, but knew the time for comfort had passed. This one meant business.

It was fight or die now.

He reached into his rucksack for the makeshift spear – a carving knife lashed to a broom handle, and crawled over to the other side of the raft. He kneeled, knowing just what he would do, silently praying that he would succeed with the first strike, and waited, the spear held high above his head in both hands. It had been a long time since he had been spear-fishing with his boyhood friends in the streams near his home. But he knew it was his only chance. The shark had tried three times, it was hungry, it meant business, it was prepared to attack a boat to get at its prey. He saw it twenty yards out, as the black fin rose out of the water and streaked towards them. He knew he had to get it before it dived to come up under the raft. He rose slowly and stood on the edge, riding the swell, his toes curled over the side to give him some purchase for the launch. He watched the shark's approach, wanting to leave his move to the last moment so it was close, but not so late that it was already diving and his strike would lose its thrust under water. And on it came, following a centuries' old attack pattern. And still he waited as it came closer and closer until he judged it was within his range and he almost sensed it was about to dive, out of his reach.

He knew it was now or never. He had to be sure and this was the only way. He crouched, took a deep breath, then launched himself off the raft towards the oncoming predator so that, for one moment, his dive took him vertically above it. He plunged the home-made spear down into the shark's left eye, deep into its brain, feeling the knife break off the handle on impact, and praying it had found its mark. The shark dived away from the pain of the injury, thrashing about as Tito surfaced in water already turning crimson red. He swam furiously for the raft, feeling the turbulence produced by the dying panic of his predator, expecting his legs to be ripped off at any moment as it sought its revenge.

'Tito! Tito! Quick! Here ... here....'

She was leaning over the raft, her hand outstretched, as he swam with all his strength for safety, reaching the craft and hauling himself up as she helped drag him on board.

'The paddle!' he cried. 'The paddle!'

She looked round as he rubbed his eyes and brushed his wet hair back, found it and almost threw it to him.

He paddled furiously, first one side of the raft, then the other, striving to get away from the assault area, waiting for the next impact, feeling none. After five minutes he slowed down, looked behind as if he might see his pursuer, then looked up at the blue sky and gasped for breath. The blood of the dead or dying shark would attract any other predators away from them, and they had put some distance between the raft and the area. They were probably OK. Until the next time. He crawled over towards Carmen and knelt beside her, his arm around his daughter, and they cried together with relief, the small raft bobbing helplessly on the swell. The shark was gone, but they were still alone, lost on the high seas, facing another dark night and another long hot day. She cradled his head, stroking his wet hair, and looked to the horizon for land, seeing only green ocean.

They slept on and off for a few hours that night, from sheer exhaustion. The shrill cry of the seagull woke him as the sun threatened to break over the distant horizon. He rubbed his eyes, and looked up at the white bird as it inspected their craft for food. He scanned the horizon, slumping down at first in familiar disappointment, before rising slowly and concentrating on one direction, screwing his eyes up, wanting to believe what he saw, not daring to.

'Carmen,' he whispered, then louder, 'Carmen, Carmen!'

He looked over to her as she stirred, then looked back, not wanting to lose it. His daughter woke suddenly, saw him standing and crawled over to him.

'Papa, Papa ...'

'Ah, *chiquita*, look, look over there. Carmen, look....'

He pointed to the horizon and they all looked to where he was pointing, and screwing up their eyes then seeing it – a long strip of land against the green-blue horizon.

'It's America,' he said, almost in awe. 'America.'

'Are you sure, Tito, are you sure it's America?'

'It must be,' he replied, 'it *must* be. We made it, Carmen, we made it.'

'Thanks be to God,' whispered Carmen, looking at her husband. He was shouting now, jumping up and down, making the raft shake. His daughter laughed at his joy and clapped her hands. His wife joined in and they enjoyed their moment until he fixed the sail and showed Carmen how to hold it, then reached for the oar and started to paddle for all he was worth, taking the primitive raft slowly closer and closer to freedom. They watched with increasing excitement as the shore became larger and moved slowly towards them, waiting to embrace them with safety and liberty.

Two hours later, as Miami awakened, they rowed up the inlet, and searched for somewhere to land. The small houses on each side gave way to bigger buildings until he spotted a suitable landing. He pulled the raft against the jetty and helped Carmen and Maria up the wooden steps.

The jogger never gave them another glance.

The elderly man, walking his dog, paused and looked at them.

'You some of those Cuban boat people?' he asked.

Tito and Carmen looked at each other, then back at him.

'I guess,' he said. 'Where are we?'

'Miami Beach.'

'Miami Beach?'

'Yep, Miami Beach. You did good.'

Tito nodded, smiling.

'You must be hungry,' the American said. 'Come with me.'

They had little choice so they picked up their belongings and followed him to his waterside house, marvelling at its beauty and comfort. He made them at home, showed them where to shower, and provided them with fresh soap and towels. His wife gave Maria cookies and Coke, then helped Carmen bath her.

After breakfast, the American took Tito aside and said, 'I've got to call the authorities now, you know?'

Tito looked at this kind man, this angel of mercy, this personification of everything he had ever thought of as American, and nodded.

'Of course,' he said, and smiled.

The good American looked at the young Cuban, and said, 'You sure?'

'Of course.'

He left and Tito turned happily back to his family and the American's wife, as she fussed over his beautiful daughter like she was her own favourite grandchild.

The Miami Beach police arrived an hour later and joined them for coffee. One of them chatted to the American, the other took details from Tito. Ten minutes later, two immigration officers rang the doorbell, spent a few minutes talking to the American and the police, then escorted the immigrants out of the waterfront house.

Within two hours, expecting to be taken to an immigration centre for routine processing and visa approval, they found themselves incarcerated behind the barbed wire of Krome Camp, South Florida, with thousands of other refugees, confused, disorientated and, as much as at any time during the previous three days, uncertain of their future.

CHAPTER 5

Anne Bell yawned, stretched, and looked up at the clock on her office wall. The digital figures showed 09.30. It seemed more like nine in the evening.

She hated the drag of quiet days. Of the eight available beds in the intensive care unit, currently only two were occupied, and these by convalescent patients due for transfer back to their rooms in the next twenty-four hours. It went like that sometimes. One day there were eight sick patients and frantic demands to admit three more. Other days intensive care became *inventive* care, as the staff sat on their hands, caught up with paperwork, cleaned out their cupboards and desks, and tried to invent other ways to pass the time as they waited for the next disaster to crash through their doors, with or without prior warning, and give them an excuse to do what they did best – work twenty-four hours a day to keep people alive after their apparent sell-by date had expired and everyone else had given up on them. But today was quiet, and at least a day like this gave them a breather, time to regroup and recoup, time to be thankful that no one was sick enough to need their attention. That had to be good news. Not that it would last. Someone would need them sooner or later. But for now, like the rest of them, Anne Bell was waiting. Only this time, she actually knew just who her next admission would be.

It would be Daniel O'Donaghue – a fifty-five year old Amtrack worker from Hartford, Connecticut, with a ventricular aneurysm of the heart.

A man in desperate need of heart surgery.

Gary Master's first case at UHSM.

It was two weeks since Masters had taken up his post, and Lester Pearson and his colleagues had given him an almost obscenely short settling-in period, or honeymoon, as the

49

politicians sometimes called it, before referring him the cases
they had selected prior to his arrival as being suitable for his
new expertise. Not to test him – a new surgeon in their midst –
perish the thought! No, solely for the advancement of medical
progress, though they were all waiting avidly to observe the
performance of the new boy. They had sent him seven possible
cases. He had worked them up and selected three as suitable.
The reasons for rejecting the other four were, in retrospect,
reasonable, and he was not judged to have lost his bottle. Now
they were all gathered in OR 7 watching him operate on
number one.

Anne Bell had resisted the urge to join them. Her place was
here, she told herself, in the intensive care unit, preparing to
look after the patient when the surgeon, a species she regarded
as a mere technician, occasionally referred to as a butcher, had
done his job. That was when she accepted the shattered
metabolic remains of what the butcher and the anaesthetist left
behind so that she and her team could pick up the pieces, and
fine tune the heart, lungs, brain, and blood to nurse the
patient's vital bodily functions through their trauma back to
independent existence. But there was another reason why she
was sitting in the quiet of the intensive care unit. She didn't like
Gary Masters much, and didn't feel inclined to grace him with
her presence as he played out his role as the new whizz kid
sent to rejuvenate cardiac surgery in South Massachusetts.

She wondered why she felt that way. She had only spent
ninety minutes or so in his company at the interview. Could
that be enough to make a judgement? She knew it could not,
and wondered about her irrational feelings as the memories of
five young years at Stanford threatened to emerge from the
protective womb of her subconscious....

She shook herself out of her reverie and stood up, seeming
undecided for a moment until curiosity overcame stubbornness
and she picked up her white coat from the back of the chair,
threw it loosely around her shoulders and made for the door of
her office.

'I'll be back soon, Trudie,' she called to her chief nurse, 'just
going down to see how they're doing.'

She walked out of her department along the corridor to the
elevator. Several other people were waiting. One of them, a
blue-eyed, dark-haired man in operating greens glanced over at

her, then smiled and moved through the group to stand beside her.

'Hello, Anne.'

His English accent sounded strangely out of place in southern Massachusetts. James Sinclair had studiously avoided adopting an American accent since his arrival from England as Associate Professor of Urology two years before.

'Hi, James. Not seen you around recently.'

'No, I've been home.'

He looked at her, wondering if she remembered why he might have visited England. She did, and nodded, knowing he had been back to arrange his official separation, prior to divorce.

'Everything all right?'

The elevator door opened. They followed the others in.

'Yes.'

The doors closed. He looked serious. But he often did. English serious. Reserved. Distant. A good friend, if you could get through the crust, the shell, the protective aura of formality. She recalled lying very drunk on a floor with him somewhere in the St Pete's Beach Rheinhart Hotel on Superbowl night after the Boston Patriots beat the Tampa Bay Buccaneers at Tampa Stadium. He hadn't been so reserved then.

He looked at her, and suddenly smiled, as if recalling the evening.

'Sure, no problem, Anne. What about you?'

'OK. Just off to see the new whizz kid perform.'

'Masters?'

'Yes. Gorgeous Gary.'

He raised his eyebrows.

'That's what the girls call him. G.G.'

He grinned. 'I feel deprived. No one ever called me Georgeous James.'

'Oh, poor James,' she sympathized. 'Not even *Juicy Jim?*'

He shook his head. The elevator stopped and two nurses got out.

The doors closed.

'*Jimbo, Bimbo?*'

He shook his head again, grinning at Anne Bell's customary humour.

'Not even salacious, sexy, super-stud Sinclair, before you

ask,' he added, 'but I'll be delighted to accompany you to the court of Gorgeous Gary and see just what all the fuss is about, if you can put up with plain James.'

The elevator stopped and the doors opened.

' 'Course I can. Let's go see how he's doing.'

They walked along the corridor to the OR and opened the door to the observation gallery above the operating room to watch through the glass walls, specially designed for the teaching and demonstration of surgery. Above them were two wall-mounted monitors, transmitting close-ups of the procedure to the TV screens.

They edged into the busy gallery, straining to get a view of the activity below, listening to the voices from the OR over the audio system.

'And that, ladies and gentlemen, is that.' The voice of Gary Masters came over the audio as they watched him turn from the table and leave the room, taking off his gloves and throwing them in the direction of a refuse bag as he went.

'Missed it all. Story of my life,' said Sinclair.

'How'd he do, Paul?' Anne looked at the paediatric cardiologist standing beside her.

'Pretty damn good from what I could see up here. Lester assisted him, and they both gave a commentary and answered questions. Best show I've seen for years. Maybe I was wrong about this guy.' He looked at her and shrugged, then turned to leave with the other surgeons and residents.

'I'd better get back down to the unit, James. Looks like we missed something good here.'

She walked back, her hands tucked into her skirt pockets, her white coat swaying behind her.

So, pretty damn good, huh? And there's you, Anne Bell, judging him before he even took up post, almost willing him to botch it up. Why so sceptical? Did Pete Dewan really hurt you that much at Stanford? So much that you'll never trust another young surgeon again? Ever?

She reached the unit.

'Trudie,' she called as she walked through the doors, 'everything ready?'

'Sure, Dr Bell, nothing else to do but check and recheck. We're double ready. How did it go?'

'Pretty well from what Paul Schering said. I was too late to see much.'

In spite of Trudie's reasasurance, she checked the bay and equipment herself, hearing the phone ring and Trudie saying 'OK' then, after replacing the receiver, 'they're on the way Dr Bell.'

Within two minutes the doors swung open and the bed crashed into intensive care, one orderly pushing, one pulling. Two nurses, one on each side of the bed, struggled to keep up with its movement, holding i.v. bags above their heads so that their life-preserving fluids continued to flow. A cardiac monitor fixed by a bracket over the patient recorded continuously his heart activity, and an array of multicoloured wires and tubes lay on the bed in what a passing stranger might have thought to be a state of chaos but which Tim Dowdall, the cardiothoracic anaesthetist, knew represented an orderly, familiar arrangement. He smiled at Anne as he saw her waiting for them. They had been through this procedure scores of times before.

'Hi, Anne. Daniel O'Donaghue, repair of ventricular aneurysm. Stable and satisfactory.'

'Bay three,' she ordered, and walked beside them, watching the monitor, inspecting the cardiac anaesthetist's familiar equipment.

'No problems, then?'

The anaesthetist shook his head. 'Just like any other routine open heart procedure. He seems pretty good, this new guy.'

They parked the bed in Bay 3 and Tim Dowdall connected the laryngeal tube to the wall-mounted anaesthetic dispensers while Anne Bell and her nurses disentangled various tubes and wires and plugged them into their monitors.

Suddenly the doors burst open once more and Gary Masters rushed in, still in his bloodstained OR greens, looked around the unfamiliar unit, then walked towards them.

'How is he?' he demanded. 'Everything OK?'

They looked up in surprise.

'Yes ... of course,' said Anne. Then more slowly, deliberately, 'We're in control.'

The surgeon looked anxiously at the monitors, the drip lines. 'Sure?'

She chewed her lip. Give him the benefit of the doubt, Anne. Just this once.

'I'm sure, Dr Masters. Now why don't you just …'

Her words were interrupted by the scream of the emergency alarm.

'Quick, quick, cardiac arrest!' he yelled.

Gary Masters pushed through the nurses to his patient and raised his clenched fist to bang on Daniel O'Donaghue's chest.

He turned in surprise as he felt the strong hand grip his wrist and halt its transit, then looked at the monitor as the familiar *blip! blip!* started up again.

'Just a disconnected electrode, Doctor,' said Trudie. 'Often happens as we transfer them.'

He looked at the monitor, the nurse, then at Anne Bell, his arm still raised, his wrist still in her grasp.

'We're in control here, Doctor. You did a good job. Now let us do ours.'

She kept her grip for just a moment longer before releasing it and turning back to her patient, inwardly seething at his interference, but determined to give him just one chance.

He stood there for a moment, then muttered, 'Yes … of course,' and left without a backward glance.

'He's keen,' said Trudie, working with the i.v. tubes.

'He's lovely, and he obviously really cares,' said Melanie Brooks, the trained nurse working alongside her, watching him leave.

Trudie's eyes rolled up as she said, 'Oh, do me a favour, Melanie. He's not that gorgeous….' She paused as the first irregularity appeared in the cardiac trace.

Anne Bell had already noticed it.

'Lidocaine, Trudie,' she said quietly.

Trudie was already moving to the drug trolley.

'It's on the way.'

Anne watched as the regular rhythm of cardiogram gave way to an irregular, weaker beat, first intermittently then, by the time the nurse returned with the syringe, constantly.

Anne took the syringe and inserted it into the administration channel of the i.v. set, injecting it slowly and watching the monitor.

The rhythm stuttered then returned to normal.

'He should have been here to see that!' Trudie said triumphantly.

Anne smiled. She was right. This was a a good ICU team. The

best she'd known. All hand-picked over the past three years, until it was just right. And Trudie was the best chief nurse she could ever have wanted. Looks like Dolly Parton, brain like Albert Einstein. One of those nurses who, had she been given the opportunity to study medicine, would have been amongst the high flyers. Instead, she did her work to a standard over and above the average, without even seeming to try very hard. Anne owed her a lot. They had virtually set up this unit together after she had been appointed to save an intensive care unit threatened with closure because of failure to meet state legislature standards. And they had resuscitated it together, until it was recognized as one of the best ICUs on the eastern seaboard.

'Set up a slow lidocaine i.v. for twelve hours and watch him carefully.'

'No problem.'

Anne Bell walked to her office and sat down to complete the initial paperwork. She would normally have gone to the residency and read the papers or watched TV. But tonight was going to be different. Tonight she would stay in her office, close to the patient, whether she was needed or not. This case was special in more ways than one, and there was no way she would allow herself to be open to criticism by UHSM's new boy for not being there if there was a problem with his first patient. Oh no, if anything went wrong, this patient would have the best possible care, and any complications would be surgical, not post-surgical. She had been burned once. Never again.

No way.

Within a week of performing his first heart operation at UHSM, Gary Masters received notification that the National Institute of Health Care had approved his grant application and awarded his department an initial sum of $1.5 million to set up the human clinical trials of his new techniques, with the possibility of further review after eighteen months. By the end of his third week, he had completed two more of his revolutionary procedures – Jennifer Pitt, a twenty-three year old heart defect, and Phil Peters, a thirty year old with the same problem. Lester Pearson was enthusiastic about his successor. He had assisted him at all three operations, marvelling at his surgical dexterity, impressed by the new technique, reassured that his choice of successor seemed to be correct. Gary Masters would put the UHSM department on the map, and Lester could leave his unit in good hands, knowing that his hard work setting up the department would be rewarded by its continuation in the top league. Word spread around the hospital of the new cardiac surgeon and his talent, and Gary Masters was made to feel a welcome addition to the surgical staff. Even Anne Bell was impressed at the lack of problems with his cases when they reached the ICU. They appeared to show the signs that mark some surgeons out as special – a notable absence of immediate post-operative complications, and a smooth passage through the minefield of the first three days after surgery.

'I may have to eat my words,' she told James Sinclair over lunch in the hospital restaurant.

'You, Anne?'

She smiled. 'You sound like Weinberg.'

'Speak of the Devil....'

She looked up to see the tall figure of Jerry Weinberg approaching them, a grin on his tanned, weatherbeaten face.

'Join you?' he asked.

'Sure,' she replied.

He sat down and rearranged the plates and cups on his tray.

'Don't let me interrupt you,' he said without looking up.

'No problem,' said Sinclair. 'We were just talking about Masters.'

'Hmm. He's hot all right.'

'Anne's about to eat her words.'

Weinberg looked up from his food and smiled as he chewed.

'You're going to eat shit, Anne?'

She liked Weinberg. The only man who could match her own acerbic wit.

'Sure, Weinberg. Watched you do it for long enough.'

He nodded, still smiling and taking a slurp of coffee.

'So, he's doing OK?' he asked.

'Seems like it,' said Sinclair. 'I got to see his second case. He's a good technician. Nice hands, good technique, precise method. Just right for a cardiac surgeon. I can't fault him in the OR.'

Weinberg looked up at his British colleague. 'Only in the OR?'

Sinclair shrugged. 'Can't comment on anything else.'

'What are you getting at, Weinberg?' asked Anne, interested.

'Oh, nothing. Just that ... well ... he is a bit brash, a bit pushy. I know you had your doubts at the interview, Anne, that came over loud and clear.'

'Yes, well, I still haven't made my mind up, it's too early. But so far, I can't fault him.'

'Me neither,' said Weinberg, 'especially since he got the one and a half big ones for his department.'

'Well, he's here to stay, I guess. I'm only too glad to be proven wrong.' Anne Bell looked up suddenly as Jerry Weinberg's knife and fork dropped noisily on to his plate.

'Excuse me,' he said, in mock apology, 'could you repeat that, Anne?'

She stood up, showed him her middle finger, and left, smiling.

It only took Tito a couple of days to reach the conclusion that Krome Detention Centre was a shithole. It was so bad he almost wished he had never left Cuba, uprooted his wife and child, taken them away from their home, subjected them to the sun, the sea, the sharks. The joy of their arrival at Miami Beach, of all places, was soon shattered by their transfer to the camp where they had been separated for a while, as the formalities of delousing, disinfecting and debriefing were completed. Eventually, they found each other again. Carmen never complained, never reproached him for bringing them there. He knew what she would be feeling. At least they had made it safe to the USA. Now they would share whatever fate might have in store for them. So long as they were together, nothing else mattered. He knew how she felt because he felt the same. But it didn't stop him wishing he could have given them something better, as one day merged into another, and they waited for news of what might become of them, the mere pawns in a bigger game being played between President Castro of beloved, wronged little Cuba and the other president of the most powerful nation on earth.

Since their arrival, they had seen daily consignments of more and more refugees, until the emergency capacity of the camp was met then exceeded. Some people got visitors from Cuban-American relatives already settled in Miami, bringing food, solace, hope. Others got visits from the authorities, usually with bad news of missing relatives who had left Cuba but never arrived on US soil. Every day brought news of empty rafts in the Florida Straits, as well as the overloaded ones intercepted by the US Coast Guard, their occupants taken back to the US naval base on Cuba at Guantanamo Bay. Rumour had it that some days there were more empty rafts than full ones. The food was awful. Plenty of it, but awful just the same. The washing facilities were designed for 500, adequate for 750, inadequate for the maximum of 1000, and inept for the current total of 1200.

During the third week, there was some excitement when a camera crew from New York arrived to film conditions in the camp.

They took some pictures, then left. The next day, they came back. This time, a group of men wandered amongst the inmates, looking, asking questions, taking notes. They stopped Tito that day, asked a few questions about him, then moved on. He wondered what it meant.

On the third day, the men and the cameras returned and filmed some more. The crowds gathered to watch. Tito took Carmen and Maria by the hand and pushed his way to the front, ignoring the annoyance of the others. He wanted to be near the action. He had things to say. He watched as the news team moved through the crowds, getting closer and closer to them, the cameraman following the producer's instructions, the front man alternately glancing at his notes, then smiling at the camera and delivering his commentary.

Closer and closer.

The producer saw them then, the tall young man with the handsome face, the pretty young wife by his side, the gorgeous little girl with the wide dark eyes holding his hand. He beckoned the team over, and the man from NBC approached them with the mike in his hand.

'Good morning sir,' he said, 'what is your name?'

'I am Humberto Juan Pereira from Havana. This is my wife Carmen, and my daughter Maria.'

'And what did you do in Havana?'

'I was a doctor. A doctor in the government service. And I have things in my belongings to demonstrate how corrupt and degraded a regime we have fled from. I can show you evidence, notes, documents. We had to flee, we all had to flee.'

The crowd around him murmured their agreement.

'Otherwise we would have perished. My name was already on a death list for speaking out against Castro, but I would not be silenced.'

The crowd cheered.

'How did you get here, Humberto?'

'On a raft, of planks and tyres.'

'How long did it take to get here?'

'Five days, I think.' He grinned. 'There were waves, and bad winds, and sharks. But nothing so bad as Castro's Cuba.'

The crowd laughed and cheered again.

'So you came here for freedom?'

'For freedom, and for Maria.'

He looked down at his beloved daughter.

'For Maria?'

The commentator indicated to the cameraman to pan to the child as he spoke.

'Yes. Maria has a hole in her heart. She gets weaker every year. Without help, she will not survive. Only your doctors can give her the chance she needs. You see, I had to come to your country, for my own life, and that of my wife, but also for the life of my child.'

He looked at the camera, and there was silence. The commentator was, for a moment, uncertain how to continue. Then, responding to the signs from the producer, he said, 'Well, we all wish you good luck, Humberto. This is Ed Berkeley for NBC at Krome Camp, Florida,' and the cameraman faded out for the commercials.

'That was great, just great,' said the producer enthusiastically. He was a lanky, dark-haired young man with thick black spectacles and an open-necked blue shirt and jeans.

'Humberto, come here,' he called, brushing his long hair off his forehead.

Tito looked at Carmen, then approached him.

'You can call me Tito,' he said.

The producer put his arm around him. 'Tito?'

'Yes. I have a brother also called Humberto, but I am the younger Humberto. So I am called Humbertito – *little Humberto* – Tito for short.'

'Well, Tito, you were just great back there. Now, what you said about evidence. Was that true?'

'Yes.'

'What sort of evidence?'

'Papers. A diary. Records of supplies, food, medicines, all diverted from the people to the black market or the dollar shops. And drugs, imported from Colombia and then sent on to Miami. And girls, for the SS.'

The producer was making notes as the commentator approached them. He smiled at Tito, holding out his hand. Tito shook it warmly.

'Thank you for giving me the chance to speak,' he said.

'You're welcome. You were just what we were looking for.'

Before Tito could ask what he meant, the producer spoke again.

'Can we see these documents? Use them?'

'Use them how?'

'On the programme. We're here all week. We could use them on tomorrow's show, make the corruption you have fled the lead story.'

'It's possible.'

The producer looked at the anchor man and back at Tito.

'Is there a problem?' he asked.

Tito shrugged. 'I have only one reason to be here. To give my family freedom, and my daughter life. Can you help with that?'

The producer sighed. 'I don't think I can spring you from this place if that's what you mean. Unless the authorities see you as important to their arguments with Castro. That might make it possible. But don't you want the chance to show your data, make your arguments?'

'Of course. But if we get sent back to Cuba, then my daughter will die. Me also, if they catch me. Especially if I show the documents.'

The producer nodded. 'I see,' he said, quietly, 'of course, you're right.'

He was silent for a moment.

'I guess it's your call, Tito. All I can say, is, this might be your only chance. Prime-time exposure on network TV. A lot of people will be watching. You might just get the break you're looking for. I'll certainly make sure the interview mentions Maria, and we'll get her in the picture, maybe fade out with her at the end. I'll have to see what you've got, but if it's newsworthy, I'm prepared to help. What do you think Ed?'

'I agree,' said the anchor. 'It's perfect. And one thing's certain, Tito, without this chance, you'll just stay an anonymous face in a big crowd.'

Tito nodded, knowing he was right.

'So let's see what you've got.'

CHAPTER 6

Gary Masters was living in a faculty house in Cambridge while he looked for more permanent and personal accommodation. It wasn't perfect, but it sufficed for the time being. He was just happy to be back home in Boston, throwing himself into his new job. Lester Pearson was working out his notice, and becoming more obviously tired and pale as the secondaries from his prostate cancer ate away at his bone marrow. Gary felt for the old man, who had been supportive and full of encouragement for his protégé, clearly delighted with his choice for heir to his kingdom. Gary gladly adopted the role of apprentice and let Lester wind down at his own pace knowing it would only be for a few weeks more.

Since the NIH had given him permission to start his project he had done three cases, and the grant was now secure. Of the three, Daniel O'Donaghue was within days of going home, Jennifer Pitt, a twenty-three-year-old student was back in her room from intensive care and beginning to mobilize, and Phil Peters, a twenty-year-old construction worker was in his third day in the ICU. Number four, Ludovico Palucci, a retired restaurateur, was in the line up scheduled for the next day or two. Now he needed to identify number five. The cases had to keep coming to justify the grant, get the research in print, crunch the numbers to the point of statistical respectability. Thirty should do it, and four in as many weeks was better than he could have dreamed of.

His new colleagues had been almost as supportive as Lester Pearson. Jerry Weinberg in particular had helped by having him over for dinner twice already with chosen staff and faculty members to help introduce him to the south Boston medical and university establishment. The paediatric surgeon, Paul Schering, was a little suspicious still, and he simply couldn't begin to fathom out Anne Bell, the ICU director. She was certainly good at her job, but she hadn't smiled at him or given him one extra word or second of her time since he had arrived. He didn't know if it was a professional thing – *respect had to be earned, not assumed* – or a woman thing. She was certainly attractive, a bit on the small side, but good figure, excellent features and complexion, and feisty – could be a real little raver on the right day, he thought. But he'd made a real jackass of himself after the first case, rushing into the ICU like a new intern after his first appendicectomy. Perhaps she just needed time to accept him as a doctor, before they became friends. Single too. Maybe she was just cautious of other single medics. He'd thought the fact that he himself was single might have come up at the interview. After all, some places want their chiefs of surgery to be a *couple*, the chief and *Mrs* – part of the old order to guarantee respectability for the post. *Dr and Mrs Respectable at the Winter Ball ... Mrs Respectable at the Cardiac Surgery Fundraising Tombola.* Too bad he was a loner. Just his style, always had been. At least UHSM had recognized and acknowledged his professional talents and skills and not bothered with all that bullshit. Unless they thought he was gay – and he was the Boston liberal establishment's obligatory gay professor of surgery....

He smiled.

Tell that to Kathryn Skiathos.

He still couldn't get her out of his head.

He had gone back to her Coconut Beach apartment that Thursday some weeks before as arranged, arriving at about 7 p.m. She opened the door wearing a loose bathrobe. Almost before he had closed it behind him she was in his arms, kissing him as she worked on his belt and zipper before sinking to her knees and taking him, bringing him up immediately and working on him until he pulled her up, stooped to enter her then lifted her up as she wrapped her legs around him and they satisfied their passionate, urgent desire for one another.

'I needed that,' she gasped eventually, as he let her down. She kissed him and pulled the robe around her before making for the living-room.

'Champagne?' she called without waiting for an answer.

He smiled, pulling up his pants.

'Sure,' he replied, doing up the zipper and following her.

A plate of smoked salmon and thinly sliced brown bread sat beside the ice bucket. She popped the cork as he sat down, and filled a glass, handing it to him before filling her own, dropping the bottle into the bucket and looking into his eyes.

'A toast?' she asked.

'Sure. To what?'

She looked at him questioningly, putting her left index finger between her lips, gently pushing it in and out then licking it. He felt the second erection rising. They stared at each other for a moment. He took a long gulp of the Bollinger, put his glass down and moved closer to her, slipping his hand under the robe to enter her, moving to stimulate her as she slid down the sofa on to her back with a groan while he kissed her neck, her breasts and her pubis, before searching for her and working on her with his tongue and his lips, as her back arched with a mixture of unbearable pleasure and pain. Just before she came he moved up to enter her, working furiously until they exploded together in a climax of mutual excitement. Ninety minutes later, they sat opposite each other at the dinner-table, sipping brandy and staring into each other's eyes.

'He's back tomorrow?' he asked, eventually.

She nodded slowly. 'When do you leave for Boston?' she asked.

'Two weeks. Will I see you again?'

She shook her head slowly. 'We leave for Athens, Monday. For a month.'

They continued looking at each other in silence, neither flinching from the gaze, both feeling the same intense emotions, both acknowledging the irresistible urge of their physical attraction, neither wanting the inevitable end to their new-found passion.

They made love for hours before falling asleep. He woke at four, wondering where he was, turning his head to see her staring at him, her olive dark eyes wide open.

She kissed him warmly, not with the usual urgent passion, but with a tenderness he had not previously felt, pressing her lips to him as if wanting him to understand an unspoken thought. Then she moved her mouth to his ear, and whispered, 'In the morning, just go. Say nothing. I want to remember it like it is now.'

Which is what he did. He woke at seven, moved gently out of

the bed so as not to waken her, dressed quietly, and left the apartment without a backward glance. Eventually he moved to Boston, got settled, worked like a dog, but thought of her every night when he climbed exhausted into bed. Since that kiss, and her warm, whispered message, he hadn't been able to get her out of his mind. She wasn't like the others. Usually he couldn't remember what they looked like, let alone their names. She was different.

He resisted the urge to call her for a whole month before he sat alone in his darkened apartment, the third glass of wine in his hand, as he called Directory Assistance.

'Area?'

'Miami, Coconut Beach.'

'Name?'

'Skiathos, Parthenon Apartments.'

After a pause, the ATT voice chanted, '305 732 9416.'

He dialled the number, his pulse racing. The phone just kept on ringing.

He took a shower and went to bed.

The next morning he flicked on the TV with the remote as he waited for the coffee to percolate. The familiar faces of Bryant Gumbell and Kate Couric hosting NBC's morning programme appeared then faded as the scene shifted to the Krome refugee camp for illegal immigrants.

'Fucking Cubans,' he muttered as he walked to the bathroom.

Taking over Florida, along with the Haitians, and the other spics and dagos. Everyone felt sorry for the refugees, but was it his problem? His country's problem? Was the USA supposed to look after anyone who arrived at its doors? Were his taxes meant for these people rather than their own poor and elderly? Last American out bring the flag. Was that the sick joke currently circulating around south Florida? It was the same in California with all the Mexicans drifting north. At least they had had the guts out West to pass Proposition 187, depriving the state's 1.8 million illegal immigrants of state benefits....

He filled the mug and sat on the sofa for a few minutes, flicking the channels until he got back to NBC.

'So, Tito, that is the evidence you have brought to confirm the corruption which exists in the Cuban administration?'

The handsome Cuban nodded.

'And why did you flee when you did?'

'I heard my name was on the death list.' He paused, then added, 'and I have to save my daughter.'

'Your daughter?'

The camera panned to Maria, standing beside him, looking wide-eyed at the camera.

'She has a hole in the heart. She is slowly dying. Only your great surgeons can save her. We had to come here.'

Gary sat up, suddenly interested. *A hole in the heart....*

'So, Tito, you fled from death in Cuba, braved the ocean, the sharks, the hurricanes, on a makeshift raft, to seek freedom here and to save your daughter?'

He nodded again, standing tall and proud, yet at the same time with an air of genuine humility.

Gary Masters watched for a few moments, mesmerized, before reaching for the telephone directory. He skipped through it till he found what he was looking for, picked up the phone, and punched in the numbers.

After a couple of rings, a voice answered, 'Hello, NBC-TV. How may I help you?'

'I'm not happy, Trudie.'

Trudie could see that. Anne Bell looked tired and pale. Her skirt and blouse were creased from a long night of work punctuated by short snatches of sleep on the chair in her office. She stood now at 6.30 a.m. in Bay 3 of the ICU staring down at Phil Peters as his respirator played out its lifegiving rhythm with a regular swish-thump … swish-thump … swish-thump.

It was the beginning of day four in the patient's post-operative status and the day on which he should have been moving out of the ICU and back to his room. Instead, after his oxygen saturation had fallen suddenly from 98% to 84%, and he had become acutely breathless, they had had no choice but to keep him on ICU, then intubate him and reconnect him to the respirator to push oxygen into his lungs. Now they stood before him, waiting for the lab to call back, Anne wondering whether or not to call Masters. She decided not to; he would be in in an hour anyway and she would have the results by then.

When they came, they didn't help. No bleeding, no heart attack, no pulmonary embolus, just some mysterious shortage of breath. She switched the oxygen up to 90%.

Masters arrived thirty minutes later. He looked at the patient, then at the results, before looking directly at Anne.

'So what the hell's going on?' he asked.

Before she could answer, Trudie pulled another print-out off the computer and handed it to her.

'Blood count and diff.'

Anne looked at it, Masters moving behind her to look over her shoulder.

'Raised count,' she said quietly, 'thirty-eight thousand.'

'Yes,' he said, 'and forty per cent lymphocytes, that's unusual.'

'Certainly is.' She turned to face him. 'Some strange infection? Rejection?'

'There are no other signs of either,' he replied. 'I don't know.'

He shrugged then said, 'I'm expected in the OR. You're doing all you can here. Keep me posted, won't you?'

'Of course,' she said, and watched him leave. She looked over at Trudie.

'I'm going for a shower, Trudie. Are you OK for a while?'

Trudie nodded, and Anne Bell walked wearily to the female changing quarters, still wondering what the hell was wrong with Phil Peters.

The NBC news crew was already setting up when he reached his office. His bemused secretary was making coffee and thinking that this sort of thing never used to happen with her previous boss. A good-looking young girl with a bleached-blonde ponytail and fresh complexion approached him, huge earphones hanging round her neck, notebook in hand.

'Doctor Masters?'

He nodded.

She breathed a sigh of relief. 'Thank God. Thought you'd gone AWOL. We're on live in ten minutes. I'm Jenny Kerr, production assistant.'

'Hi. No sweat. Just show me what you want me to do.'

She looked at him. 'You're cool,' she said, 'done this before?'

'No, but it's no problem.'

I suppose not, she thought, not after you've operated on someone's heart....

'OK,' she said, taking his arm, 'come over here and let's get a little make-up on you.'

She sat him down in a chair and another girl appeared from

nowhere, threw a sheet over his shoulders, and started working on his face with a massive powder puff, as Jenny Kerr kept talking.

'I want you to sit behind your desk, so we get the professional image. We'll hook into Krome, and into the New York studio, cutting to each as appropriate. As you talk, we'll zoom into you to get close ups. Just say what you want to say, keep it natural, we'll do the rest.' She pulled off the sheet and ushered him to sit behind the desk. She looked over her shoulder. 'Carl, how's it looking?'

The bearded cameraman in the faded jeans, T-shirt and scarlet sweatband continued chewing furiously, peering through his lens, waving a finger in the air, before looking over the camera at Gary and Jenny and grinning. 'It's cool.'

'OK, hit the lights, Carl, get ready, thirty seconds and counting. Gary, you OK?'

No one in the room looked cooler than Gary Masters.

She put on her headphones and looked at the monitor. Bryant Gumbel gave way to Krome Camp and he greeted the local reporter.

'Hi, Ed.'

'Bryant, this is Ed Berkeley at Krome Camp, Florida. I have here the family you met yesterday, Dr Tito Pereira, his wife Carmen and their daughter Maria. Maria is the little girl with the heart defect who braved the Florida Straits with her parents to seek refuge and treatment here in the US.'

The picture split to include Bryant Gumbel in New York.

'Well, Ed, I have a surprise for you and the Pereira family down there. Jenny Kerr, you there in Boston?'

The picture split into three to include Jenny Kerr, microphone in hand, standing in front of Gary Masters' desk.

'I'm here, Bryant, and I'm in the office of Professor Gary Masters, chief of cardiac surgery at the University Hospital of Southern Massachusetts. I believe Dr Masters has some news for Dr Pereira.'

The camera slowly zoomed towards Gary, his image alone filling the screen. He played it like Cary Grant.

'Yes. Dr Pereira, I believe Maria has a heart defect, and that one of the reasons you needed to come to the US was to seek help for her. I would like to offer my services to you and your family. If the immigration authorities will permit it, I will admit

Maria here for tests, evaluate her case and, if the tests support it, perform the surgery here in Boston for no fee.'

The screen split into three again and Bryant Gumbel spoke.

'Well, Tito, what do you make of that?'

Tito Pereira stared unspeaking into the screen, his mouth slowly opening, no sound coming. He looked at Ed Berkeley, then back at the screen. The reporter took his arm, breaking the spell, and said, 'Tito, did you hear that?'

Tito looked at him, then back at the camera, and said, 'Yes. I heard. Doctor … er....'

'Masters,' said Ed.

'Masters. Thank you, sir. Thank you for your offer. We knew everything would be all right if we got here. We knew. Thank you, thank you.'

The picture cut to Bryant Gumbell.

'Professor Masters, is this offer within your power? Can you deliver on this?'

'Of course. This is my department, my unit. I'll need to clear things with Admin, but I'm sure they will come up with the hotel and other fees, and I know my team here will be only too happy to help little Maria in every way we can. I hope the immigration authorities will recognize the urgency and humanitarian importance of this offer.'

Case number five, he thought to himself. With mega-publicity.

The camera showed Tito and his family again, then faded to the New York studio before splitting to include Gary Masters.

'Well, I'd like to thank you, Professor Masters, for your generous offer. We'll be following this story real close, and doing everything we can to help that beautiful family. Do you have anything else to add?'

'No sir. I'm here, we're ready, let's do it for the little girl.'

'Thank you sir,' said Bryant, turning to face the camera. 'We'll be back after a station break.'

Jenny Kerr almost ripped the headphones from his ears. 'Great! Great, Doc. Just great! You're a natural!' She beamed at everyone in the office. 'Now that's live TV. What do you think, Carl?'

'It was cool, baby, real cool,' chewed the cameraman, packing up his gear, and swinging the camera on to his shoulder as if it was a Winchester '73.

They left, Jenny talking animatedly, Carl chewing noncha-
lantly. Gary looked at his secretary, who looked back at him
seriously before they both burst out laughing.

'Cool, Professor.'

'Now that's live TV,' he responded as the phone started to
ring. His secretary picked it up, and looked over at him.

'It's Doctor Weinberg for you.'

He took the receiver from her.

'Hi, Jerry. How can I help you?'

'Gary, can I come down there and talk with you for a few
minutes?'

'Sure. I have a case scheduled for nine-thirty.'

'This won't take long.'

Jerry walked into the office within three minutes. Gary rose
from the desk and walked towards him.

'Hi, Jerry. How's it going?'

'Good Gary. Just caught your TV slot.'

'Oh yes? What did you think?'

Jerry looked down at him, from his six inch height
advantage. 'Maybe you should have cleared it with someone
first?'

Gary looked surprised.

'There was no time.'

'No time.'

'I spoke with NBC yesterday. They wanted the piece
immediately.'

'Gary, you can't just go round offering illegal immigrants in a
Florida holding camp free cardiac surgery here in Boston
without clearing it. I mean, who pays?'

'The OR time and consumables will come out of my research
funds. My fee is waived. I'm sure the hospital can find it in its
heart to waive the day-to-day accommodation and housekeep-
ing costs.'

'Oh yes? And the drug bill, the post-op time, ICU expenses,
further costs if complications ensue?'

'Those will be offset by the PR advantage. Hell, Jerry, think of
the publicity for the hospital, the unit, the research. This is
high-profile stuff. This is a gimmick if you like, but nonetheless,
something that propels a department into the public eye.'

'Gary, we don't need this kind of publicity. It will stir up a
hornet's nest. They're illegal immigrants. You want to have

them released, operate on the child, let the parents go free, and have the state pick up their tab. Are you serious?'

'Oh, come on Jerry.' Gary was getting exasperated. 'This family fled oppression in Cuba. On a raft, for Christ's sake. If Bill Clinton hadn't changed the status of Cuban immigrants on a whim because the Governor of Florida was panicking, this family would have become US citizens the moment their feet touched US soil. They got here a day late.'

'And that qualifies them for treatment here?'

'Why not? I'll fly them up, do the tests, operate for free and pick up the operating costs. All the hospital has to find is some accommodation for the parents and the extra expenses. In return for the PR.'

'You should have discussed it first. What happens when the people here see what you're doing and say, *hey, man, free surgery? Yeah. Me too. Where's the line up?* then find out this service is only available for illegal immigrants, not indigenous Americans? Like I said, you should have talked it over.'

'With who?'

'The CEO and myself.'

'Oh, sure. And he would have agreed?'

Jerry was silent for a moment. Part of him wanted to slap Gary on the back, and say *good for you, boy. Just do it. Go out and get it organized. Fuck the administrators. Cure the kid, get the publicity, build your department and its reputation.* The other side of him saw the problems such maverick behaviour landed on the directorate desk.

'Look Gary, this one's launched. We can't call it back now. All I'm saying is you've had my support since the day you started. We want you to succeed here. Don't go and screw it up by going off on a one-man crusade and shitting on everyone else in the process.'

'Sure, Jerry, sure. Now who do we talk to in Admin to sort out immigration?'

Weinberg knew there was no point berating him further. He left, saying he would sort it out, and made for the chief executive's office. He found David Meeson pacing the floor, hands deep in pockets, an exasperated look on his face.

'Holy shit, Jerry,' he said immediately, 'what the fuck's going on in cardiac surgery? I've just had Washington, *Washington,*' he repeated as if to emphasize the enormity of the matter, 'on the phone, wanting to know who authorized this hospital to operate on an illegal immigrant's kid from Cuba. My ears are bursting – creating precedents ... regulations ... legal ramifications....'

Jerry held up his hands to silence him.

'You said you wanted a high-profile, energetic, thrusting young surgeon to put this place on the map, David. Looks like you got what you asked for. Can't get higher profile than the Today programme.'

'This isn't funny, Weinberg.'

'I know. I've already spoken to Masters. He's determined to see the kid and if she's suitable to fund the surgery from his research grant. I know it's irregular David, and I know he went about it the wrong way, but think of the positive PR for the hospital. And the Administration, for that matter. With all the bad feeling going on between them and the Cuban community, this could help sweeten things a little.'

The administrator moved behind his desk and sat down, still fuming, but listening to the surgeon.

'What will it cost us?'

'Accommodation charges, if all goes well.'

'What do you mean?'

'If it goes smoothly, without complications, we'll have to meet the costs of the child being here, and probably have to find somewhere close by for the parents. Once they're discharged, it will be for the state or the government to sort them out. If there are problems, there could be ICU charges, a longer hospital stay, unexpected drug charges....'

Meeson ran his hand over his smoothly shaven chin, then looked up at Weinberg.

'What do you think we should do?'

'I think we should go with him. He's gone about it the wrong way, but he has the skill and the technique to cure the child. It could bring this hospital into the national, even international forum. I think it's a golden opportunity.'

'But what if it goes wrong? What if the kid dies?'

He looked up at the tall surgeon with a look of anguish on his face, as if seeing himself facing the world's Press on the steps of the hospital to tell them the worst possible news.

'That's the risk, David. That's surgery. And if we pull out now when it's already gone public, Mass. General, or Cornell, or Montefiore could snap up the chance and make us look like chumps. Only they don't have Gary Masters. If we handle it right, get the Administration's co-operation, muster support from the Cuban community, it could be a really good medical coup for Gary and the hospital.'

The administrator relaxed a little, seeing some of the positive aspects of the mess the new professor of surgery had landed him in.

'OK, Jerry. I'll get back to Washington and say we're serious about this. No doubt Gary will be on the seven o'clock news, the ten o'clock news, Today tomorrow, tomorrow today, until the media and public opinion make the scheme irresistible....'

He reached for the phone and Jerry Weinberg left, smiling quietly to himself.

In the ICU, Anne Bell worked on Phil Peters.

She checked his bloods, altered the respirator, fine tuned the intravenous infusion, repeated his chest x-ray and ultrasound scans, got neurology to check his brain status, repeated the bloods, and watched helplessly as his white cell count went up through 62,000, his blood oxygen saturation dropped through 84%, 80%, 75% to 66%, as his pupils became fixed and dilated and he slipped into irreversible brain death.

She called the operating suite. They told her Gary Masters was busy. She told them to make sure he got back to them as soon as possible. She put the phone back on the hook and slumped on to the desk, her head in her arms, asking why? What did I miss? What did I do wrong?

Later that evening, Gary Masters sat in front of the TV set, whiskey glass in hand staring at the screen, seeing only the image of the attendant leaving the ward with the body of Phil Peters hidden in the mortuary trolley, removing him from the area of the living to the room of death to await his post-mortem. He too went over the operation in his mind, wondering where he had gone wrong, questioning his technique, his performance, his aptitude, before coming to the conclusion that nothing he had done in the operating room could have been responsible for his patient's death. What killed Phil Peters happened after his operation, during his recovery in ICU. He would find out what it was, whatever it took. And who was responsible. He had done a good job, and someone, somewhere, had screwed up and let him and his patient down. His depression was already shifting a gear towards anger when the phone rang, interrupting his thoughts.

'Yes?' he barked.

'Dr Masters?'

The voice sounded familiar.

'Yes?'

'This is Kathryn Skiathos. I need your help.'

CHAPTER 7

Kathryn Skiathos was not used to asking for help. A deprived childhood in the backstreets of Athens had taught her the rules of survival. If your father beat you, and abused you, your mother and your sisters, if you starved unless you begged on the streets, if your future looked like your past and there seemed little hope, then you had two choices: accept it, or change it. She chose the latter. Before she was fifteen she had run away from home, scraped, scrimped and sold her best assets in downtown Athens for money until she made enough to advance herself up the hooker's career ladder. Eventually her spectacular looks, self-confidence and ambition took her out of the call-girl circles and through more respectable hostess assignments into the circles she had always coveted.

Circles which included Anthony Skiathos.

He was a well-known figure in Athens and beyond, with his international shipping and business interests, a regular in all the best places and, more importantly from her perspective, recently divorced from his second wife. From the first time she saw him in the tabloids, she had him targeted. No matter that he was twenty years her senior, grossly overweight, and heading for his second heart attack. So what? He was a true fat cat, and a part share of his billion drachmas would do her fine. So she followed her destiny, working double shifts to buy the right clothes, using the right people to get her into the right crowd, making sure she was at as many functions as possible which Anthony Skiathos was listed to attend.

It was only a matter of time before he noticed her.

It was at a New Year's Eve gala ball of the Royal Hellenic Yacht Club. She went with a junior government minister she had been cultivating solely for the purpose of getting to the ball. A dork, but a useful dork nonetheless. Once there, before dinner, she made sure she was always within sight of her quarry, occasionally catching his eye and smiling in his direction. Five minutes before dinner was announced, she knew she had him. Two groups were monopolizing the reception area, his, with the hangers-on, the fawners, the parasites, and hers, with the tryers, the roués, the guys who saw her as a spectacular lay, tailor made for them....

Some hope.

But when he looked across at her, thinking she looked familiar somehow, exactly as he was supposed to after all her efforts to be at the same functions as him for the past three months, she saw the look in his eye and she hooked him as deftly as the most expert deep sea fisherman. The smile, the direct look into his eyes, followed by the transient bashful downward glance to let him feel he had the upper hand before looking up directly at him again with a look that said *take me any time – I'm yours* – had the desired effect. All through dinner, she saw him watching her from two tables away, occasionally acknowledging with glances to let him know she understood, know they were sharing a common feeling, possibly the start of something. She sensed the excitement of the chase, and knew he was feeling the same. It was only two days before the telephone call, two weeks before their first date, two months before they became acknowledged as an entity in the gossip columns. They married, amidst international media attention, on a beach in Kos.

The marriage was never consummated.

She didn't know he was impotent when they married. After the initial shock she didn't really care. In some ways, it was a relief. She was disappointed but not devastated. She had caught her meal ticket for life. She could at least show him some understanding. So they loved each other in different ways, as he took pride in showing her off to society, and she demonstrated to the world that Kathryn Skiathos had arrived, and that the rich powerful man beside her had the most beautiful woman in the world on his arm.

She never enquired about his business and he never discussed it with her. She wasn't interested. All she cared about was keeping him happy, whether it was in their Athens home, their Nea Makri villa, or their Miami apartment. She especially enjoyed the Miami visits. Anthony had a lot of business there, and used it as a base to travel across the USA and down to South America, leaving her alone to enjoy the city. And the occasional, very occasional, man. But never anyone like Gary Masters. No one, *no one*, had ever been back to the apartment even once, never mind twice. It would be too risky. Until him. She just hadn't been able to resist it the first time, and then she had to have him for one more night. And it had been worth the risk. Well worth the risk. It had probably been the best night of her entire life. But now, events had intervened, unexpected problems had forced themselves upon her, and she didn't know how to deal with them. She was confused, frightened, and the irony of the situation was not lost on her, yet as soon as she realized what she had to do, there was no hesitation. So she called him, not as a lover, not as a friend, but as a woman wanting a favour from the only person in the world she knew had the means to help her. The rest would follow. For now, only one thing mattered.

So she dialled the number, heard his voice, that beautiful deep voice, swallowed hard, and said simply, 'This is Kathryn Skiathos. I need your help.'

Anne Bell needed help too. Ludovico Palucci was only twelve hours out of surgery but already he was behaving irrationally on the respirator. Patients coming out of heart surgery, or any surgery for that matter, were controlled totally by the ICU system. Their breathing was passive, dictated by the respirator. Their blood composition, oxygen levels, electrolyte balance, were all controlled by the intravenous infusions. Their blood pressure was monitored and manipulated by drugs to keep it just right ... the patient was no longer anaesthetized, but was in suspended animation, like a 747 being taken gently from cruising height on automatic pilot, to begin its long, slow descent and landing. And just like the 747 pilots, the ICU specialists watched the monitors, checked the data, corrected for variations, kept the patient on an even keel until they were extubated, conscious, alert, and ready to leave their care. If the ICU had been the cockpit of a 747 at this moment, there would have been a considerable degree of concern.

'Melanie, are those gases back yet?'

The nurse looked up from the computer screen behind the nursing station.

'No, not yet.'

'Well call the lab and tell them to get them to us stat.'

Anne Bell looked up at the monitors on the wall over the patient's bed, talking quietly to herself.

'BP one hundred over sixty, pulse ninety-eight per minute. Is he bleeding? Nothing in the drains. Is it a pneumothorax – air in the pleural cavity instead of the lungs, compressing them and starving them of oxygen? Good breath sounds, normal air entry, normal chest x-ray. Has he had a heart attack? Normal ECG.

'Trudie – page Dr Masters, make it a five five five,' – the most urgent call.

He was there within five minutes.

'What is it?' he asked breathlessly.

'I'm not happy. His obs are all wrong and I can't find an ICU explanation. Would you go over him, see if there's a surgical explanation before I start the ICU protocol?'

Gary walked into the cubicle, looked down at the patient to get a general impression of his condition, then felt his pulse, looking at the monitor, before taking his blood pressure and again looking at the monitor. His own readings matched those of the hi-tech. Pulse 100 per minute, blood pressure, 90/60. He put the stethoscope on the patient's heart and listened.

Thubb ... dupp. Thubb ... dupp. Thubb ... dupp.

The classic heart sounds, just as one would teach them to students. No added sounds. No murmurs. Just *thubb ... dupp*.

He listened to the chest. Inspiration, expiration, pause. Inspiration, expiration, pause. NAD. No abnormality detected.

He checked the drains. Nil drainage. He checked the urinary catheter. Excellent output. He looked at the lab tests – haematology, biochemistry, pathology – normal. He looked at the ECG – normal.

He walked back into Anne Bell's office.

'Nothing,' he said, 'I don't know what's wrong. I'll get a Doppler scan and an angio if that's normal.'

She nodded, relieved that she'd not missed anything. He turned to leave, then called out, as an afterthought, 'By the way, he's got temporal arteritis; we gave him an extra dose of steroids with the pre-med; give him an extra dose with the next drug round. And call me if there's any change in his condition.'

He walked away from the ICU towards his office, deep in

thought. Another problem. Four patients, one dead, two OK, one getting sick. What if this one died too? Christ! Even in cardiac surgery you can't go round with a 50% mortality rate. It was irrelevant that he had done seven CABGs – coronary artery by-pass grafts – cabbages as they called them for short – and three valve replacements as well as the four trial cases, and they had all done fine. That was the bread and butter stuff, and he was a good surgeon. No, it was the trial patients everyone was watching and upon which he would be judged. So what was going wrong? He had done a good job on Phil Peters, but now he was on his way to a meeting with his tearful parents to explain what every surgeon hated trying to explain – the operation was a success but the patient died. And so it happened. And five minutes later they wanted to know why.

'You told us everything had gone well.'

'It did.'

'That the surgery had worked.'

'It had.'

'But he died.'

'The cause of death had not been identified yet, even at autopsy, but the post-mortem did show that the graft was intact.'

'So why did he die?'

'We just don't know.'

'You said this is a new technique.'

'It is, but it's been fully evaluated in animal experiments, and Phil was the third one. The other two are alive and well.' He didn't mention the fourth....

'Was there an alternative procedure available for Phil?'

'No, the defect was too large, that's why he was getting worse.'

'What would have happened if he hadn't had surgery?'

'He might have had three to five years. No more.'

Logic exhausted, emotion and grief inevitably reasserted themselves.

'Poor Phil ... my poor baby ...' and the tears began to flow.

That was when he sat there, watching Mom's shoulders shaking, as Pop's comforting arm went around her, his eyes moistening also, Gary feeling like he wanted to hug them both, cry with them, tell them he knew how they felt, for he felt the same way; they had lost a son, he had lost a patient, and a trial case....

But he sat there, leaning forward slightly towards them, his hands clasped together on knees, waiting for the emotion to subside a little before saying, 'Phil knew the risks, Mrs Peters. He was a brave boy. He wanted to have a normal life, but he saw his chances ebbing away as he lost his job, lost his energy, had the attacks of breathlessness. We had one chance, and we took it together. I'm only sorry, very sorry, that he didn't make it. We did our best.'

Pop nodded slowly, as if understanding. Mom just continued weeping. Her baby was dead, and no words were going to bring him back, especially words from the man who had taken him away.

Gary stood up. 'If there's anything else I can do ...?'

Pop shook his head slowly. He tried to smile but his face just collapsed into a crooked grimace. Gary left.

God, how he hated these interviews. But the question still remained. Why did Phil Peters die? Was there something wrong with his technique? Or was there a problem with the ICU? Now Ludovico Palucci was showing signs of distress also. Were they going to be able to sort it out, or was he going to die too?

50% mortality rate.

He continued walking to his office, his thoughts racing, an empty feeling in his stomach. He sat at his desk, picked up the phone and called radiology.

'I need an urgent, and I mean urgent, Doppler on a patient in ICU – Mr Palucci. Call me with the result when it's ready please. Dr Masters, extension 5484.'

He put the phone down. It rang immediately.

'Yes?' he barked.

'Dr Masters, it's Helen.' His secretary sounded surprised at his tone of voice.

'Yes, Helen?'

'Mrs Skiathos has arrived. Shall I show her in?'

Mrs Skiathos. Kathryn! How could he have forgotten?

'Of course, Helen.'

He walked over to the wall mirror and checked his tie, combed his hair, turning abruptly as he heard the door open, aware that his heart was thumping.

'Mrs Skiathos, Doctor.'

His secretary paused as Kathryn walked past her into the

room. She stood before him as they waited for Helen to leave the room, facing each other even after the door had closed.

She was dressed entirely in black except for the emerald green silk scarf tied loosely around her neck. The double-breasted jacket gave her a formal look, countered by the tight pleated short skirt, short enough to show off her perfect tanned thighs. He wanted to rush to her, hold her in his arms, take her there and then.

Her polished leather shoes clicked on the pine floor as she moved towards his desk, and sat, uninvited.

He watched her for a moment, surprised, expecting something different, something more, before he moved to the other side of the desk to sit, facing her.

He cleared his throat, hiding his confusion, and said, 'Can I get you something? Coffee?'

'Yes please.'

He pressed the intercom. 'Helen – coffee please, two, black, no sugar.'

He knew how she liked it.

'How are you?' he asked.

'I've been better. You?'

'Not bad.' Been better too, he thought, like when I was with you.

'You have settled in?'

'Yes.'

Silence. Then, 'You said you needed help.'

'I do. It's Tony....'

They paused as Helen brought in the tray, laid it on the table, then left with a backward glance at the elegant dark woman sitting in her chief's office.

She took a sip of her coffee, put the cup back on the saucer, and sat back, crossing her long legs, and looking at him with her black eyes.

'It's Tony,' she repeated.

Anthony Skiathos. Her husband.

He waited for her to continue.

She took a deep breath, her breasts rising beneath the black silk, her wonderful cleavage reminding him of another time, another place.

'We went to Athens as we had planned. I went to the villa at Nea Makri. Tony had business, important business, in the city.'

She paused for a moment, then continued, her voice quiet. 'Dangerous business, with dangerous men. One of these men didn't like Tony's suggestions and, apparently, he decided to make his point. He stabbed Tony in the heart.'

Gary sat forward, intrigued.

'He was taken to an emergency department, then to a private facility where he could get the best possible care. They took him straight to the operating room. Later the surgeon spoke to me. He told me he wouldn't last the night. The stiletto had pierced the heart itself. They had had to try the best they could to repair it. He needed six hours' surgery and twenty-seven pints of blood before he got back to intensive care. Even then they expected him to die. They didn't know Tony.'

He felt almost jealous as she spoke of him, yet she said it without affection.

'He recovered well, eating and drinking again within three days, never showing signs of pain, laughing, joking with everyone, complimenting the doctors and nurses. Until the second week. Then he started to get breathless, had attacks of blueness, gasping for air, needing oxygen at times. They did some tests but they were negative. I think they thought he had a clot of blood on the lung or something. Anyway, the cardiologist eventually did a … Doppler and an … angio – I think those are the terms – and told me he had a weakness, a bulge, in the heart, which might rupture at any moment.'

'Did he have a medical name for this bulge?'

'Yes, but I can't remember it.'

'Was it an aneurysm?'

'Yes. That's right. An aneurysm.'

'So what was his advice?'

'He said there was nothing he could do.'

'So what did you do?'

'I chartered a 747 and flew him to the Miami Cardiac Institute.'

'Dr Rodriguez?' His old chief in Miami.

She nodded.

'And?'

'He ran his own tests, then confirmed the diagnosis. He said he needed a transplant, but that there was no guarantee that a donor could be found in time.'

She paused, watching his reactions, then added quietly, 'Then he said there was only one other possibility.'

'Yes?'

'He said there was a doctor, working in Boston, who had pioneered a new technique which might just save Tony. That his name was Dr Gary Masters, and that he would call him tomorrow after the next Doppler. I decided to come and speak to this doctor myself.'

They sat facing each other in silence. Eventually he said, 'How is he now?'

'Breathless, on oxygen a lot of the time.'

'Is he fit to travel?'

'I don't know. But if he must come to Boston for surgery, then he must travel. I still have the 747 on standby.'

'Unless I come to Miami, do it there.'

'Is this possible?'

'I don't know. If I can operate, I'd prefer to do it here. But if he's not fit to travel....'

He was thinking only of the case now, the professional considerations, the surgical practicalities.

'I'll have to come down and see him for myself. There's no other way. I'll bring the equipment down with me, so that if he's not fit to come up here I can get on with it there.'

'Then you'll help him?' she asked quietly.

'Of course.'

He looked into her black eyes again, feeling an irresistible urge to get up, move around the table to her, take her in his arms, in spite of the fact that they were discussing his role in performing life-saving surgery on her husband. He was about to get up when the door burst open and a tall, balding, well-built man walked in, looked around the room, saw Kathryn and walked towards them.

'Mrs Skiathos, I'm sorry ...'

'It's all right, Menos, everything's all right. This is Dr Masters. He's going to help us.'

Gary watched the big man approach Kathryn and take her hand in a protective manner, as he looked across at him with the air of a professional assassin making a deadly judgement before looking back at her.

'Good. That is good,' he said, looking back again at Gary.

Masters watched the newcomer's performance, and remembered her words.

Dangerous business ... with dangerous men ... he stabbed Tony in the heart ... business in Miami and South America....

He felt the perspiration prickle on his brow, like it did sometimes during surgery when something unexpected occurred, when he knew there was trouble ahead before anyone else in the room had a clue, and he tried not to believe what he was thinking.

Menos walked towards him, held out his hand, and said, 'I am Menos Stafanopoulos, Mr Skiathos's business manager. I would like to thank you for what you are doing for my boss, Doctor. I can assure you we will be very grateful if you can get him through this crisis.'

His mouth smiled, but Gary looked straight into his eyes, and the eyes were not smiling.

'I'll do my best,' he said, a small part of him wondering if he really meant it.

On the waterfront, a half-mile away from the lights of Bayfront, the thin man leaned against a wall in the darkness, finishing off the cheap cheroot. His white suit was grubby from the journey, but he was glad to have made it into Miami without difficulty and to have found the lodgings which had been arranged for him. A movement caught his eye and he watched the water rat climb over the dockside and search furtively for scraps of food before disappearing again over the side of the dock.

The thin man smiled, and reached slowly down towards his right ankle. After a few seconds, the rat reappeared and, more confident this time, searched a little further afield before disappearing again. The thin man's arm moved slowly up from his leg as he waited, motionless, in the dark. Within a minute, the rat was back, searching for food, this time finding the scraps he wanted, sitting on its haunches like a squirrel, nibbling the rancid meat. The thin man's arm moved swiftly. The rodent looked up suddenly, seeing the glint of movement, but was too slow for the flying steel, as the knife went through its heart and pinned it to the wooden dockside in a grotesque posture of crucifixion. The thin man smiled and took a last deep inhalation of the cigar, before flicking it into the dirty water. He walked up to the dead rodent and retrieved his knife, wiping the blade on a piece of litter and replacing it in the ankle sheath. He looked down at the rat, 'You are dead, *hombre*,' he said quietly, then placed the toe of his grubby black shoe against it and kicked it into the dirty water.

'Dead,' he added, then walked slowly away.

CHAPTER 8

The restaurant was already full when Anne Bell arrived. She paused at the entrance to wait to be seated, but spotted Siobhan O'Connor almost immediately and made her way to the table. Siobhan stood up as she approached.

'Hi,' said Anne. 'And sit down, you don't have to be formal for me. Not late am I?'

'No, I was early.'

Siobhan O'Connor was a tall, elegant woman in her mid-thirties with long auburn hair falling loosely on her shoulders, and green eyes which sparkled like the emerald pendant around her neck. There could not have been more of a contrast with five foot four inches Anne Bell with her sparkling blue eyes and short blonde hair. The two of them had met when Siobhan had been to some hospital functions with James Sinclair, and they had made a date to meet for dinner some weeks before.

'So how's the legal business?' asked Anne, taking her seat.

'Booming,' Siobhan replied in her English accent. It was her first year in Boston, working on international law with a major firm of attorneys in Copley Square. 'What about intensive care?'

'Very intensive at the moment.'

The waiter appeared with the menus.

'Cocktail, ma'am?'

Anne looked at Siobhan's glass. 'Chardonnay?' she asked.

Siobhan nodded.

'Same for me please.'

The waiter moved off.

'So why so intensive?'

'We had a death a few days ago, an unexpected and so far unexplained death in a very special case who had had a new kind of operation. We see a lot of death on ICU, but either we're expecting it, or at least we know why it happened. In this case, we don't know either. And now, another of the patients is showing the same signs.'

'Hmm. That's not so good.'

They ate dinner, the conversation easy. Eventually, Anne asked, 'So why Boston, Siobhan? Promotion? Prospects not so great in the UK?'

'All those,' she replied then, after a pause, 'and a boyfriend who loved me so much he wrapped his car around a tree and died on me.'

'Oh, I'm sorry, I didn't mean to pry.' Anne Bell was embarrassed.

Siobhan smiled. 'It's OK,' she said. 'At least I can talk about it now. It was awful at the time, and pretty bad for a few weeks after I got here. James Sinclair's been a great help.'

'Yes, he's a good guy. In fact, him and Jerry Weinberg, the other urologist, are two of the nicest people at UHSM. Did you know Jim back in England?'

'A little.' She didn't elaborate, or tell her friend that she had known him pretty well – had, in fact, defended him in the High Court against a vicious accusation of serious professional misconduct and attempted rape, a court case which had all but wrecked his marriage and precipitated his emigration to the USA. As well as propelling Siobhan even higher in the pecking order of renowned defence attorneys. 'Just good friends,' she added. 'So how did you get into intensive care?'

Anne took a sip of wine and smiled. 'Long story,' she said. 'I was a l'il ole farm girl back in Idaho, you know.'

'Oh, how lovely. You grew up on a farm?'

'Well, not anything like your picturesque green English pastures. It was a potato farm mainly. Even so, the folks were pretty pleased when I got into Boise College to study nursing.' She looked into the golden Chardonnay, and focused on its colour, remembering....

She had qualified as a nurse, to the delight of her parents, and taken a job on the children's ward at the city hospital. She enjoyed it at first, but soon became tired of the repetitive nature of the work, the bureaucracy, the paperwork which took her away from the patients. After seven months, she was bored stiff. One day, she spoke to one of the attending physicians about her chances of getting into med. school. She had expected a rebuff, and was surprised when he had sat her down in the coffee room and told her there was every chance.

'You're a bright girl, Anne. Most medical schools set aside a certain number of places for mature students with other degrees, and people like dentists, physios, nurses, who want a career change and are serious about it. You just have to fill out the forms, send in your CV, take the entrance exams and go for the interview. Why don't I get you the forms from my old college at Stanford?'

Stanford University, San Francisco. She couldn't believe it when the forms arrived. Not that she had much to put on them, her c.v. must have been the thinnest in the entire USA. *Farm girl, nurse*, that was about it.

She left the form in her bottom drawer.

The following week she was on the night shift when the intern turned up at 6 a.m. to do the chemo round. She followed him from room to room with the drug trolley. In the fourth room he said, 'Vinblastine a hundred thousand units. Draw it up please.'

She looked at him as he bent over the child, checking the i.v. line, smiling reassuringly.

He turned to Anne. 'Well, is it ready?'

'No,' she whispered, 'look, do you really mean a hundred thousand units?'

'Of course. Draw it up immediately.'

She moved slightly to put herself between the doctor and child.

'Are you sure you don't mean ten thousand units? That's what the intern gave yesterday.'

'Are you questioning my orders, Nurse? Just do what I say, will you?'

'Only if you check the chart first.'

'Then I'll do it myself,' he said, making for the drug trolley.

She slammed the lid shut, pulled out the key, and put it in her pocket, standing defiantly before him.

'Not till you check the chart,' she said, you jumped up, fucking jerk, she thought.

They stood facing each other, until he grabbed the chart from the top of the trolley, flipped through the pages till he found room four, looked down the regime then blanched before blushing. She was already opening the trolley and reaching for the syringe.

She handed it to him without comment, and he turned to inject it into the cannula as the little girl continued watching the TV. It was not her first course of chemo.

The round ended. She was clearing up in the clean utility room when the intern appeared. She turned, eager to accept his apology, glad to have helped him avoid a serious error.

'Nurse Bell,' he said coldly, 'don't you ever, *ever* humiliate a doctor like that again, or question his orders. You're lucky I don't report you. You just remember your place here, Nurse.' He almost spat the word, before turning and storming out.

She stood, rooted to the spot, furious, trembling with rage. But she knew there was nothing she could do. It would be his word against hers. And he had given the correct dose. Thanks to her. He would deny the entire episode. She would be accused of questioning his competence. Someone would probably say she must fancy him, been jilted by him, or some such bullshit.

That morning, she sealed the envelope and mailed the application form to Stanford. Two months later she took the entrance exam. Within six weeks she was heading home to tell her parents she was going to medical school to try to become a doctor.

'Wow,' said Siobhan, 'some story. So how did you make it through to head of ICU?'

Anne smiled. 'Oh, that's another tale.' She looked for the waiter and, catching his eye, indicated for the check by writing an imaginary signature with her right index finger on her left hand.

'Now, my treat. OK? That way we have to do it again so that you can treat me.'

Siobhan smiled.

'Sounds good to me,' she said.

It had rained solidly over most of southern Florida for thirty-six hours, and Krome camp was even more intolerable than ever. As day followed day, Tito Pereira became more and more disconsolate. So when a guard appeared at the door to their hut and shouted 'Pereira, visitors' room, Tito Pereira,' he jumped up with hope and anticipation.

'Who could it be Tito? Doctor Masters?'

'No Carmen, he will not come here, he is a busy heart surgeon. It could be the immigration people, though, maybe to tell us yes ... or no.'

'Don't be negative, Tito. We will be all right. I know it. I've known it since we reached Miami.'

He shrugged and made for the door. Since the TV interview and the offer from the Boston cardiac surgeon, they had heard nothing. Perhaps it had just been a trick by the NBC crew, just to get a story, to see his documents. But to be fair, they had promised nothing, only said they would do what they could. So he didn't know what to expect when he followed the surly guard across the muddy compound to the visitors' building. The Kind American was the last person he expected to see waiting for him.

He was a big man with close-cropped, steely-grey hair over a weatherbeaten tanned face. He stood up from the chair and held his hand out across the wooden table.

'Hello, son,' he said, 'how're they treating you?'

Tito shook hands with him. 'What are you doing here, sir?'

They sat, facing each other.

'Well, Tito, I saw you on TV the other day. Ethel and me were sitting there half watching Today while we ate breakfast then Ethel shouted JT, JT, look quick, it's Tito, and Carmen, and it sure as hell was, the two of you, and little Maria. She OK?' Tito nodded.

'Well, as soon as the interview was over, Ethel went and packed some things for you – food, clothes, things for the youngster.' He leaned his head to indicate the suitcase on the floor. 'It's been OK'd with the authorities here. You ... you don't mind? You'll take it?'

Tito smiled, realizing that he was wondering if he would be too proud to accept charity. He was not.

'Of course. I don't know how to thank you. Right now, we need all the help we can get,' he said.

The Kind American breathed a sigh of relief. Ethel would have been so hurt if they rejected it. She had fallen in love with that family, with Carmen and Maria especially. Since their own daughter had been killed in an auto accident when she was eight months pregnant, they had been alone, childless, with no hope of grandchildren. Ethel had never got over it. When he had brought home the dishevelled Cubans that day, it had been like she had snapped out of years of grief, found a new family to help, to look out for. When they had been taken away by the immigration authorities, Ethel had written to every government agency she could think of to support their case. She had even contacted the Cuban movements to see what she could do to help. Then she had seen them on TV.

'Is she here, your wife?' Tito asked.

'No. They would only allow one visitor, and we agreed I should come first. To make sure you … didn't mind, you know?'

Tito nodded again. 'Please thank her, from all of us. And you too. I don't know what to say. You had no reason to help us.'

'That's OK son. We'd like to assist you. You know, the Cuban groups in Miami are rooting for you. They see you as a cause, an example of your people's suffering. There's a lot of pressure being put on the government to make an exception of you and help you. Especially with Maria's heart problem and the Boston offer. I think you're going to make it.'

'I hope so. It's awful here. I could stand it, but Carmen and Maria … there are not many women here, you know. Most of the refugees have been young men, fit to make the journey, leaving parents and even wives behind. I don't know how long Maria will survive in these circumstances without becoming ill.'

The big man nodded. 'Well, we just want you to know, Tito, that if you do get to Boston for the surgery, and you need somewhere to be afterwards, or some evidence that you will have a place to stay, Ethel and me decided that you can come and stay with us for as long as you like. I've already written to the immigration authorities and the camp people here to tell them.'

He reached into his shirt pocket and brought out an envelope. 'I've written it down, with our names, address, all that. In case you need it.'

Tito sat motionless, staring at the man opposite him. Eventually he spoke. 'What is your name, sir?'

'James T. Powell. Folks call me JT for short.'

Tito stood up and held out his hand. His eyes were moist. 'Well, Mr JT,' he said, 'I have never known such kindness in my whole life. You know nothing of us, yet you offer us everything. This will mean so much to Carmen. Please, come back again and visit, if you have time. Bring Mrs JT to see Maria. You make me believe a miracle might happen after all. *Gracias.*' He gulped, and swallowed, trying not to lose control as the kindness of the American weakened his resistance.

'*De nada*, Tito. I'll do just that, and we'll keep on working from the outside. So long for now, son.'

They shook hands, and he left. An hour later, as Tito and Carmen were unpacking the suitcase, the guard came into their hut again and barked, 'Mr Pereira, another visitor.'

Carmen looked at him, hope in her eyes. Two visitors in one day. Something must be happening now.

It had stopped raining, and the sun was bringing steam up from the soaking compound as they walked again to the visitors' room. A tall young man was standing behind the table. He got up as they entered.

'Dr Pereira?' he asked.

'Yes.'

'I'm Dr Masters, from Boston.'

He smiled and held out his hand. Tito grasped it in disbelief.

Gary turned to the guard. 'I need to see the whole family,' he said. 'I have clearance.'

The guard smiled. 'That's OK sir. The warden himself has gone over to get Mrs Pereira and Maria and take them to the hospital block. He reckoned you'd want to examine the child properly.'

'Good. Well, Doctor,' he said to Tito, 'let's find the patient and see if we can help.'

Tito and Gary followed the guard outside, chatting about Tito's background, the journey. Gary was relieved the way to the hospital was paved, as he looked at the mud in the compound, the wooden huts, seeing visions of other distant camps in Poland, and Korea, and Vietnam, and Sarajevo.

In the hospital, Tito introduced him to his wife and daughter. The governor had arranged for the camp doctor and a nurse to be present and, after the introductions, left them alone, asking for Gary to call into his office before he left.

So Gary examined Maria, gave her a full physical, a cardiogram, and then sent her for a chest x-ray before sitting down with the family. He looked grave.

'Mr and Mrs Pereira, Maria certainy is poorly. She is all right at the present, but she has two heart defects, one atrial septal defect and, more seriously, one ventricular septal defect. Alone, either might cause a problem, especially the VSD. Together, she could deteriorate at any time, with disastrous consequences. She needs surgery, and she needs it soon. I intend to speak to the authorities in the next day or two to insist on her transfer to Boston for further tests and surgery. The longer she stays here in this disgusting environment, the worse the prognosis. Do I have your permission?'

'Yes!' Tito and Carmen said it at the same moment.

Gary stood up. 'I'll be in touch,' he said.

'Thank you, sir, for coming down here, for seeing us, for everything.'

'It's a pleasure. I have other business here also, so it was convenient to see you now. See you again soon. In Boston, I hope.'

He left, a wry smile on his face.

I have other business here also....

After Kathryn Skiathos had left his office in Boston, he had gone to check on his patient, Mr Palucci. To his surprise, the old man was looking better, obs stable, cardiogram normal. He went back to his office, cleared the pending tray, and rearranged his schedules to allow him a two-day trip to Miami. He called Krome, Washington, the Miami Cardiac Institute, Delta Airlines and Avis. He reached Miami at 11 p.m., slept over in the Airport Marriott, and hit the road for Krome at 6 a.m. Now his business there was finished. It was 2 p.m. when he walked through the familiar doors of the Miami Cardiac Institute and made for cardiac surgery, walking straight into the office of the Chief of Cardiac Surgery, Dr Geraldo Rodriguez. Two women were typing in the outer office. They looked up when he entered and one of them, a large middle-aged black lady with full red lips and bright smiling eyes leapt to her feet with surprising agility and rushed towards him. 'Dr Masters, how *are* you?' she cried, smothering him in a bear-hug as Gary gave a bemused smile at the other secretary who was watching them with amusement.

'Fine, Beth, just fine. Least I will be if you don't squeeze me to death first.'

'But we *missed* you.'

'You behaving yourself these days?'

She held him at arm's length for a moment, then let him down.

'Me? You serious?' she asked, before hugging him again. The office door opened and a distinguished grey-haired man in OR greens walked in.

'Put her down Gary, you always were a bad influence round here.'

Beth let him go with an embarrassed look on her face and walked back to her desk, as Gary turned to face his old boss.

'Geraldo, how are you?'

'Good. Come in.'

They walked into his large office and sat down in two easy chairs in the corner, away from his work desk. Beth appeared within seconds with a tray of coffee, which she put down on the table between them, flashing Gary a huge wink as she left.

'If you ever fire her, Geraldo, send her to Boston.'

'No chance, Gary. So, how are things shaping up there?'

'Not bad. Getting there.'

'Got all the local support you need? Colleagues ... ICU ... OR staff ...?'

'Yes, all those. They're really supportive and eager to help me settle in. No jealous prima donnas, hard cases.'

'You're lucky,' his old chief said with feeling, remembering how difficult it had been for a Puerto Rican immigrant to rise to Chief of Cardiac Surgery in Miami's Cardiac Institute.

They sipped their coffee for a few moments before Gary got down to business.

'So, what's the scene with Mr Anthony Skiathos?'

Rodriguez's eyes clouded for a moment.

'Hmm, Tony the Greek.'

Gary felt a twist of familiarity in his stomach.

'Tony the Greek?' he repeated. 'You make him sound like a Mafioso.'

Rodriguez was not smiling. 'I have no proof, but that's the word around these parts. And the people surrounding him and looking out for him here don't leave much to the imagination.'

'What business is he involved in?'

'Officially, shipping, export of Greek produce, GVK electronics – he even sells *us* computers. Unofficially, he visits South America a lot. Colombia, especially....'

Gary shifted in his seat.

'But officially he's clean,' Geraldo continued. 'Big shot in Miami society. Friend of the mayor. You know the scene.'

'Looks like someone tried to repay a bad debt.'

'Sure did. Almost a very good job. Inferior approach, through the epigastrium in front of the stomach, up through the diaphragm, into the left ventricle. Four inch tear in the myocardium, six inch tear in the pericardium. They patched him up well in Athens – seven hours of surgery, twenty-seven pints of blood. They didn't think he'd make it. He did OK for ten days or so, then things started to go wrong.'

'As the aneurysm developed?'

'Yes. And it's still developing. Slowly but surely getting bigger, and weaker, all the time. Two millimetres a week at present, but it could go anytime.'

'Anything else?'

'Angios show a partial single vessel stenosis, right coronary. Otherwise he's in surprisingly good shape. But he's going to die without a transplant. Or the Masters patch. How many have you done now?'

'Four.'

'Doing OK?'

'No. One died within a week of surgery. We don't know why. The patch was fine. There were no signs of rejection.'

Rodriguez rubbed his chin. 'Hmm, the others?'

'They're OK.' He crossed his fingers mentally, hoping Palucci was continuing to recover.

'Well, short of Tony the Greek putting out a contract on someone with identical tissue typing and ripping out his heart for a transplant, you're his only hope.'

'Are you serious, Geraldo, about him being a Mafioso?'

The older man shrugged and smiled. 'I don't know. I wouldn't speak like this outside this room. For all I know, he is a pillar of society. But this is Miami, and there are rumours. It's irrelevant anyway. For now he's just some poor *capo* with a heart that's slowly rupturing.'

'Is he fit to travel?'

'Fifty-fifty. It would be better if he didn't. If he must....' He shrugged again.

Masters drained his coffee cup. 'So, let's go see him,' he said.

Geraldo Rodriguez stood up.

'One more thing,' he said. 'Mrs Skiathos. When the Athens

team said they couldn't help, she chartered a 747 – a 747 mind you – and a medical team, and flew him straight here. When I ran the tests and told her there was nothing we could do short of a transplant, she created mayhem. When I told her there was a slim chance someone might be able to help, she wanted your office number, address, the works. Said she wanted to see you personally.'

'She did. She flew up yesterday morning.'

'She doesn't hang around. She must really love the guy. What did she have to say?'

'Just what you'd expect. Like you said, she'll do anything to save him.'

'Quite a looker, huh?'

Gary nodded. Is it good? he thought.

'What money will buy,' mused Geraldo as they walked to the elevator to the third floor and the ICU.

Anthony Skiathos was indeed a big man. Some of it was fat, but most of it was muscle on a huge frame. The front of his head was bald, but he had a luxuriant beard and long hair down the back of his neck to his shoulders, and the remainder of his body was covered in dark hair. Gary thought he looked like a moderately intelligent ape, and wondered for a moment what she saw in him, before remembering he was rich and impotent.

He had an oxygen mask over his mouth, and was breathing with some difficulty.

Kathryn Skiathos was at his side, holding his hand. She stood up as they entered the cubicle.

Geraldo spoke first. 'Mr and Mrs Skiathos, I want you to meet Dr Gary Masters from Boston. As I explained, Dr Masters is pioneering a new technique in heart surgery which might, just might, be applicable here. Gary?'

Gary walked to the bedside, and took the huge paw the sick man stretched weakly out to him.

'So … welcome Doctor … welcome to the only man who can save me now….'

Gary withdrew his hand, and looked at Kathryn.

'Mrs Skiathos,' he nodded.

'Doctor Masters,' she replied.

He turned to the patient. 'I want to examine you, sir, then I need to go and look at your tests. Only then can I say if I can help.'

'I ... understand.' The big man made to move, but Gary put his hand on his shoulder.

'No, don't move, it's OK. Keep your strength. Just leave it to me.'

He looked at the entry wound in the left 4th 5th intercostal space, knowing from previous cases the havoc which could usually be found beneath that almost innocent looking wound. There were a lot of knives in Miami. He examined the surgical wound, stretching like a thin red pencil line from the umbilicus to the top of the breast bone. Then he took out his stethoscope and listened intently for several minutes, hearing the heart sound, the murmurs, the ebb and flow of blood taking an abnormal route through the damaged chambers of a dying heart. Finally he gently eased the big man forward and sat on the bed beside him, listening to the back of his chest.

He stood up.

'Now I'll check the tests, then I'll come back and speak to you again, give you the verdict.'

'Or the sentence....'

Gary smiled grimly and went to the office with Rodriguez.

'He's not so good, is he?'

The older man shook his head. They looked at the scans and x-rays, and Rodriguez ran the movie of the angios on the video. They watched the heart, outlined with the iodine dye infused into it from a cannula in the femoral artery, as it beat, weakly, occasionally irregularly, and saw with each beat how the usually tight, powerful left ventricle wasted most of its contents into a large thin-walled sac, which looked as if it might burst at any moment.

'Hell, Geraldo, this is bad. We've got to do this soon or it will be too late.'

Rodriguez nodded. 'Here?'

'Yes. He'd never survive the trip to Boston. I brought the gear with me – it's in cold storage in the medical centre at Miami International. Can you get a team together, a good team?'

'Sure.'

'Doris to scrub?'

He nodded.

'Endor for by-pass?'

He nodded again, smiling. Every surgeon has his favourite team.

Gary grinned too. It would be like old times to operate in Miami again with some of the friends he'd left behind.

'Seven a.m.?'

'I'll fix it now,' said the chief of surgery, reaching for the telephone, 'and I'll get you a good assistant. Me!'

Gary walked back to the ICU cubicle. Kathryn Skiathos stood up once more as he entered, concern on her beautiful face.

'Well, doctor ...' her husband said quietly, 'am I a dead man?'

'Not yet, Mr Skiathos, but time is running out. The aneurysm on your heart is weak. It could burst at any moment. You have to understand that I don't even know if I can save you. All I know is, no one else can. With your permission, at seven a.m. tomorrow morning, I'll try my best.' He looked at Kathryn. 'Seven a.m. in the morning. If you both agree.'

There was silence, until Tony the Greek spoke.

'You ... have my permission ... Doctor ... and may God be at your elbow.'

Masters nodded, and turned to go. He paused in front of Kathryn Skiathos, who held out her hand, and looked directly at him, her black eyes piercing his soul.

'Thank you,' she said quietly, holding his hand a moment longer than necessary. 'Please do your best.'

He nodded and left.

CHAPTER 9

David Meeson rose from his desk as Jerry Weinberg walked into his office, dressed in OR greens.

'Jerry,' he said, 'thanks for coming. Coffee?'

'No thanks, David. Bit pushed for time.'

'OK, I'll make it brief. I've just come off the phone with the Department of the Interior and the Immigration Office. It seems the Pereira case has got to the very highest level, and I mean the very highest level.'

He paused for effect. David Meeson loved politics.

Jerry Weinberg was not impressed. He hated politics. He waited for him to continue.

'The decision has been made to let Masters go ahead. Apparently there's been intense pressure from the Cuban-American lobby, not only in Miami, but in other major cities – New York, Boston, all up the East Coast in fact. Maria Pereira and her parents have grabbed the imagination and sympathy of these people.'

'I'm not surprised,' said Jerry. 'They have a genuine case, these boat people. They're escaping from tyranny, and if they hadn't all decided to come at the same time, the Pereiras would have got in under the old rules. They'd be American citizens now, and we wouldn't have got landed with this problem.'

'Well, we've got it now. The President himself has looked at the case. He's granting the family a temporary visa, subject to renewal, on medical and humane grounds to let the little girl get out of Krome and get her surgery. Apparently, there have been offers to take the family in after discharge, and not just from Cubans. From all-American families who normally don't approve of the immigrants.'

'That's good. So what arrangements need to be made from this end?'

'First transfer of the family from Florida to here. My secretary's fixing it up with Delta. We'll have them met at the airport. Better do it properly – there's bound to be big media interest, especially after the Today coverage. I've arranged for them to stay in one of the married doctors' apartments in the medical residence. That way, they'll be within the campus, close to the child.'

'Seems like you've got everything covered. Does Gary know all this?'

'No. Apparently he's gone off to Florida to see a patient down there. Doctor Jet-setter. He was expected back this morning but he hasn't shown up yet. His secretary's making enquiries.' His voice sounded bitter, like administrators sometimes did when confronted with successful doctors who put them in the shade, instead of clocking in and out like regular blue-collar workers.

'So it looks like we're on countdown for surgery,' said Jerry.

'It sure does. Let's hope and pray it goes all right.'

Weinberg nodded. 'Anything more we can do?'

'No. I just wanted to keep you posted.'

He left to get back to the OR, but detoured via the ICU to speak to Anne Bell. He found her slumped over her desk, her head on her folded arms.

'You all right, Anne?' he asked.

She looked up, bleary-eyed, then let her head slump back down again.

'Hi, Jerry. I've been better. What can I do for you?'

'I was just passing, wondered if Gary Masters was here.'

'I've not seen him. What is it anyway?' She looked up at him this time.

'They've given the go ahead for the Cuban child's transfer up here.'

'Oh, great,' she said, in a tone of voice which left him in no doubt how she really felt about it.

'You don't sound too impressed.'

'I'm not, Jerry, not impressed at all. You heard about Masters' third case, Mr Peters?'

'Yes. That was sad. A bad break.'

'I thought so too. A real bad break, but it happens. It's just that usually we know when to expect it, or at least what caused it. In Peters' case, we know neither. His autopsy just showed some fluid on the lungs they couldn't explain. Non-specific pulmonary exudate, Wellbeloved, the attending pathologist, called it. No heart failure, no pulmonary oedema, no pulmonary embolus, no nothing.'

She was clearly upset.

'It happens sometimes, Anne. It's not your fault. Probably some undetectable cell level metabolic death.'

She was on her feet now, walking around her desk to look up at him.

'No, Jerry. You see, the fourth case got sick like Peters, but this time only twelve hours after surgery. He rallied for a while; we thought we'd got it under control. Masters called last evening and they told him he'd stabilized. Well, an hour later his oxygen saturation started dropping, just like Peters' had, his breathing got worse, and he went downhill fast.'

She paused and, for a moment, he thought she was going to cry. 'He died twenty minutes ago.' She leaned back against her desk.

'Hell Anne, that's terrible. Two out of four.'

'I know it's terrible, Jerry. Terrible for the patients, terrible for the relatives, terrible for Gary Masters. But it's terrible for me and my staff too, because it's here in my ICU that they're dying. They're coming out of the OR with everyone saying *it went like clockwork, he did a great job, brilliant surgeon*, then they get sick here and die and no one knows why. All Gary said about Peters was *it wasn't surgical*, implying it was *our* fault. It's fine that all his pigs lived, Jerry, but the humans are dying.'

'Some of them.'

'Fifty per cent so far.'

'You know, Anne, in surgery, after taking all the necessary precautions, doing all the experimental work, training yourself to the hilt, leaving nothing to chance, when you actually start a new technique there are unexpected casualties. It happened with transplants, it happened with the laparoscope, it happened to me when I started doing radicals, the complications in the second ten were nothing compared with the first ten.'

'Death is a pretty serious complication, Jerry.'

He nodded. It was.

'Are you working up to something here, Anne?'

She stood up to her full five-four, dwarfed by his six-six.

'We're good pals, aren't we?'

He nodded. 'Of course.'

'And good professionals. I rate you as the best urologist I've ever come across, and I hope you think I know something about intensive care.'

'Everyone knows you're the best on the East Coast, Anne.'

'Well, I want you to consider a moratorium on Gary's experimental cases until we know what's going on.'

Weinberg whistled, slowly. 'Hell, Anne, that's a bit premature, isn't it?'

'Premature?' Her voice was raised. 'Jerry, two out of four. Fifty per cent mortality. Can UHSM live with figures like that?'

'Now look, Anne.' Weinberg was walking around the office now, thinking on his feet. 'This may just be the bad run. He may do another twenty now with no problems. Then you're looking at eight per cent. Then another twenty, four per cent. And these are sick people, not breast augmentations or toe-nails. If we call a halt now, this technique might never get off the ground. Or some other unit will do it and steal all the credit.'

'Patients don't die on my ICU without me knowing why, Jerry.'

'Are you saying you'll refuse to take them?'

'I'm saying don't put me in that position.'

'Hell, Anne, I'll have to think this through.'

'Then get started Jerry, because from what you told me earlier, you're going to be asking me soon to put a little Cuban kid on my ICU while the eyes of the world are watching. Will you explain to Bryant and Katie on the Today show why she died and of what, or will you expect me to do that?'

The thought had already been formulating in Weinberg's mind as she said the words.

'Anne, I'm expected in OR. Let me think about this and get back to you.'

She nodded.

'And when Gary shows up, tell him I need to speak to him, will you?'

He walked out of the room, leaving Anne Bell feeling very alone.

Gary was not going to show up. At least not for another day. As

Jerry Weinberg spoke with the frustrated, exhausted chief of intensive care, Gary Masters was leaning over the huge frame of Anthony Skiathos as he lay on the operating table in OR 1 of the Miami Cardiac Institute, Florida. The big man's chest was open, and his blood was being diverted away from the heart through the by-pass machine so that the heart would lie quietly dormant, to allow the cardiac surgeon to do his work.

'Christ!' he muttered, shooting Geraldo Rodriguez a glance over his green mask. 'This wouldn't have lasted much longer.'

They looked down at the heart in general, and the left ventricle in particular, the chamber whose task it is to pump the oxygenated blood returning from the lungs to every tissue in the body. Anthony Skiathos's left ventricle would have been like any other if it were not for the fact that its normally thick muscle was deformed by a huge, thin-walled, almost transparent sac they called an aneurysm.

'Doris, give me a sixty ml syringe and some saline.'

Slap! It was in his hand almost before he finished speaking.

'Watch this,' he said, and he pushed the syringe into the ventricle and started slowly to fill it, occluding its exit up into the atrium or out through the aorta with his fingers. They watched in fascination as the aneurysm slowly filled, jumping when it burst, spraying saline into the field.

'That could have happened at anytime,' Gary said, grimly, clearing the saline with the sucker. 'Tomorrow, today, five minutes from now. Only it wouldn't have been saline, it would have been bright red blood pouring into his chest. Scissors!'

He started to dissect the wall of the aneurysm sac off the muscle of the left ventricle. Thirty minutes later, when it was completely free, he handed it to the scrub nurse and said, 'Send it to pathology. It won't tell us much but we'll need it for the records.'

They looked down at the gaping hole in the patient's ventricle.

'Patch please,' Gary ordered.

The nurse leaned over her trolley of gleaming instruments and reached with a non-toothed forceps into a bowl of clear fluid, taking from it a rectangular piece of thin flat tissue. She handed it to him and he placed it over the defect, then trimmed the edges to fit the hole. Next, he took the needle holder and suture from the scrub nurse and started meticulously to suture the membrane to the heart, using small, strong, interrupted sutures, about 1/8th of an inch apart, slowly but surely making his way around until he came to his starting point.

He leaned up, straightened his back, and looked at his work.

'Neat,' said Rodriguez with admiration. 'Looks like it's always been there.'

'Syringe and saline.'

Gary repeated the previous manoeuvre when the aneurysm had ruptured. This time, the membrane didn't budge, holding as firm as the surrounding muscle. He noted a few small spurts of saline between the sutures, and placed a few more reinforcing sutures to seal them off before closing the incision in the heart.

The surgeons looked at each other, without speaking. They knew the real moment of truth had arrived.

'Defibrillator!'

It was time to start up the heart again, to awaken it from its slumber, to see if it would beat again for them and pump the blood round Anthony Skiathos's huge body, instead of short-changing him as it filled and stretched the aneurysm as it had for the past ten days. And ultimately, to see if the Masters Membrane would hold, would stay taut, would allow the ventricle to function again.

He put the electrodes on to the heart.

'Clear!'

Everyone stood back. The body of the huge Greek jumped as 200 joules shot through his body.

The heart stayed flaccid.

He shocked him again. Still nothing.

'Give me four hundred,' he ordered. The pump technician leaned over and turned the dial.

'Clear!'

Again the heart jumped, then resumed its stubborn slumber, as if to say *you made me like this, smart guy, now you work it out.*

'Ten ml of calcium chloride and one ml of one in one thousand adrenalin,' he ordered.

He injected the two drugs into the heart and waited for a moment.

'Clear!'

Shock!

Jump!

Beep ... beep ... beep....

'You've got sinus rhythm, Doctor,' said the anaesthetist. They knew it already, as they watched the heart beat once more, strong and regular.

'Get him off the pump, Endor.'

And they watched some more, as the heart started to pump its scarlet life-giving fluid around Tony the Greek, and the patch stayed firm and dry.

'Close him up, please, Carl,' Masterson said to the resident who had assisted them, and he and Geraldo Rodriguez walked in the direction of the surgeons' room.

'Thanks Doris,' Masters called back as he went.

'Thank you Doctor. Take care of yourself up there in Boston.'

'Good work, Gary,' said Rodriguez, pulling open the changing-room door and standing back to allow Gary to go in first.

'Thanks, Geraldo,' Gary replied, pulling off his cap and mask. 'I owe it all to you – your training, your support. You've backed me all the way.'

'I only back winners,' Geraldo replied, slapping Gary on the back.

Gary pulled off his shirt. 'I'll stay to check him into the ICU then go and speak to his wife,' he said.

'Sure. How long are you staying?'

'Tonight. I'll see him at six tomorrow, then get the early flight north. I should make it to Boston for late morning.'

'Good. We'll have dinner together tonight, and I'll drive you to the airport in the morning. Don't worry Gary, I'll watch him like a hawk, and get daily reports to you. I'll call if there are any problems. But I can't see there being any.'

So long as he doesn't do a Phil Peters on me thought Gary, as he pulled off his trousers, threw them into the dirty-linen bag and stepped into the shower.

He met her in the visitors' room. She was sitting with the tall man, Menos.

The *consigliere*?

She stood up anxiously as he entered.

'How is he?'

'He's stable,' said Gary. 'It went OK. No problems. Now we have to get through the next few days to make sure the heart recovers, the patch holds, he develops no other complications like rejection, pneumonia, blood clots. He's not out of the woods yet, but he's stable and I'm happy with him.'

'Thank God,' she said quietly. 'When can I see him?'

'In an hour or so. They'll be busy in intensive care transferring him to his bed, hooking him up to the monitors, all that stuff.'

Menos moved forward and held out his hand to Masters, gripping him in a powerful handshake while he said, 'We are very grateful to you, Doctor Masters. I know that Mr Skiathos would want me to say that, and also to say that we will demonstrate our gratitude to you if ... when ... he pulls through this.'

He kept his hand in his grip a moment longer, then released it.

And what if he doesn't? mused Gary, looking again at Kathryn. God, how beautiful she was. He wanted to take her in his arms right there, make love to her like they had in the hallway that evening. Hang the fact that he had just performed heart surgery on her husband. Hang everything. He wanted this woman more than he had ever wanted anything in his life. But her demeanour was distant and correct, with no sign of familiarity, no hint of wanting to see him before he left for home, no suggestion that they meet again. And the *consigliere* was sticking to her like they were Siamese twins. He hadn't seen her out of his company except when she was with her husband.

Her voice interrupted his thoughts. 'You will be in tomorrow?'

'Yes, but early. I have to get back to Boston.'

Was that a flash of disappointment on her face, or just concern for her husband?

'Back to Boston? But you can't.'

'I have to, Mrs Skiathos.'

'If it is money, Doctor, we will pay anything. Name your price.' Menos was also concerned.

Gary was almost tempted. 'It's not that, sir. I operated here because he was not fit to move to Boston. I've done the operation, that was all I had to do. I was the technician. The cardiac and ICU teams here can take over now. There's nothing special any more, just routine post-cardiac surgery care, and they do that here better than anywhere.'

For some inexplicable reason, a vision of Anne Bell flashed across his mind.

Menos nodded slowly. He understood. Kathryn still looked apprehensive.

He smiled at her. 'Really, Mrs Skiathos, I mean it. And if there should be a problem that needs my attention, I'm only a few hours away.'

There was silence. Then her face suddenly lost its taut, anxious expression, and she smiled back. 'If you say so. Thank you for everything.'

There was silence again. Gary wondered if Menos sensed the electricity between them. There was so much he wanted to say. Did she fell the same? Or was he just a two-night stand to amuse her while her husband was away, before he became her husband's physician, no more, no less.

She turned to Menos. 'We should go up to ICU to wait,' she said.

'I'll show you the way,' Gary said, 'check him over before I leave.'

He called in again with Geraldo after dinner. Anthony Skiathos was fine. Kathryn was nowhere to be seen.

The next morning at 6 a.m., he made his last visit. This time she was beside him, holding his hand. He was still unconscious, on the respirator.

'Doing good,' said the ICU resident. 'Should have him off the respirator by noon.'

'He's doing OK,' he told Kathryn Skiathos.

She nodded, without looking up at him. He left without further words, just as he had left her bed some weeks earlier, quietly, without speaking, so she would remember it like it was. Like he remembered it.

Is it good?

Yes it was. It was.

The Pereiras were the lead story on the NBC evening news.

They also featured on CBS, ABC, Fox, Eyewitness News, Channel 7, CNN and plenty of other local stations, especially those dealing with Hispanic issues.

Maria Pereira and her parents were being freed from Krome

Camp and flown north, at government expense, for little Maria to have heart surgery. The pictures showed Tito and Carmen, with Maria in her father's arms, leaving the camp, getting into a limo, and being taken to Miami International to board the flight to Boston. They walked through the other internees who, with the generosity of spirit and love of family they shared, parted for them, clapped their hands, slapped their backs, and wished them luck. Just before he got in the car, Tito turned to the others behind the wire and shouted, 'Freedom, comrades, freedom for Cubans in this great country, freedom for Cubans in Cuba. Freedom for Cuba.'

They left to cheers.

In Boston, Gary Masters watched it gloomily. Tomorrow it would be him they wanted to film, as they jostled and pushed and shouted for him to turn and give them a good picture, or a good quote. The surgeon who had rescued the little Cuban girl from the horrors of Krome Camp and was going to repair her heart. For free. UHSM would become the focus of the nation's news, the world's news, as they followed every temperature check, every pulse reading of the little angel saved by the dashing surgeon.

While Phil Peters lay in the South Boston Cemetery.

While Ludovico Palucci lay in pieces on Jules Wellbeloved's mortuary slab.

While Anne Bell tried to blame him for their deaths, and Jerry Weinberg threatened a moratorium on further membrane procedures. And while Kathryn Skiathos, caring and devoted wife, sat with her husband in Miami.

Life's a bitch, he thought.

CHAPTER 10

'I've called this meeting because we have a serious problem which has to be addressed.'

Jerry Weinberg looked in turn at Anne Bell, Gary Masters, Paul Schering and Jules Wellbeloved sitting around the table in the hospital boardroom. The wall clock showed one minute after noon. 'I've deliberately not involved management because I see this as a clinical matter, not an administrative one.'

David Meeson would be furious when he found out.

'We're here to discuss the NIH cardiac surgery study in general, and some specific aspects of it, not least the young Cuban patient transferring in here today for work-up. As you all know, Gary has done four cases now, and there have been two deaths, one a young ex-construction worker who died four days after surgery, and the other a sixty-six-year-old retired restaurateur who died twenty-four hours post-op. Neither left the ICU. As far as I can see, surgery was uncomplicated and technically successful in all cases and they arrived at the ICU in good shape. No case had to return to the OR. As I understand it, no firm cause has been found for their deaths at autopsy. Those are the facts. I want to work backwards through them, starting with you Jules.'

Jules Wellbeloved, the pathologist, puffed his pipe, raising clouds of sweet-smelling Dutch smoke. He had been blocking out the smell of death that way since he had left Edinburgh twenty years before to take up the appointment of chief of pathology at UHSM. No one objected. In truth, it was doubtful if any of them had ever seen Jules Wellbeloved *without* a pipe in his mouth. He was a small dark man with a bushy black celtic beard under a mop of untidy hair.

'Och, there's not much to report. Brain, nothing. Heart, nothing. The membrane looked good, suture lines intact, no signs of rejection, just a thin exudate on the surface. Chest, nothing, just a similar thin exudate on the surface, so far analysis of which shows non-specific inflammatory characteristics only. Nothing special. Abdomen, nothing. We're running some pleural and lung biopsies, and further analysis of the exudate. Don't hold your breath though.'

'Both patients showed the same exudate?'

'Yes.'

'On the membrane and the lungs?'

'Yes, but like I said, don't hold your breath. We see this sort of thing in lots of cases as an incidental finding. There's usually another certain cause of death.'

'OK. Anne, can you take us through their ICU behaviour?'

She cleared her throat. 'Like you said, Phil Peters came out of surgery stable. Tim Dowdall gassed him, said there were no per-op problems. There were no complications for the first three days. Not even any dysrhythmias or irregularities. Then, on day four, he dropped his oxygen concentration for some inexplicable reason, just when we were thinking he'd be back in his room by nightfall. We hooked him back up to the respirator, oxygenated him, but he just went down and down until he faded away.'

She paused.

'And Mr Palucci?'

'Same status on arrival at ICU, same progress, same mode of death, only sooner. He started with problems twelve hours after surgery and died more quickly.'

'And nothing, x-rays, scans, blood tests, cardiograms, encephalograms – nothing gave you a clue as to what was happening?'

'That's correct.'

'Signs of rejection?'

'No. Too quick in Palucci's case anyway. We saw no such signs, and neither did Jules at autopsy.'

'Gary, can you take us through the surgery, and any similar problems you might have seen in your animal work?'

'Sure.' He looked tired after the two-day Miami trip. He'd heard about the meeting from Weinberg the night before, and had slept badly.

'These were cases three and four. One and two followed the same technique I perfected in the pig studies. The surgery was straightforward, case three was a septal defect, case four a small aneurysm. 'Very small, he thought to himself, a pin-hole compared with the chasm he had repaired in Miami.' Surgery was unremarkable. They left the OR in good shape. As regards your other question, I can't recall any of the pigs dying in this way. If they had, we'd have investigated it and hopefully would have the answers already.' He shrugged. 'That's it.'

'Is there any significance in the fact that they were consecutive cases – third and fourth? Did you change your technique, membrane preparation, anything?'

Gary shook his head. 'Same technique, same membranes, same source, same sutures, one young patient, one old patient, different heart problems....'

'So, what do we do?' asked Jerry Weinberg. He looked around, waiting for comment.

They listened to the old boardroom clock ticking.

Gary Masters spoke first. 'Nothing,' he said. 'These were bad breaks, two sick people died after major revolutionary heart surgery. It happens. We just carry on, while we search for the reason, and hope for better luck.'

'Better luck?' asked Anne Bell icily. 'Gary, we've got two deaths in as many days. Don't you think it would be wise to do that in reverse order? Search for the cause, *then* carry on? Stop and reappraise?'

'The only thing we need to reappraise, Dr Bell, is the ICU performance. These were patients who left the OR well, and who died in the ICU later. I want to know why. Don't you think we need to look at ICU performance, protocols, procedure? Do a bacteriology screen of the apparatus, the piping, check the leads, the monitors, the respirators? Let's look at the environment where the patients died, where things got screwed up, instead of adopting the old anaesthetic knee-jerk response of blaming the surgeon.'

Jerry could see Anne's hackles rising. Before she could retort he said, 'Jules?'

'I don't want any more customers, Jerry. The autopsy shows the surgery went OK. I agree with Gary. We need to look more closely at what happened afterwards.'

He avoided eye contact with Anne Bell.

'Paul?'

'I agree. There's no evidence that these are surgical

complications. Something else is going on after surgery, and that's where our investigations should be directed.'

'Right. With your co-operation, Anne, I'll get that moving. Meanwhile do we suspend the programme?'

'Yes!'

'No!' Gary Masters' fist hitting the table almost drowned out Anne Bell's response.

'No!' he repeated, only slightly less loudly. 'You can't stop a trial like this just because of a few setbacks. Otherwise progress would never be made. Check the ICU. That's where the problem is. Until you find out what's wrong up there, *every* patient passing through it will be at risk, not just mine. I've just been the unlucky one who copped for these first two unexplained deaths.'

'That's not fair!' Anne Bell's voice was raised now. 'And it's not proven. We had no other unexplained deaths like these two. Our figures are the best in Boston.'

'Until *now*!'

'Until *you* came here.'

'Hold it!' Jerry's calm, firm voice broke into the verbal scrap. 'Come on, you two. We've got to work on this together or we've got no chance. Gary, have you got any more cases scheduled?'

'Two – Philip Farkas, sixty-seven year old aneurysm tomorrow; Russell Anderson, eighteen year old heart defect still going through evaluation.'

'And Maria Pereira,' Jerry added quietly.

There was silence again.

'What do we do about her? The eyes of the nation, the world maybe, will be on us for that one. Is she at risk Gary?'

'Without the surgery, she's a goner within a year. We have no choice.'

'We do have a choice,' said Anne. 'If her life is not in immediate danger, I would strongly advise we delay her, find the cause of the problem, see how the next two do if you're determined to go ahead with them, *against my advice*, and schedule her later.'

'Oh, sure,' said Gary, sarcastically. 'And let the whole of Boston, the entire nation even, know that we've got an ICU problem the director can't solve. That it's a fifty-fifty chance if you get into this ICU that you won't get out alive. Sure, let that leak to the media and watch our referrals for *all* sorts of major surgery dry up. Is that what you want, Jerry? To hand it all to Mass. General on a plate?'

'It's only *your* patients who are dying, Doctor,' said Anne icily.

'So far,' came the reply.

'Jules?'

'I'm with Anne. I've had two bodies on a slab already. I'd like to know why before a third appears.'

'Paul?'

'I disagree. We've got to carry on. Christ, I'm all for caution, but any delay could throw doubt on our entire service. Gary's right. These are sick people. Without Gary's technique, most of them wouldn't stand a chance anyway. Get real. This isn't nose job stuff, this is the sharpest end of life-saving surgery. I'll assist Gary personally with the next two, and with little Maria Pereira if he'll let me. Two senior guys, no residents, no questions for the Press to ask. Maybe I'll spot something. I doubt it. I really believe this is an ICU problem. Sorry, Anne.'

'Any more comments?' asked Jerry.

There were none.

'Right. We'll put ICU under the microscope, run a complete technical, computer, microbiological check, but carry on with the programme.' He looked at Gary Masters. 'Including Maria Pereira after her evaluation, which could, I guess, take a few days longer than necessary, Gary?'

Masters nodded, understanding his meaning and flashing a triumphant look in Anne Bell's direction.

The meeting broke up and they left in silence.

'I love you, Anne.'

She could hear his voice as if it were real, feel his urgency as he felt under her short skirt, feel her fear and desire mixed into one, confusing her, making a rational decision impossible. Part of her wanted to say no, no, not now, not yet, but a more dominant part told her that it was time, that there was no reason to resist it.

At 24, Anne Bell was a virgin. She joked around with the other students, bragged along with them from time to time, but generally tried to avoid girlie sessions when sex was the topic of conversation. What you didn't have, you didn't miss, she told herself. When it happens, it happens. But now she was with Pete Dewan, the senior surgical resident, the guy all the girls lusted after. It was she, Anne Bell, whom he had singled out to go with to the faculty dinner dance. It was she who had agreed to go back to his apartment afterwards. It was she who now felt she should say no, but instead kissed him harder and attempted to love him back, letting him lead, responding to his movements, trying to enjoy it as he pushed her on to the bed, their bodies still entwined, and entered her. It was over surprisingly quickly. Within a couple of minutes of thrusting and panting she felt him climax and he relaxed suddenly with a groan, falling motionless on top of her in a dead weight. He was asleep within seconds, snoring loudly. She lay still for ages, not daring to move, wondering what would happen next. After a few minutes, he turned on to his side, bringing a gasp of pain to her lips as he left her, still snoring but more gently and regularly now.

She waited a full twenty minutes before slipping out of his bed, gathering her clothes, and dressing in his living-room. She left without delay, walking quickly down the unfamiliar streets until, with a feeling of intense relief, she saw the cab and went back to her quarters.

She sat in the shower for half an hour before she climbed exhausted into bed and tried to banish the confusion from her mind to let sleep take her.

The next day was Saturday. She waited for his call and stayed in for the evening so as not to miss him, but he didn't make contact. It was the same on Sunday. She agonized over what to do, whether to call him, to go over to his apartment. Instead, she decided to wait for rounds on Monday, to play it cool, as if everything was fine.

After all, he'd said he loved her....

As usual, the doctors and students gathered in the conference room on Monday morning to begin the preamble to the rounds. She looked anxiously for Pete but couldn't spot him. She was wishing she'd called him, wondering if something was wrong, when the chief of surgery's voice interrupted her thoughts.

'I'd like you all to greet Dr Martin Backhouse, our new senior resident. Many of you will know that Pete Dewan has taken an associate professorship in Wisconsin, and is on terminal leave.

I'm sure all our good wishes go with him, and to you too Doctor Backhouse. Welcome.'

There was a muted round of applause and then business began. Business as usual. Anne stood, rooted to the spot, until one of her friends gave her a nudge and said, 'Come on, Anne, move it along. You OK?'

She nodded, but spent the morning in a daze, going through the motions. *Wisconsin? Pete? But he'd said nothing to her, nothing....* At lunchtime, she called a cab and went over to his apartment, not even able to remember which one it was, only the block itself. She stood outside, as if he might appear through the front entrance, then walked up to the mailboxes and looked at the names. The name *Dewan* was still in the slot for apartment 904. She pressed the bell. There was no answer. She didn't see the janitor come up behind her as she pressed it again, jumping at his unexpected voice.

'You looking for Dr Dewan, ma'am?' he said, leaning past her and opening the slot with a key. He took out the card bearing Pete Dewan's name and shut the door. 'He left, Saturday. Packed everything, and set off for Wisconsin. He's got a big job there, he told me. You a friend? You want the forwarding address?'

She looked at him, blankly, and shook her head, walking slowly away, realizing what a fool she'd been. What an impressionable, childish, silly little girl. She found it hard to concentrate for a few days, but eventually got things together and threw herself into her studies. When her period didn't start on the expected day, she felt a transient minor panic but reassured herself that it would come the next day. It didn't. Nor the next. She went to a doctor in town rather than the student health centre, fearful of what they might say or do if they found one of their final-year medical students was pregnant.

The test was positive.

She walked back in a daze to the campus after hearing the result and sat on a bench in the wooded picnic area by the lake, watching the ducks and swans without really seeing them. The feeling of panic had given way to a vacuum, so that she felt she was somewhere else, watching this drama unfold, watching this person immersed in a situation so hopeless there could be no acceptable escape. She shivered and pulled her coat closer as she contemplated her future.

Could she continue her studies, or would she have to give them up? Abandon her life's ambition to become a doctor, return home to her family, taking with her the shame and the hurt they would feel?

Or should she go to the health centre, get counselling, see what the chances were of getting an abortion ... *kill* her baby, Pete's baby.

Or find a quiet clinic in town that would do the job for a couple of hundred bucks and ask no questions?

Or should she call Wisconsin, tell Pete Dewan he was going to be a father and ask him what the fuck he was going to do about *that*? She sat for hours before reaching a decision, but when she stood up, her right hand unconsciously found its way on to her abdomen for an instant, as if reassuring its tiny occupant.

As the weeks went on, her decision not to make a decision began to weigh in favour of doing nothing. The thought of an abortion was abhorrent to her. She had made the mistake, not the little being inside her and it would be a greater sin to remove it now. She was a little scared about how her parents would react, and didn't want to hurt them, but she would cross that bridge in due course. She would take time out, have the baby, then resume her medical studies later. As the decision slowly made itself for her, she began to feel more comfortable with it, and felt happier with life. Indeed, she took some pleasure from the secret of the new life within her as she went about her duties.

So the miscarriage came as an even greater shock than finding she was pregnant. She was in the library when the first pain came, doubling her up over the desk, and bringing a gasp from her lips. Some of the students around her looked up.

'It's OK, something I ate, I guess,' she whispered, taking a deep breath, and collecting her books. She walked unsteadily out into the quadrangle, holding her lower abdomen, and made for the students' residence, stopping twice more as the cramps came. She had just made it to her room when the bleeding started. She dropped her books and dashed to the toilet where she sat, watching the new life drain from her, crying from grief, guilt and loneliness....

The empty tumbler fell to the wooden floor with a loud bump, waking Anne Bell with a start. She looked around her living-room, remembering her frustration of the day past, and the two large vodkas that had sent her off into her reverie on the sofa in front of the warmth of the fire. She stared into the flames suddenly realizing why she disliked and distrusted Gary Masters so much. He reminded her of Pete Dewan. He was the same kind of man – handsome, smart, confident, ruthless, willing to use people to get his way. He didn't care if he was right or wrong, probably didn't ever consider that he could be wrong. The blame for the ICU deaths could not possibly be his. So he shifted it on to someone else. And now Anne had seen her own colleagues, people she had worked with for years, line up against her. Even Jerry Weinberg had failed to support her. Well, she would show them who was right and who was wrong. She would co-operate with the enquiry, demonstrate that her ICU was beyond reproach. She had been shafted once in her life by a conceited, arrogant man. She was not going to let it happen twice.

CHAPTER II

Gary was at his desk when the call from Miami came through.

'Dr Rodriguez on line two.'

He grabbed the phone.

'Geraldo. How is he?'

'Calm down, Gary,' said Geraldo Rodriguez, sensing the urgency in his voice. 'He's fine. All obs stable, normal cardiac function, normal echo-scan, sitting up and eating like a horse.'

'No fever?'

'97.6 and steady as a rock.'

Gary breathed a sigh of relief. 'Excellent,' he said.

'Certainly is. Now, when do I let him home?'

There was silence for a moment before Gary replied.

'Seven days, and then back for review five days later. Is he fit for that?'

'He's already asking when he'll be discharged,' replied Rodriguez. 'This is one strong man, Gary. Anyone else would have been dead weeks ago. This one's asking to go home.'

'Well I hope the man who put him there isn't waiting somewhere with his stiletto for a second attempt.'

'From what I can gather, that's unlikely to happen.'

Gary's thoughts turned to the rumours of mafia connections, the *consigliere*, Menos, and Kathryn Skiathos. He shook his head imperceptibly, as if to dismiss her from his consciousness.

'Good,' he said. 'Keep me posted.'

'Sure. Everything OK with you?'

'Yes, fine. I'm just about to start another aneurysm.' He didn't mention the news that had greeted him on his return from Miami, the news of the second death.

'You're galloping along then, crunching the numbers.'

'They're coming in a steady stream.'

123

'When have you scheduled the little girl I keep seeing on TV?'

'She's just arrived in town. We'll be working her up for the rest of this week.'

'Well, good luck with that one *amigo*. The eyes of Miami will be on you.'

'Thanks Geraldo. I'll let you know how it goes, if the *Miami Herald* doesn't tell you first.'

He put down the phone. The eyes of Miami, and most of the rest of the Eastern United States, he thought. But NBC had made him a good offer for an exclusive, and agreed to pay a substantial amount to the Pereiras when it was all over to try to help their case for immigration. With NBC behind them, they would have enough publicity to pull it off. The phone rang again. It was his secretary.

'They're ready for you in OR.'

He replaced the receiver, stood up and stretched, before making his way to the operating suite. He passed ICU on his way and wondered what would be the fate of his next patient, Mr Philip Farkas.

Inside the ICU at that moment, four beds were occupied, one was prepared for the arrival of Mr Farkas, and the other three were screened off. Behind the screens, a microbiologist was taking swabs and samples from the masks, the tubes, the respirators, then removing the detachable parts to be taken away for further analysis, as one of the ICU technicians put in replacements in preparation for the next case which would occupy the bay. Meanwhile, other technicians from the medical electronics department tested the monitors, the recorders, the pulsimeters, the oximeters, in fact, every meter, computer and recorder in each bay to check for malfunction such as inaccurate display of oxygen saturation, inaccurate delivery of gases, anything that could explain inaction or erroneous action on the part of the medical attendants as a result of instrument malfunction.

Anne Bell watched over these processes while she also set her nurses to work checking the stock, recording the expiry dates on the intravenous fluids, the i.v. giving sets, the cannulas, everything that might be inserted or injected into the bodies of the patients arriving on ICU.

While Gary Masters put in another membrane repairing an otherwise inoperable and ultimately fatal aneurysm.

At 1.30 p.m., they wheeled Mr Farkas into the ICU.

Tim Dowdall looked unusually flustered.

'Tricky one Anne. He lost a lot more blood than the others. There were problems with the membrane and he had to go back on by-pass a second time. Then he arrested when we took him off. V-fib. He responded to the first shock. He's stable now, but he'll need watching. The others were easy. This one copped for all the complications.'

They changed him over to the ICU connections. Anne Bell watched and the thought suddenly occurred to her that it was all very well checking the ICU equipment, but the patients arrived in ICU already hooked up to similar equipment from the OR. The OR apparatus and stock needed the same rigorous check. She made a mental note to call Jerry Weinberg and widen the testing to include the cardiac OR.

Trudie did her usual expert job of connecting Mr Farkas to his ICU lifelines, and they watched as the monitors lit up.

'Stable,' Anne said, almost to herself.

'I've got another case at Brigham, Anne,' said Tim Dowdall. 'If you have a problem, call me.'

She looked up at him. He was watching her intently. To her surprise, he touched her arm and said, 'I know none of this shit is down to you, Anne. This is the best ICU I've ever worked in.' He looked almost embarrassed for a moment, then turned and walked towards the exit. He looked back and mouthed *call me* before disappearing around the corner.

She watched him go, grateful for his support before turning back to the patient, watching the monitors, checking the drains for blood, watching the urine output, looking for signs of trouble. Four hours later her patient was still stable.

She sat with Trudie at the nurse's station sipping coffee.

'So far, so good,' she said.

Trudie nodded. 'You staying over tonight?'

Anne shook her head. 'I would have if he'd shown any signs of trouble, but it looks like all of that happened in OR. I'll be at home. I've got a stack of things to do. Who's in charge tonight?'

'Melanie Brooks.'

Anne smiled. 'That's OK. She'd die for Gary Masters. I'm sure she'll take good care of his patient!'

'Funny he hasn't looked in yet,' said Trudie. 'You must have really frightened him off that time he dashed in and tried to take over.'

'I don't think he scares that easy, Trudie. He'll be down.'

But he hadn't appeared by the time Anne decided to call it a day. She spent a further hour on the unit before leaving for home. Trudie would be on until eight. The ICU resident was competent. Melanie was on for the night. There was no reason to stay. But she left with the familiar uncertainty of whether the phone would wake her later to summon her back before morning.

'Pinch me.'

Carmen Pereira looked at her husband.

'Que?'

'Pinch me. I need to know this is real.'

She smiled. 'It is real,' she said walking towards him and reaching up to kiss him, then turning her head suddenly to bite his ear.

'Ouch!'

'See, you are awake. It's real, Tito. You did it for us.'

This time, she kissed him full and long on the lips.

'Come to the window,' she said, leading him to walk beside her. They stood in the hospital residents' apartment and looked out over the green gardens surrounding the UHSM, and the Boston skyline beyond.

They stood in silence for a moment, Tito looking back briefly towards the second bedroom where Maria was sleeping. It had been a busy day.

After they left Krome camp, with the sound of their cheering countrymen ringing in their ears, the limo had taken them to the administration wing where they were given a full new set of clothes, spare garments and bathroom necessities, and $200.00 in cash. They were told there would be further provisions made available to them in Boston, and they would be given $200.00 a week for petty cash. The hospital would provide accommodation and food free of charge for the duration of their stay. An immigration officer would be available to them for advice, and they were not to leave the hospital grounds without first telephoning his number in Boston. The camp governor bade them farewell in person.

'Good luck, Doctor Pereira, I'm pleased for you and your family. I only wish I could let the others go with you.'

Tito looked at him closely, realizing he meant it and taking his hand.

Within minutes, they were back in the limo, heading north to Miami International Airport.

The flight attendants made a fuss of them all, but especially Maria. At Logan, an army of reporters was waiting as they left arrivals, but the immigration officials hurried them through the mêlée without giving Tito time to respond to the cacophony of questions. Within thirty minutes they were at the hospital. They were greeted by David Meeson, who ushered them through the imposing front entrance as security kept another batch of reporters at bay. They walked to the end of the main corridor, and across a leafy courtyard to a modern apartment block where they were shown to their quarters – two bedrooms, a bathroom, a living-room, and a kitchen. There was a phone and a TV in the living-room. They stood in awe and appreciation as they were shown around, before thanking David Meeson. One of his assistants showed them the kitchen which had been stocked with groceries, and asked Carmen to prepare a list of requirements over and above those provided. She showed Tito a map of the locality, emphasizing that he must call the immigration office if they wanted to leave the hospital grounds. She also emphasized that they were not prisoners, but were guests of the government and the hospital and, as such, had to observe certain rules.

Then she left also, and they were alone.

Alone in Boston, Massachusetts, USA.

They really had made it and it seemed a million miles away from the poverty of Cuba, the makeshift raft, high seas, sharks. But there was still uncertainty about their future, and the fate of little Maria who, they now knew, had two holes in her tiny heart.

They made love on a soft bed that night, as Maria slept in the adjacent bedroom. It was like a honeymoon for them, almost intoxicated with their freedom. When they woke the next morning, neither of them knew where they were for a few moments, before the realization sank in and they embraced and held each other. After a few moments, Carmen crept into Maria's room, to find her lying on her back, sucking her thumb, her eyes wide open.

'Is this America?' she asked.

Carmen nodded. 'Do you want to come into our bed?'

Maria nodded enthusiastically and leapt out to take her mother's hand.

They stayed in bed for another hour as Tito tried to prepare his daughter for the days ahead, the tests, the evaluations. At eight, they rose, and Tito shaved while Carmen made breakfast. At nine, the phone rang, making them all jump. It was Gary Masters.

'Hi, Doctor Pereira. Welcome to Boston. Are you settled in? Got everything you need?'

'Yes, sir. Thank you.'

'Well, I'm just calling to let you know we have Maria scheduled for lab tests, lung function tests, and an echo – an ultrasound scan of the heart – tomorrow. A Spanish-speaking nurse will come and collect her. One of you, you or your wife, can be with her most of the time. That will be all for tomorrow. The next day, she needs an angiogram. That will be a little more upsetting for her, but I hope that after today, she'll feel less of a stranger, more familiar with the nurse, and less antagonized by her surroundings.'

'I understand. I will speak with my wife to decide who comes.'

'This week will just be tests. I don't intend to schedule surgery before sometime next week,' he said, thinking let's see how Mr Farkas does first.

'I understand,' Tito repeated.

'I've spoken with the immigration people. So long as you clock out and back in again, they're fairly relaxed about you all. I think they realize you're not going to do a runner. So why don't you get out and look around the city between Maria's appointments? You'll enjoy it, I'm sure.'

'We would love to do that. I think we'd feel like tourists.'

'I guess. But if this pans out OK, Doctor Pereira, I'll do what I can to make sure you're considered for permanent immigration status. I hope you won't have to feel like a tourist for long.'

Tito felt the same lump in his chest he had when Mr Powell, JT, had turned up at Krome with the parcels and offered help. He made a mental note to call him and let him know they were in Boston although he had possibly seen it on the news by now.

'Thank you Doctor Masters. I hope you know how much we appreciate your incredible help.'

'Sure. We all do, and we're all rooting for you. If I don't see you before, we'll get together Friday and I'll update you with the test results. OK?'

'Of course. Thank you again.'

The phone went dead, and Tito related the conversation to Carmen.

'So,' he said, 'shall we have a look around?'

David Meeson's assistant had suggested that they leave and enter through the side door to the hospital gardens, and had provided them with a key. There would be reporters hanging around the front entrance for days from now on, and it would be better for everyone if there were no unofficial interviews. So they let themselves out of the gate an hour later, and followed the signs for downtown and Quincy Market, using the tourist map with which they had been provided. They wandered around the financial district, the shopping areas, the harbourfront, Quincy Market, mingling with the tourists and feeling the joy of freedom. They drank coffee at a pavement café in the market. At one point, as Maria drank her Coke watching a mounted policeman canter by, Tito noticed Carmen staring down at her daughter, and saw her eyes misting up.

'Are you all right?' he asked softly, as a single tear ran slowly down her cheek.

She nodded, wiping the tear away and indicating for him not to draw Maria's attention to her.

They had a wonderful day, taking it slowly, Tito often carrying Maria so as not to tire her, thinking it was possibly the happiest day of their lives. When they got back to the hospital, Tito called in while Carmen fixed supper. Later, when Maria had been put to bed and Tito and Carmen sat drinking coffee, Tito asked gently, 'What were you crying over this morning?'

She looked at him, then knelt before him, her head on his lap. 'I was just thinking.'

'What?'

She looked up at him, her eyes once again moist. 'I was thinking how awful it would be if, after getting this far, Maria ...' her voice trembled a little, 'Maria didn't make it through surgery. I just couldn't bear being so happy today but thinking how sad I would be if anything....'

She was sobbing now, her head once more on his lap, her shoulders shaking.

He stroked her soft black hair.

'I know,' he said gently, 'but remember what we left behind. I would have been arrested, you would have been alone, and Maria could have got sick anytime.'

She looked up at him. 'I know, I know. It was just that, seeing her today, she seemed so well, so normal. I just wanted it always to be like today, but instead kept thinking of the ordeal she has to face.'

He nodded. Freedom was not yet theirs, and the future was not secure at all. Uncertainty was still their constant companion. He wiped away her tears.

'Everything will be all right,' he said softly. 'I promise you. I have always believed it.'

Carmen accompanied her for the first tests. Tito wanted her to be with Maria for the more daunting angiograms the next day also, and felt it would be better that they both went through the first day together. He stayed in the apartment for a couple of hours after they left, then decided to venture out for a while. He called the immigration number.

'Yes?'

'This is Doctor Pereira, at University Hospital of Southern Massachusetts. I would like to go out for an hour or two.'

'Doctor Pereira? Southern Massachusetts? Hold on for a minute, let me see if I can locate your reference.'

Tito sighed. Bureaucracy was the same the whole world over.

He waited for five minutes and nothing happened.

He wondered what to do next then, being a surgeon, decided to ignore the bureaucracy, replace the receiver, and go for a walk through the hospital and its grounds. He walked through the ground-floor corridors, through the gardens, along the lakeside. He got back an hour later. There was no sign of Carmen and Maria.

He switched on the TV and flicked through the channels quickly, sitting up suddenly and staring at the screen in disbelief.

He was seeing himself, Carmen and Maria leaving the airport and being ushered into the car. Then the scene shifted to the frontage of the hospital as they entered the front door, before Krome Camp appeared on the screen.

'*Meanwhile, back at Krome Camp, life goes on ...*' drawled the commentator's voice. '*There is no resentment here that the Pereira family was granted permission to leave, only a fervent hope amongst the inmates that little Maria Pereira comes through her surgery safely, and that one day soon, all of these Cuban refugees can walk through those same gates, to freedom. This is Ed Berkeley, Krome Camp, South Florida.*'

The news continued as Tito sat staring at the screen. He made a mental note to watch the bulletin again later with Carmen and Maria.

Suddenly the door burst open, and Maria ran into the room, looking around, seeing her father and running towards him. He plucked her up and swung her around looking over to Carmen, his eyebrows raised questioningly.

She smiled. 'She was as good as gold,' she said, putting her bag on the sofa and joining them, pulling Maria's leg gently, 'weren't you?'

She nodded.

'Did they tell you anything?' he asked.

Carmen shook her head. 'They just did the tests.' She sighed. 'I need a cup of coffee.'

'I'll do it,' Tito said, swinging Maria from side to side.

'Want to help me make the coffee for Mama?' he asked.

She nodded and he carried her to the kitchen. 'And later, we'll all watch TV together, because I've got a surprise for you both.'

For Anne Bell, the surprise was that she woke at 6 a.m. without having been disturbed overnight. When you went to sleep knowing that there was a difficult case on the unit, a case which might go off at any time, and yet you got a full night's sleep, it meant one of two things, depending who was on duty. Either everything was fine, or something was wrong but no one had spotted it yet. But Melanie Brooks had been on last night, so there was probably nothing to worry about. Anne smiled as she got out of bed. Melanie Brooks. Thunder Thighs as they called her. Two-time loser in the marriage stakes, and on the lookout for a man who could handle her, with Gary Masters firmly in her sights. But a damn good ICU nurse. She walked to the kitchen and flicked on the percolator, then moved to the living-room and pulled back the curtains. It was a grey day in Boston, with threatening clouds moving down from the north. Not what the brochures usually depicted as fall in New England. But she had got used to the unpredictability and mixture of Boston's weather, the city lying at a junction of different atmospheric influences from the warm south, the variable westerlies, and the cold air from Canada. When these three met over Boston, anything could happen. She brushed her teeth and showered, then poured a cup of coffee, idly watching the television in the kitchen as she sipped the first caffeine fix of the day, a necessary addiction for most ICU doctors. She watched the footage of Maria Pereira's arrival at UHSM, feeling butterflies in her stomach when she thought of the media microscope which would be on them all when that case came through. Normally she would have enjoyed the publicity for her unit and her hospital. Now, with two unexpected, unexplained deaths, and Gary Masters running amok, blaming everyone but himself, and mainly her, she felt a foreboding about the little girl she could not shake off, and a vulnerability that was alien to her. She was known always to be in command. But things were happening which were outside her control, which she was unable to influence, but for which she was being blamed, held responsible. Her doubts turned to a feeling of anger as she remembered the meeting with Weinberg and the others, remembered Gary Masters' accusations and blame, supported by all of them. She turned off the TV and refilled her cup. Well, if they wanted a fight, they'd come to the right place. She would spend the next few days searching herself for the cause. She would dissect every document, every report, every clinical result of all the patients who had come through the ICU since Gary arrived until she found an answer. She knew it had to be something unique to him and his work. And she would find it, show them all that they were wrong to blame her and her staff. She felt more positive as she left the apartment and made her way to the metro station to catch the train to work.

CHAPTER 12

'I just don't know what to do about it, James.'

Jerry Weinberg sounded fed up. He was sitting at the bar in Mulligans, one of Boston's best known Irish bars, and the one which staff from UHSM, as well as an assortment of local cops, fire department personnel, office workers, bankers and others, tended to regard as their 'local'. It was also a favourite with followers of the Boston Patriots NFL football team.

James Sinclair looked at his friend then took another thoughtful mouthful of his Bud Ice. He was a man in his mid-forties, medium height and good-looking, with dark hair just beginning to turn a little grey at the temples, and deep, blue eyes, a contrast to his big, blond Viking-like companion.

'Well, if you don't know, Jerry, there's no hope for the rest of us.'

Jerry Weinberg looked at his friend, his tanned features breaking into a grin. 'Thanks, Jim, boy. You know you're partly responsible for putting me in this position.'

'Me?'

'Yes, you. You and Anne Bell both persuaded me to take on the director of surgery job. Now look what you've landed me with.'

'You were the best man for the job, Jerry. Everyone knew that.' They sat in silence, glancing up occasionally at the TV.

'How's the investigation going?' Sinclair asked eventually.

'Too early to say. The equipment's all been passed A-1. Bacteriology is culturing swabs from everything and everyone. Meanwhile, all the patients coming and going through the unit are doing as well as they always did.'

'Until the next one?'

Weinberg shrugged. 'Maybe. Seems like we're just waiting

for the next disaster without knowing what to do to prevent it.'

'Or even *if* it will happen.'

'Exactly.'

'I feel sorry for Anne.'

Jerry looked pained.

'Me too. Suddenly it seems like she's in a corner with no one on her side. I guess in a way she asks for it – you know what she's like. There's no one more confident, capable, self-opinionated, dedicated. She looks on that unit as her baby, protects the staff, fends off anyone who tries to butt into her work. Trouble is, this time, all the evidence points to the ICU as the source of the problem. She just won't acknowledge that.'

'She's co-operating with you isn't she?'

'Yes, but reluctantly. And it's obvious she feels let down by us all, feels we're siding with Gary.'

'Which you are.'

'What?'

'You are, Jerry. This ICU has an unbeatable record. Anne Bell is probably the best doctor I've ever worked with. Both the deaths are Gary's patients. It's a new technique. I'm surprised you haven't at least slowed the programme down a little. Instead, he did another yesterday. And the little Pereira girl's waiting in the wings.'

'Tell me about it. But two isn't enough, Jim. It takes three points to draw a straight line. People die in intensive care. We've just got to hope there are no more.' He sighed. 'Want another?'

Sinclair nodded. He knew Jerry liked Anne a lot, and was uncomfortable with the fact that her work was under suspicion. If he had not been director of surgery, he would probably have been in there pitching for her, fighting off Gary and anyone else who dared to threaten her. He understood his friend's dilemma.

Jerry walked over to the bar, and ordered two more Buds. He looked over to his left to where a crowd of regulars were gathered, homing in on their conversation. Every now and then, a cheer erupted from the group.

'What's going on, Pat?' he asked the barman.

'Joe Kennedy's up to his tricks.'

Weinberg smiled. He knew Joe Kennedy. A local cop. And a local character.

'It started with him naming five Boston beers, now what

were they ... Samuel Adams Lager, Tremont Ale, Goat Island Light, Waves Boston Brew and Black Dog Ale. Then Jimmy Mills challenged him to name five regional brews, and he came up with Pete Wilkins from Minnesota, Dixie Jazz Amber from Louisiana, New Amsterdam Amber from New York, Anchor Steam from California and ... er ... yes, Wild Goose Ale from Maryland. Now he's got a twenty dollar bet with Barney Callaghan. Says he'll name a beer from any twenty US regions or countries anyone calls out. Any twenty. He's up to eleven.'

'Twenty countries. That's ambitious. I didn't know Joe was a globetrotter.'

'He isn't, I think Washington DC's the furthest he's ever been. He likes his beer though. Maybe he majored in brewing at college.'

'What's he got so far?'

'Oh, all the easy ones – Bud, Coors, Killian's Red, Fosters, Amstel, Stella, you know?'

Weinberg nodded. Another cheer broke out from the group. Jerry caught James Sinclair's eye and beckoned him over, handing him his beer and leading him towards the group.

He recognized some of the faces. Patriots people.

'Singapore,' someone called out.

'Tiger lager,' Joe Kennedy responded, bringing another cheer from the group.

He was a man just on the right side of fifty, with a tanned face and a lop-sided grin, the result of two scars, one beneath his right eye and one on the right side of his chin, mementoes of his career as a Boston vice cop. His hair was greying, and cut short. His eyes were a striking light blue. When his friends were in a benevolent mood, they had been known to liken him to Paul Newman.

'New Zealand?'

'Steinlager.'

'Santa Fe?'

'Black Cloud Porter.'

'Mexico?'

'Corona.'

'Spain?'

'Sol.'

'You sure you're not making these up Joe?' called one of the group.

'That's for you to find out, Barry,' Kennedy responded with a grin. 'Come on, you guys. Jeez. You can't even think of twenty countries, let alone their beers.'

'Thailand?'

'Singha.'

'Italy?'

'Nastro Assuro.'

'Jamaica?'

'Red Stripe.'

'That's nineteen,' Pat announced from behind the bar. 'Reach for your wallet, Barney.'

There was silence around the bar, until Sinclair's English accent broke it.

'Manchester.'

Kennedy looked over. 'Oh, hi, Doc. Docs,' he corrected himself, seeing Jerry also. 'Is that Manchester, New Hampshire, or Manchester, England.'

'Manchester, England.'

There was silence again. Barney paused, his hand on the wallet in his back trousers pocket, sensing this might be a tough one. The silence continued, the group waiting for Joe to respond, feeling that the English doctor had saved Barney his money at the last minute.

Joe looked thoughtful, took a gulp of his Miller Lite, then looked up at James Sinclair shaking his head slowly with a serious expression on his face.

'That's not easy, Doc, and not fair. Manchester is a city in another country, not a country. If you said, England, I'd say Watneys, or Courage, or Stones. If you said Ireland I'd say Cafreys, or Smithwicks. But Manchester, England....' He rubbed his chin.

'Manchester, England,' he said, almost to himself. Then a grin slowly spread over his face as he looked around the group, and back at Sinclair.

'Why, that would have to be Boddington's Bitter, Doc.'

Sinclair smiled, then nodded, and a cheer erupted over the bar followed by applause from the locals. Barney Callaghan handed over a $20 bill, and the group returned to their conversation and drinking. Joe Kennedy walked over to Weinberg and Sinclair.

'How are you, Doctors?' he asked.

'Good,' said Jerry. 'Didn't know you were into party games.'

'Oh, just a little information I've accumulated over the years. But you know, I still prefer Miller Lite to any of those others. Though, to be fair, I've never tasted Boddingtons.'

'The Cream of Manchester, they call it,' said Sinclair, almost wistfully.

'So how's vice?' asked Jerry Weinberg.

'Search me. I'm in homicide now.'

'Homicide?'

'Yeah. The chief reckoned I was spending so much time doing their work, I might as well move over and do it officially. I moved six weeks ago.'

'The *Painter* murders?' asked Sinclair, remembering their involvement in a series of racially motivated murders the year before.

Kennedy nodded. 'And the Laura Rheinhart affair. Remember that, Jerry? Remember bursting into your house that night, not knowing what we were going to find, finding the Boston Rapist laid out on the floor dead as a dodo, with Mrs Rheinhart and your wife?'

'Only too well,' said Jerry. 'You still owe me for the back door you kicked in! So let me rephrase the question. How's homicide?'

'Quiet, I'm glad to say. But that doesn't mean you guys have got to go out there and find me more work. Like you usually do!'

'Don't worry, Joe. We've had enough of that stuff too,' said Jerry, wondering for a moment if Joe Kennedy might be able to solve the mystery of the ICU deaths, then immediately dismissing the thought from his mind, as if ashamed to be thinking that those deaths could be anything other than natural causes.

That night, she waited until 4 a.m., the lowest point of the shift, the point where all anyone wanted to do was nod off, take a nap, go home, the point where most of the work was done and they were ready for a break before starting the 6 a.m. rounds. She had prepared everything already, the 2 ml syringe with the 400 mg of scoline, the 5 ml of saline to wash it through the cannula so it left no trace. She had selected the case, a sixty-nine year old bronchopneumonia, extubated yesterday, due for discharge back to the ward tomorrow. All she had to do now was wait for Susie to go make the coffee. The bays were still bright, and there were people at work in three of them, but the far end was Susie's and hers, so no one would see. The old boy was sleeping. He was out of danger. Or so they thought. She knew better. She knew that he was in mortal danger, that he had a role to play, an important role, a role which he should be happy to accept, since it would rescue and protect one of the greatest talents in the whole country from the suspicion that was surrounding him and threatening to destroy his career. She knew how dedicated he was, how much he cared. Perhaps later, when the pressure was off, she would be able to get closer to him, show him how much *she* cared. But first, she had to make sure that he was going to be around, that he was not going to be suspended, or moved.

She felt the two syringes in her pocket, and walked out of the office.

'Want to make some coffee, Susie?'

'Sure. Two minutes.'

She went over to the bay next to the old man's, and checked the lines, the monitors, watching Susie in the next bay out of the corner of her eye, eventually seeing her walk off in the direction of the kitchen. She moved slowly into the next bay, taking out the smaller syringe. She looked down at the sleeping patient. He was old anyway, she told herself. A vagrant, off the streets. It would only be a matter of time before he was back in again, this time with a fatal dose of something else. She switched down the volume control on the monitor alarm, and took the small syringe from her pocket, sliding the needle smoothly into the rubber bung of the i.v. tube. She emptied the syringe, put it in her pocket, then connected the second one to the same needle and emptied that, withdrawing the needle and syringe in one smooth movement, putting the guard over the needle, slipping it off the syringe and putting them into her pocket. She left the old man and walked purposefully into the adjoining bay as if to check things there before moving slowly towards the nurse station, stretching as she went, as if she were as weary as the others.

'Tired?' asked one of the nurses emerging from Bay 1.

'No more than usual. Susie's getting the coffee.'

It ought to be working now, she thought to herself. Scoline's quick, very quick. Smooth muscle relaxant. Paralyses the patient in preparation for anaesthesia, stops spontaneous breathing within a minute in preparation for inserting the endotracheal tube. Got to get that in quick after scoline, got to artifically inflate the lungs, get the oxygen down there. Otherwise....

Susie appeared with the tray, and they sat down. It was only a matter of seconds before she leapt up, spilling coffee over her notes and yelling 'My God, Bay 6, he's flat.'

She looked at the sixth screen along. While the first five were showing the regular, healthy peaks and troughs of normal cardiac activity, the trace on six was moving along monotonously on the baseline. The others put their mugs down and rushed after her to the old man.

'This can't be, I was with him a second ago.'

They worked fast. She grabbed a laryngoscope and tried to get a tube down while the other banged on his chest, counting. 'One-two-three-four-five-six' ... pause ... look at the monitor ... flat ... 'one-two-three....'

The nurse from Bay 1 put out the crash call.

'I can't get this goddamn tube down.' Not surprising. Everything will be in spasm now. I'll just have to ram it in as hard as I can. It's not going to matter anyway.

'Where's that crash team?' someone demanded of no one in particular.

'There!' she said triumphantly, as the tube slid in. Just hope it took long enough. Long enough so that we're not too good at the CPR.

'Good work. One-two-three-four-five-six' ... pause ... look at the monitor ... flat....

Flat.

Twenty minutes later, the resident told them all to relax.

'You all did your best. He's gone.'

They exchanged glances, like they always did at moments like this, the glances of any arrest team when the immediacy and intensity of the co-ordinated effort is rewarded by failure. They felt cheated.

The doctors melted away, leaving the detritus of the failed resuscitation for the nurses to clean up, leaving the dead vagrant lying naked in a pile of used syringes, soiled dressings, bloodstained sheets, useless failed electrodes, lubricating jelly.

She started clearing up with Susie.

'This is terrible,' Susie said.

She nodded.

'I know he was a vagrant, he'd probably be back sometime, but he wasn't that old. I mean, sixty-nine....'

She busied herself taking the electrodes off his chest.

Susie stopped what she was doing, and looked at her. 'My God,' she said. 'Who's going to tell Dr Bell? Another death on the ICU....'

She nodded. 'Only one good thing about it,' she said. Susie looked up at her and she met her gaze. 'At least it's not another of Dr Masters'.'

When she turned away, there was a hint of a smile on her face.

Anne Bell woke with a start, sitting bolt upright in bed. She listened to detect what might have disturbed her. There was nothing. Only silence. She looked at the radio clock on the bedside table. It showed 4.45 a.m. She lay back, wondering whether to get a drink or turn over and go back to sleep. She did neither, just lay there, letting the ICU problems drift through her mind, wondering where to go from here, the old feelings of loneliness and isolation surfacing.

She decided to get some orange juice. Halfway to the kitchen, the phone rang.

She walked into the living-room and picked up the receiver.

'Anne Bell,' she said.

'Hello. This is Doctor Menendez, ICU. I thought you should know. We've had a death.'

Anne Bell felt weak, suddenly. She sat down in the chair. *Farkas*, she thought to herself.

'A death?' she asked.

'Yes. Joseph Pelegrino, sixty-nine year old pneumonia. Looks like cardiopulmonary arrest. We tried for thirty minutes. It was no use.'

Pelegrino. Not Farkas. Not one of Gary's. That's good. But hang on, good for Gary maybe, but not so good for ICU. The third death in a few days, and now a non-cardiac patient. So that means....

'Dr Bell?'

'Yes, sorry, I heard. Thanks for letting me know. I'll come in early. Put all the records on my desk so they're there when I get in. Thanks for letting me know.'

She put the phone down and stared into space. Another death. Only this one broke the pattern. Now the focus really would shift to ICU.

And her.

CHAPTER 13

Gary knew something was wrong as soon as he walked through the door of the ICU. After years of surgery you develop a sixth sense for trouble, and trouble was in the atmosphere today. You could almost smell it, feel it.

Melanie Brooks saw him enter and made towards him.

'Mr Farkas?' he asked, anxiously.

She smiled, and touched his arm, lightly....

'No,' she said. 'He's fine. It was one of the others, an elderly pneumonia case.'

Gary gave a sigh of relief, and returned her smile. 'I'm sorry,' he said, giving her arm a squeeze in return, knowing it must have been a bad night for the staff, appreciating her attention and relieved at the news. He made for Mr Farkas in Bay 2.

'Everything OK?' he asked the attending nurse.

'Absolutely, Doctor, all obs stable, saturation excellent, needing very little sedation. I think he'll be ready for extubation later today.'

'Temperature?'

'Ninety-eight point four.'

'Urine output?'

'Eighteen hundred.'

Gary took out his stethoscope and listened to Mr Farkas's chest and heart sounds. He stood back, taking the tubes out of his ears and putting the 'scope back into the pocket of his white coat.

'Very good. Thank you nurse. I'll be back later.'

She nodded, and watched him go. Almost worth being up all night for, she thought to herself.

As he left, Gary caught a glimpse of Anne Bell in her office, poring over the charts of the deceased vagrant. She looked awful. He felt a pang of pity, and almost went into the office to give her some comfort, but the thought was quickly replaced by the memory of her attempts to stop his programme. He walked on with a feeling of relief and apprehension. Relief that this death was a non-cardiac case, apprehension that it was yet another death on ICU, proving his theory that the previous two were not cardiac specific, but reassuring him not one bit about the safety of the unit for his patients. He made for the ward to meet his resident and intern to make rounds.

'What?' Jerry Weinberg shouted down the phone. 'Another? I'll be right down.'

He almost ran to the fire exit stairwell and took them two at a time up to the ICU level, walking quickly through the doors and straight to Anne Bell's office.

She looked up at him, her face serious.

'What happened. Is it another of Gary's?'

'No, it was an elderly pneumonia case, a vagrant they took off the streets.'

Jerry looked at her thoughtfully, turning over the implications in his mind, glancing at the charts on her desk. They sat down.

'Coffee?' she asked.

He nodded, and she went to her filter machine and poured them both a cup.

'Was it expected?' he asked, when she had sat down again.

'No, he was getting better.'

'Did it have any of the features of the other cases, you know, the fever, the dropping oxygen saturation, the breathing difficulties?'

'No, none of those.'

'So, what happened?'

'It looks like a respiratory arrest. There are no warning changes on the ECG, no signs of infarct. Could be a pulmonary embolus, I guess.'

'So, your initial assessment is natural causes?'

'Looks like it.'

'Not the Gary syndrome?'

'No evidence clinically. We'll have to wait for the autopsy.'

'Does this let Gary off the hook?'

Anne looked at him and shrugged. 'It's another ICU death this week. If the autopsy shows the same findings as the others, maybe it does. Maybe there is something wrong here....'

She looked away, not wanting to admit it. But it was another sudden unexplained death. If it had been a solitary, isolated occurrence, she might have accepted it as just that, a fact of ICU life. But coming so soon after the others, she knew it might be regarded as part of the pattern.

'Nothing else?'

'I don't think so. I've not finished going over the papers yet. I'll call Jules Wellbeloved in pathology at nine and arrange an urgent autopsy. Jerry, I think this was just an old man pegging out. It happens. You mustn't read too much into it.'

'You're beginning to sound like Gary Masters,' he said.

Neither of them could manage a smile. Jerry got up to leave.

'Oh, Jerry, there was one strange thing.'

He turned to face her again.

'Melanie Brooks said the alarm didn't sound. There might have been a short delay between the arrest and their attending it. A matter of seconds, but that alarm was checked just yesterday. It should have sounded. I'll have the unit sent down to electronics.'

Jerry nodded and left, calling by David Meeson's office. He walked through the reception area. The secretaries were not in yet. He knocked at Meeson's door, and walked in.

'Morning, David. Can I see you for a moment?'

'Sure, come on in. Not trouble I hope.'

'Well, maybe. There's been another death in the ICU.'

'What?' Meeson rose as he spoke, his pen dropping on to the desk. He stood staring at Jerry Weinberg, as if expecting him to say *Chill out, Dave, only joking....*

Jerry sat down on one of the two chairs in front of Meeson's over-large desk, wondering what mousse he used on his slicked, black hair.

'Yes, but not one of Gary Masters' this time. This was an elderly vagrant, brought in with pneumonia.'

'What happened?'

'We don't know yet. There's an autopsy, probably this afternoon.'

'I can't believe this. Three in ten days. I've never known this happen in my time here. That unit has always been one of the jewels in our crown. It can't go on.'

'We all know that, David. But it's being investigated. And at least it's not another heart case.'

'That doesn't matter. If anything, it proves Masters' point that something's wrong with the ICU. Should we close it?'

'No. This was a sick old man, David. It may not be part of any trend.'

'Well I sure as hell want to see the director.'

'I think you can leave that part to me, David.'

'No, Jerry, I can't. If there's a problem with ICU, I want her to know she's got to root it out, or her job may be on the line. Christ, why did this have to happen now, with the Pereira kid and all.'

'David, you can't threaten Anne Bell with the sack. She *built* this unit, rescued it from oblivion. She lives for it. She wants this resolved as much as we do.'

'Maybe. But she's the director, she carries the can. I've backed off this so far, Jerry. Didn't interfere when you had your private meeting the other day. But enough's enough. If this gets out, referrals will dry up, the Pereira case will bomb on national TV.'

Jerry got up and faced the administrator.

'David, I warn you, you shouldn't blame Anne, threaten her. It won't accomplish anything.'

Meeson rose also, picking up a sheaf of papers from his desk. 'Jerry, I already have a law suit here from the Peters family against the hospital and the ICU. *Not* against Gary Masters, you appreciate, but against *me*, and against Dr Anne Bell and her unit, citing excellent surgery without adequate backup facilities. This could mean mega-millions, Jerry, especially when they ask about other deaths, of which there are now two. And with the Pereira kid, there'll be no place to hide. I don't care what you say, I'm going to haul Anne Bell's ass in here and read her the riot act, along with anyone else who needs to sharpen their practice. There's something wrong here, and it's up to your medics to find out what it is. So far, people just keep dying.'

'We are trying, David. Everything possible that can be done is being done.'

'Well, I may have to think of bringing in some outside help here.'

'What kind of outside help? From where? David, there aren't any better people around than those in your own hospital. Unless....'

Meeson looked him directly, eye to eye.

'You think there's some foul play here? A cover up? Or worse …?'

'I don't know, Jerry. But sometimes, self-regulation doesn't work.'

'David, give us a little longer. The effect of bringing someone, possibly someone less qualified or respected, from another institution to investigate this hospital's staff could be very counter-productive.'

Jerry was beginning to hate himself and his role as clinical director. What was he doing almost pleading with this jumped up administrator when what he really wanted to do was punch him on the nose, and tell him to get off the case and leave Anne Bell alone. It only took him a second or two to decide that this line of action might be counter-productive. So instead, he simply said, 'David, I strongly recommend against this course of action at this time, at least until the autopsy results are through. I'll get them up to you as soon as they're available, then we can talk again, rather than now, in the heat of the moment.'

Meeson sat down slowly. 'As soon as they're available Jerry. But I'm determined to do something about this. My job's on the line here, just as much as anyone else's.'

Jerry left, deciding not to tell Anne of the conversation. Six hours later, he got a call from Jules Wellbeloved.

'Sorry, Jerry. Not much to find. Looks like a respiratory arrest. His lungs were shot from years of living on the streets. So was pretty well everything else for that matter. No exudates on his lungs. I've got some blood samples cooking, routine stuff. But I can't give you a precise cause of death here other than respiratory arrest.'

'Thanks, Jules.' Jerry was disappointed. He had been hoping for a good old-fashioned, straightforward myocardial infarction.

He gave a sigh, and picked up the phone again to call David Meeson.

Gary Masters was watching the pro-ball pre-season analyses on TV, the can of Budweiser balanced on the arm of the sofa. Occasionally he yelled at the screen.

'Rubbish! Brad Ryan's the best quarterback we've had for years.'

'Course he can take us to Superbowl again!'

'Crap!'

The phone interrupted his appreciation of the experts' football knowledge. He picked up the receiver.

'Gary Masters.'

There was silence for a moment.

But he knew it was her even before she spoke.

'This is Kathryn.'

He sat up. 'Where are you?'

'Boston. The Ritz-Carlton. Room 1208. Please come.'

He put the phone down without answering. Within seven minutes he was on the Main Street Bridge over the Charles River. Twenty minutes after the call, he was knocking at the door of room 1208.

She was wearing a hotel white terry towel bathrobe, tied loosely at the waist. She stood back to let him in, and closed the door behind her, leaning back against it for a moment to watch him, before she moved towards him, her lips parting, her arms reaching.

The kiss was long and deep, as if making up for the missed kisses of the past few weeks. She pushed her pubis against him to make the signal clearer as he responded to the moistness of her lips, the urgency of her tongue. She felt him rising and pushed harder, her robe falling open. He reached down for his belt but she was already there, working on it, ripping open the button and zipper on his jeans, tearing at his briefs and gasping in anticipation as she felt him break free and search for her, penetrating almost immediately and thrusting deep inside her. She groaned and her head went back as she responded, gripping him round the neck, and wrapping her legs around his back. He eased off his shoes and and kicked off his jeans and briefs as she clung on, feeding off him, taking the passion she had wanted so much, and he walked slowly towards the bed, holding himself inside her then falling on to her but never disturbing the rhythm of her movements. To his surprise, after a few moments, she moved to his side then on top of him, still thrusting her pelvis in response to him, murmuring *deeper, deeper*, then taking over, dictating the speed and rhythm herself until they both felt the explosion coming and cried out with the intensity of the climax. He flipped her over on to her back, then started up again, slowly, deeply, so as not to lose the erection, feeling the blood rush in again after the initial threat of detumescence, aware that her orgasm had not subsided, keeping it going until neither of them knew if she was having multiple orgasms or one continuous one. Her tongue searched for his ear, as if in gratitude, as if to keep him aroused, as if she never wanted this moment to end, as he continued minute after minute for what seemed like an eternity before he came again. But still she was not satisfied, as she moved from under him, kissing him with her full wet lips, brushing her hair away from her face, and moving down over his chest, and his muscular belly kissing and licking him all over before going down on him until he thought she would swallow him, then withdrawing again and repeating the process, again, and again, slowly, oh so slowly, so that he prayed it might go on forever. But he felt he was spent, felt he would not climax again without some respite, yet she would not stop, she just went on, and on, and on, slowly, methodically, with an occasional groan, on and on until he began to tremble and shake as she took total control of his body before taking him out of his mind with the uncontrollable intensity of the climax. He felt her shudder with pleasure at the same time. She stayed there for several minutes before leaving him. When she returned, she lay beside him, putting her mouth to his ear and whispering, 'I missed you, Dr Masters.'

He moved to face her and they kissed again, a slow, more tender and emotional kiss.

'Me too,' he said eventually, holding her tight.

They lay in silence until he could not resist asking her for any longer.

'How is he?'

'He's OK.'

He nodded his head slightly.

'How did you get away?'

'I told him I wanted to stay with my friend in West Palm Beach. He realized the stress I'd been under. There was not a problem.'

'You're taking a big risk.'

'It was necessary,' she whispered, as if that made it OK.

They lay in silence for a long time after that. He wondered if she was asleep, but when he moved a little to see her face, he saw that her black eyes were open, looking at him.

'How long?'

'I must go back at lunchtime tomorrow. You are working in the morning?'

'No, I've arranged things.'

She kissed him again, with a slow intensity he had never experienced, then moved off him and walked into the lounge of the magnificent suite returning with a bottle of champagne and two glasses. She sat down beside him on the bed, opened the bottle expertly and poured. He sat up beside her and took the glass, and they drank a silent toast.

To what, he wondered? To passion? To danger? To illicit, unbridled, simple uncomplicated sex? Or to love ...?

She interrupted his thoughts.

'You were wonderful with Tony. Thank you.'

He shrugged his shoulders. 'It's my work and I'm good at it.'

'No, in spite of us, you and me, you gave him life when he was dying. You gave him his confidence back. He was a shell, a skeleton, fading away before my eyes, losing hope, losing life. Now, he is almost himself, strong, vital. He values your work highly. I know he will not let it go unrewarded.'

'Unless he finds out about us.'

'There is no reason why he should. Maybe it would be better if this had not happened, but it did, and I....' There was an uncharacteristic pause. 'I cannot get you out of my mind, my soul ... I have no regrets.'

He hugged her to him and said, 'During Tony's illness, I thought it was over. You were so ... formal ... cold.'

'It was necessary,' she said again. 'Tony was dying. That was the only priority at that time. In any case, Menos would have picked up any hints.'

Menos.

'Now,' she continued, 'Tony is better. Now, I need you again. But we have to be careful.'

No kidding? he thought to himself. Careful of the *consigliere* in case he reports back to his boss that his surgeon is having an affair with his wife. Careful of his hospital, who might find such a liaison somewhat below the standard of behaviour demanded of their staff ... yes, they had to be careful, that was not in doubt. There was a lot at stake for him. But there was a lot at stake for her too. More than for him, in some ways. Why was she risking it all? Just for good sex? Or was there more to it?

He leaned over and kissed her, and she moved her face into the kiss, pressing against his lips, as if telling him she knew what he was thinking, knew the risks they were both taking.

They finished the champagne, then made love again, less urgently this time, more measured but with no less passion. Eventually they lay back in each others arms.

'Kathryn?' he asked after a few minutes.

'Yes?'

'When will I see you again?'

'I don't know. Tony is talking about going back to Athens soon for a while. I don't want to go, I hate it there. But if he insists....' She gave a Mediterranean shrug. 'If I can stay here, we can meet again. Maybe even spend some days together, go away somewhere.' She sounded excited by the thought and hugged him tightly. 'But if he insists....'

'Does he have an appointment to see Geraldo?'

'Yes. In two weeks.'

'Maybe I could come to Miami to see him at that time. Could we meet then?'

'It would be difficult. He would want to be with you, maybe take you to dinner. It would be difficult for me to get away, too obvious perhaps.'

Menos might notice, Gary thought to himself.

'Unless ... unless you came down early, and I got away for the day before the appointment. That might be possible.'

There was silence as they both thought through the possibilities, until he whispered, 'Kathryn, let's do it. I need you.'

He could hardly believe what he was saying. He had never needed anyone. She leaned towards him for a moment, her perfect breast resting on his chest, her lips full and red even without make-up, her eyes dark and deep but suddenly tender.

'I need you too, Gary,' she whispered.

So, like the participants of a Greek tragedy, they sealed their tryst, knowing but ignoring the lessons of logic and sense and history, instead allowing themselves to be drawn along by their feelings, and their own passionate momentum, towards the inevitable.

While down in Mulberry Street, a shadowy figure leaned against a lamp-post and took a long deep draw of his cigarette before flicking it into the gutter, glancing at his watch, and walking slowly away with one last backward glance up at the darkened windows of room 1208 at the Ritz-Carlton Hotel.

CHAPTER 14·

Anne Bell sat down in front of David Meeson and waited.

The Chief Executive Officer (Surgery) of the University Hospital of Southern Massachusetts sat watching her, his elbows on his chair arms, his fingertips together in front of his face.

'So what's happening on the ICU, Doctor?' he asked benignly.

'What do you mean exactly?' asked Anne, in her most co-operative voice.

'Well, I hear there was another death down there last night.'

'A patient died, yes. It happens on intensive care units, from time to time.'

'Three times in two weeks?'

'Occasionally.'

'So you're not concerned?'

'Of course I'm concerned. We're turning the whole place over to see if there's an identifiable problem. So far without success. Maybe it's just a bad run.'

'That's not been your opinion up to now though, has it?'

'What do you mean?'

'I heard you wanted the cardiac membrane programme halted because of the first two deaths.'

'That's correct.'

'And now?'

'That's still my opinion.'

'In spite of this latest third case?'

'I regard this case as a run-of-the-mill death on ICU of an elderly, unfit, sick old man like we get all the time. It was unexpected, sure, and we're looking into it. I still believe there may be a basic flaw in the heart technique.'

'That's not how I see it, Doctor Bell.'

'Oh?'

'The cardiac technique has been thoroughly investigated and assessed, and passed by the NIH. What I see is three deaths in one ICU in two weeks, and that smacks to me of sloppy performance or poor control.'

Anne Bell had already decided to remain calm under any circumstances, not to let this interview upset her. So instead of saying what she really felt, she responded, 'That's your interpretation.'

'Yes it is, and I want you to know that I'm not happy. I have here ...' he rustled some papers on his desk top, 'notice of a lawsuit being brought against this hospital by the parents of Phil Peters. You remember Mr Peters?'

'Of course.' How could she forget?

'Well, we're getting our ass sued, Dr Bell, thanks to you and your unit.'

'Hey, hold on a minute....'

'No, *you* hold on, Dr Bell. I want you to know that if there is another death on the ICU in the near future, or if another patient of Dr Masters has problems on your ICU, I will be suspending you from duty.'

Anne stood up. 'You can't do that, you have no right....'

Meeson was on his feet now. 'Watch me, Doctor. I have the right, I have the power, and I sure as hell have the inclination. I have disapproved of your attitude, your treatment of your colleagues, your language, for some time. Oh, sure, everyone tells me you're a talented doctor, but I'm not sure you are the best advertisement for this hospital. I've tolerated it because of the good figures your unit produces. Now, things are different. You're on borrowed time here, lady, unless you clean up your act and your department.'

Anne stared at him, clenching her fists, wanting to respond as her inclinations told her she should, but suppressing her emotions, determined not to give him the satisfaction of an excuse to suspend her there and then.

'Is that all?' she asked coldly, through clenched teeth.

'For now,' he replied.

She turned without a word and walked out of his office.

Gary Masters met with the Pereira family Friday afternoon as planned. His secretary showed them in.

'Coffee?' she asked. They nodded. She put her arm around Maria.

'And for you, Maria, how about a cookie and a Coke?'

The little girl nodded her head enthusiastically. She understood Coke, even in English.

Gary smiled. He was tired, but who would be surprised at that? He had left Kathryn Skiathos at 9.30 after they had shared breakfast in bed. This time she had walked to the door with him, and held him tight before he left.

'Soon,' she had whispered.

'Soon,' he replied.

He had gone back to his apartment for a shave, shower and change of clothes before going to his office. He spent the early afternoon on paperwork, then gathered all Maria's test results together for the meeting with her parents. He made small talk until the drinks arrived, then got down to business.

'The tests are all through now,' he started. 'They show that, although Maria is to all intents and purposes well at present, her heart is losing its reserve, and it is only a matter of time before she develops serious symptoms. These symptoms will comprise breathlessness on slight exertion, associated with a blue appearance as she struggles for breath ...'

'Excuse me, Doctor,' Tito interrupted, 'I'm sorry, but she has already had two of these attacks.'

Masters sat back.

'So, it's already happening,' he said. 'Untreated, these attacks will get worse, and will occur more frequently. They will put an immense strain on Maria's heart, and on her lungs. Ultimately, perhaps within a year, she ...'

He looked at Carmel. She looks so frightened, he thought. And she's gone through so much. But she has to know the truth. He took a deep breath to continue but, before he could speak, she rescued him.

'It's all right Doctor Masters. I know. Tito and I have talked about it many times. What do you recommend?'

'Surgery is her only hope. I can repair the small hole by conventional methods. The big one will require a new technique which only this hospital can offer. I must tell you though that, although we have tried and tested this technique in animals to perfect it, of four patients in whom we have done it so far, two have died.'

'From the surgery, or the condition?' asked Tito.

'We don't know, but we don't think it was from the surgery. That went well in all cases and there were no problems. Like Maria, they were both desperate cases. Without surgery....' He paused, to let them draw their own conclusions.

'When would you do the operation?' Tito asked.

'Next Tuesday.'

Gary almost surprised himself with his decision. But he had seen the angios, seen the cardiac pressures, seen the life-giving blood being shunted all over the place rather than to the tissues where it was needed, seen the weakness of the heart muscle as it struggled vainly to compensate for the holes in the heart siphoning off the blood from the aorta. This little girl would not last till Easter, maybe not even Christmas, unless something was done soon. And anyway, he'd had the producer of the Today programme on the phone again this morning asking for an update. They could not delay it indefinitely, in spite of the ICU problem. Christ, he thought to himself. If only I could have done it in Miami, got them out of the camp into Geraldo's unit, put her in his safe ICU afterwards....

Tito interrupted his thoughts. 'How long will it be before she is fit again?'

'Fit? For what?'

Tito looked down at his hands, then back up at Gary.

'To return to Krome, I suppose I mean.'

Gary shook his head.

'If everything goes well, she'll be fit for anything in six weeks to three months. But forget Krome. Leave that to me. We'll sort it out, one way or another. But as far as I am concerned, neither she, nor you, will ever go back to that place.'

'Is she strong enough for the surgery, Doctor?' Carmen still sounded scared.

'Yes, of course. But I must emphasize again, we have no choice. If we don't operate, there will be only one end. If we do, then she has a chance of life.'

Maria nibbled at her cookie, oblivious of the discussions on her future.

Gary flashed them a reassuring smile. 'We'll admit her to her room in the hospital on Monday afternoon in preparation for Tuesday morning,' he said, 'I'll make all the arrangements.'

They nodded. Gary looked at the three of them.

'Anything else?' he asked.

Tito and Carmen exchanged a quick glance, then shook their heads.

'No, sir,' said Tito.

Gary stood up, and they followed suit. He held out his hand.

'Tuesday, then,' he said.

They shook hands, solemnly and the Pereiras left.

Back on the ICU, Anne Bell was letting her anger out as she told her chief nurse what had transpired in David Meeson's office.

'Honestly, Trudie, I nearly went for him. What a rude, jumped-up, pathetic, limp-wristed, arrogant, ignorant, miserable, inane, fucking apology of a man. Of a *human being*.'

'Come on, Doctor Bell, don't mince your words, tell me what you really feel about him!'

Anne looked at her, and they both burst out laughing.

'I'm surprised you kept your patience,' Trudie said.

'Not as surprised as I was. I just had to get out of there and think things through. I came close to saying "Fuck you your ICU and your fucking hospital" and leaving him to clear up this mess. Jesus, those administrators, they think they know all the answers when they don't know anything. "Get someone else in to check things over", he said. Oh sure. Like who? The Brigham team, or someone from Mass. General? Hell, Trudie, we've got the best brains in Boston looking into this right here. We're going to crack this problem, not anyone else. I ...'

The phone rang, interrupting her tirade. She picked it up and barked 'Yes' into the mouthpiece.

'Och aye, young lady, no need to bite my head off.'

The Scots accent was unmistakable. Jules Wellbeloved, the Director of Pathology.

'Oh, hello Jules, sorry, it's been a bad day, and it's only nine fifteen. What can I do for you?'

'It's about the two cardiac cases. I've started analysis on that lung exudate we talked about, you remember?'

'Of course. And?'

'Well, Anne, it's a bit more complex than I first thought. It's quite viscous, not just aqueous and watery, and it's full of abnormal cells, like it might be some antigen-antibody reaction.'

'Hmm, that is interesting. Have you seen anything like it before?'

'Not really. Not in the lungs. I'll keep at it, call you back in a few hours if I get anywhere. Thought you'd like to know the story so far. For the time being though, think immune response, short of rejection.'

'Thanks,' she said, and then, as an afterthought, 'Oh Jules ...' – she took a deep breath – 'was there anything, anything remotely like this in the third case?'

'No, Anne. Nothing. That one was totally different, usual run-of-the-mill stuff.'

She put the phone down with a feeling of triumph. So the two heart cases *were* special. There *was* something about the membrane technique.

'OK, Trudie,' she said, flashing her chief nurse a determined look, 'you carry on out there. If you want me, I'll be in here. There's something in these records that has the answer I'm looking for. I just know it, and I'm going to find it.'

It was a hot, humid night in Miami, and the pierside disco at Bayside was throbbing. He stood at the bar, watching the bodies moving on the dance floor, eyeing up the girls as they passed. It was to be his last night in Florida, and he had decided to enjoy it. He had received his instructions, and was heading out the next day. So tonight, he decided, he should have a little fun in Miami. He sipped his bourbon slowly, enjoying the music, the lights of the city across the water, the sense of freedom. No wonder they flocked here from Puerto Rico, from Haiti, from Cuba. Better this than a hovel in your homeland. Not that he could complain. He was good at his job, it paid well, and it enabled him to travel occasionally. Why should he worry?

His attention was drawn to a disturbance to his left. A crowd of local boys, students maybe, were baiting a young Hispanic girl whom they had surrounded, separating her from her companions. She was a pretty young thing, long sleek black hair, laughing black eyes, laughing now with a hint of fear in them as she looked nervously over at her friends, attempting to get to them, the boys blocking her way at each step. One big fellow was particularly aggressive, slouching up to her, pressing his chest against her, pointing his finger at his thick lips as if to indicate she must kiss him to escape.

The man in the white suit put his drink down on the bar, wondering whether to intervene.

He took just one step towards them when he saw her put her hand on the bottom of the lout's cup of beer and push up on it suddenly, throwing it into his face, then dart past him as he rubbed his eyes in surprise, which quickly gave way to anger. He made to lunge after her, but his friends restrained him. He wiped his face with the palm of his hand, glancing at the retreating figure of the laughing girl and her friends, as they congratulated her on her action, looking back occasionally at the group of men as if to reassure themselves they were not being followed.

They walked out of his sight and he looked back at the burly American boy. 'Pig,' he said quietly to himself, as he returned to his drink at the bar. Lucky for him she had the balls to sort it out herself. He ordered another drink, and was about to take a sip when someone bumped into him, pushing him against the bar and almost spilling the bourbon. He turned angrily, to find the same young man beside him.

'You fucking spic, watch what you're doing, get out of my way. Barman!' he shouted.

He looked at the young man.

'Be a little more careful, *señor*. You nearly spilled my drink.'

'What, I nearly spilled your drink? You stupid little prick, if I meant to spill your drink I would have done it. Like this.' And so saying, he deliberately tipped the glass over so that the bourbon spilled on to the bar. 'Now, you want to make something of it?'

'*Señor*, I suggest you buy me another drink.'

'Oh do you. Well you can just go fuck yourself.'

'Do you mean you will not buy me another drink?'

'You bet your Spanish balls, Diego. Barman! Get over here.'

'*Señor*, I give you one last chance to make up for your behaviour.'

'Look, just fuck off will you? I'm trying to get a drink for myself here. Christ, you fucking spics, you think you own Miami.'

The man in white looked at the young man with a resigned expression on his face, and slowly walked away.

'Yeah, that's right, you get out of here, go back to wherever you crawled out from!' He turned to the barman. 'Whiskey!'

Terry Monaghan laughed to himself. He had always been used to getting his own way. From school bully, to arrogant drop out, he was big and strong enough to get his way by force whenever he wanted. He knocked back his drink, then asked for another.

'Don't you think you've had enough, sir?' asked the barman.

Terry leaned over the bar and leered at him. 'No I don't. Now do your job and get me another.'

The barman didn't want trouble, so he did as he was asked, while Terry shook his head.

Christ, what is this place coming to? he thought. Some little Spanish creep tries to pick a fight with me, and this Spanish fucking barman won't serve me. Fucking Miami. It was like this every day, good white American boys having to kowtow to immigrants. It was enough to make any honest American join the Ku Klux Klan, or the White Supremacists or one of those other groups trying to keep the country pure. He decided he would have to think seriously about looking into membership of the KKK.

He finished his drink, and walked out of the bar along the wharf towards the parking lot where he had left his car. The sounds of the disco faded as he left the well-lit crowded Bayside area, passing deserted alleys to his left, the dockside to his right. He glanced idly up each alley as he passed, stopping when he reached the fourth.

'Well, well. What have we here?' he said to himself, stopping and turning to face the dark cul-de-sac.

Standing in the alley, was the man from the bar.

'You want something, *amigo*?' he asked.

'I want you to tell me you're sorry.'

'For what?'

'For forcing yourself on that young girl, for spilling my drink, for insulting us because we are not American.'

'You have got to be joking.'

'I think you should apologize, or else you will be very sorry.'

The other man laughed. 'Oh, yeah?' he said, walking into the darkness of the alley, clenching his fists. 'So show me how tough you really are, Diego.'

He knew he was six inches taller, a hundred pounds heavier, and immensely better at beating up smaller people than this creep ever could be. He would show him who was in charge of this city.

He never saw the knife. He heard the switchblade spring open and wondered about the noise. Within two seconds, the man in the white suit had reached him, and plunged the knife into the left side of his upper abdomen and up under the rib cage, directly into his heart. He held it there for a moment, enjoying the look of shock on the big man's face, before putting his left arm around his neck and pulling him further on to the blade in a deadly embrace as he worked his wrist, making sure the havoc inside Terry Monaghan's chest would guarantee that within ten seconds, he would never again threaten a young Cuban girl. Or insult a stranger in a bar.

He withdrew the knife and let the now limp body sink to the ground. He bent, and wiped the bloody blade on the dead man's trousers before snapping it shut and putting it back into his jacket pocket.

He stood over the lifeless body of Terry Monaghan for a moment, then spat on to his corpse.

'I warned you, *amigo.*'

He walked away, in the direction of the discotheque, to see if he could find a girl for the night. He felt good. It was his last night and he had been determined to have a little fun in Miami. So far, things had turned out pretty well.

CHAPTER 15

Maria Pereira's body lay naked and unconscious on the operating table as they prepared her for surgery. Gary and the surgical team painted her neck, chest and abdomen a dirty brown colour with the iodine solution. After covering her with sterile green drapes, and connecting the diathermy and the sucker as the anaesthetists put on the cardiac electrodes, the temperature probes, the pulsimeters, the oximeters, preparing for by-pass, Gary took the scalpel offered to him by the scrub nurse and made a long, midline incision from her neck to her upper abdomen, before splitting the breast bone in half with the electric saw to enter her chest. Next, they connected her to the by-pass machine, to divert her blood away from the heart to be artificially oxygenated, and fibrillated the heart, leaving it functionless and motionless for the surgery to proceed.

He opened the atrium to gain access to the interior chambers, examined the hole between the two atria, and gently and carefully mobilized and refashioned, then sutured and closed it. He then turned his attention to the major problem, the ventricular septal defect – the hole between the two main pumping chambers of the heart. He inspected the hole, measured it, and took the patch from the nurse, trimming it to the right size then placing it over the defect, before suturing it slowly, carefully, tediously, obsessively into place. He looked at it, then asked for another length of suture, peering at his original stitch line, then putting in another single suture here, another there, until he was satisfied that he had a watertight join. Eventually, he closed the heart muscle, took the electrodes from the nurse, and shocked the heart back into activity, looking for leaks. There were none; it stayed dry. He asked the pump technician to take her off by-pass before closing the breast bone with staples, and the skin with a thin, almost invisible, cosmetic subcuticular suture.

The procedure took four and a half hours.

Tito and Carmen waited by the phone in their apartment where Gary Masters had promised to call them as soon as it was over. It was the longest four and a half hours of their lives. They sat, looking at each other, looking at the phone, holding hands, hugging occasionally, telling each other that everything was going to be OK.

Waiting.

The reporters and TV crews also waited across the road from the front entrance to the hospital. The impending operation had been announced by Bryant Gumbel on the morning NBC show, and all the other networks and national dailies were catching up with the action.

David Meeson sat in his office, waiting to achieve the sort of national exposure most big hospital CEOs could only pray for. Good for you, Dr Masters, he thought to himself, bringing such prominence to UHSM, putting us on the national, probably the world map, giving me the chance to star on every network in the country as the CEO (Surgery) to announce that the operation had been a complete success. So long as that cocky little bitch in ICU didn't screw up again. He had been surprised at her attitude when they met in his office, expecting her to lose her temper, swear at him, give him the chance to suspend her immediately. But she had kept her cool. No matter. He would sort her out later. But meanwhile he was hoping and praying that the Pereira girl at least got through surgery, at least got through to the point where he could play the starring role on the six o'clock news, taking all the credit for him and his hospital as if *he* had done the surgery himself.

Gary Masters walked out of the OR with Paul Schering.

'Nice work, Gary. I'm very impressed.'

'Thanks, Paul. And thank you for assisting and being here today. In this case it was very important to have a top team of experienced guys. Just in case there are any problems later....'

'Glad to help. Perhaps I could assist you with a few more paediatric cases, and learn the technique?'

'Of course. That would be good.'

They reached the changing-rooms, and started to peel off their OR greens.

'Paul, can I ask you something?'

'Sure, Gary.'

'What is your honest opinion of Anne Bell?'

Schering threw his sweat-soaked shirt into the dirty-linen basket and sat down on the wooden bench that ran the length of the wall of the changing-rooms.

'She's good, Gary. I'm sorry you and she don't seem to have hit it off. I know there's a conflict over these bad cases, and you know you have my full support over this, especially after seeing your handiwork today. But, Bell is good. Aggressive, rude occasionally, outrageous on occasions, but so far in this hospital, very good. That's why we put the kids' intensive care as a four-bed annexe on the main ICU. Anne did two years at the Boston Children's, you know, and she wanted all the ICU facilities centralized on one block. It made sense. It's worked fine.'

Gary nodded. Schering had assisted well today. He respected his work and his help. He wondered if he had misjudged Anne Bell, been too quick to blame. But then, Phil Peters ... Ludovico Palucci....

Unlike Paul Schering, who changed into his suit, Gary put on clean OR greens.

'I guess you're sticking around for a while?' Paul asked, looking in the mirror and doing up his tie.

'Yes. At least until she's stable. Anyway, the media likes a surgeon to be seen in his greens!'

Paul nodded. He had never in his life been interviewed by the media. He looked at Gary with a mixture of admiration and envy. Was he really a top surgeon, he thought, with a revolutionary new technique, or was he simply an adequate surgeon with charisma and a gimmick of a procedure? The NIH had given him a grant. His technique today had been faultless....

He concluded that he was probably a bit of both. An excellent surgeon, with a media presence. Lucky guy! Wish I had some of it, he thought. He finished dressing and turned to Gary.

'If you're away in the next few days and want me to cover, it's no problem.'

'Thank you, Paul, I appreciate that. I may be away for just two days next week, so that would be useful. Hopefully, by then, she should be running around again. And thank you again for your help today, and your support.'

'Pleasure. See you around.'

Paul walked out of the exit door, leaving Gary alone in the changing-room. He sat on the bench, exhausted, his thoughts filled with images of the interior of Maria Pereira's chest, the moment when they took her off by-pass and shocked her, the little heart beating again, repaired, new, all the leaks mended, all the blood going where it should go. He suddenly felt elated. This was the first child he had done, and he thought about how, instead of giving someone ten more years, or thirty more years, he was giving this beautiful little creature maybe sixty more years.

And she *was* beautiful. In spite of his prejudices, born of working in Miami and seeing the worst of its social problems, this little girl had captivated him and won him over, along with her humble and grateful parents. He was beginning to readjust his opinion of Cuban immigrants.

He stretched and sighed. So now it was done. Now it was time to wait and see what happened next. Was Maria Pereira going to be one of the lucky ones? Or was she going to suffer an unexplained, unexpected drop in oxygen to the lungs, and die a death on the ICU from shortage of breath as if he himself had placed the pillow over her mouth and smothered her?

He got up and made for the ICU to see how his small patient was doing. Fifteen minutes later, he called Tito and Carmen and asked them to come over. He met them in the visitors' room outside ICU.

'Relax, folks,' he said, seeing their anxiety. 'Everything went fine. Her little heart is beating perfectly and all the holes are repaired. She's got a way to go still, this was a major procedure, but at this point, everything is satisfactory.'

Carmen almost slumped into Tito's arms with relief. He held her with a strong arm around her waist as he looked at Gary.

'No complications? No surgical problems, no bleeding?'

Gary remembered that this man was himself a doctor.

'No, sir. None.'

Tito nodded. 'Can we see her?'

'Follow me.'

He led them into the unit, through the adult ward into the paediatric annexe. Anne Bell was at Maria's side.

'Doctor Bell, this is Doctor and Mrs Pereira, Maria's parents.'

Anne turned to them and smiled. 'Hello,' she said, holding

out her hand. 'Nice to meet you at last.'

'Everything OK?' asked Gary.

'Sure.'

'Good. Well, Doctor Pereira, I'll leave you now. I'll be in and out to see Maria and we'll keep you updated.'

Tito nodded. 'Thank you,' Carmen nodded through grateful misty eyes and turned back to her small daughter, seeing only tubes and lines and bottle and monitors and praying to God that this good doctor was right.

Gary left and went to his department.

'There were three messages,' said his secretary as he walked through the outer office, 'they're on your desk.'

Gary nodded, walking into his office and closing the door behind him. He looked at the message slips his secretary had written. One from the NIH, one from Jerry Weinberg, and one outside call. Area code 305. Call back before 3.30. He glanced at his watch. It showed 3.25. He dialled the number.

'Yes?'

He recognized the voice immediately.

'It's me.'

'Hello, me.'

'Hi, I … I missed you.'

'Me too.' He was surprised, but he knew it was true.

'Monday OK?'

'Yes.'

'Penthouse suite five, Doral Hotel, Miami Beach. Know it?'

'Yes. I'll be there. Did … Tony get the message about the follow-up?'

'Yes. He's expecting to see you and Doctor Rodriguez at ten on Tuesday at the hospital.'

'Good.'

There was silence for a moment.

'I want you,' she whispered, then the phone went dead.

He put the receiver down slowly.

'I want you too,' he said quietly.

Between checking on Maria Pereira and her other patients, Anne Bell spent time in her office, poring over the notes of Daniel O'Donaghue, Jennifer Pitt, Phil Peters, Ludovico Palucci and Philip Farkas, searching through every comment, annotation, blood test, x-ray report, cardiogram, searching for a common link, making notes as she went. Her door opened and Trudie popped her head in.

'Marilyn called in sick, Anne. I'll work late and I've organized an agency girl.'

Anne raised her eyebrows. Trudie smiled. 'No, I know this one. She's OK.'

Agency nurses could be of variable quality. Trudie made to go, then turned again.

'Oh, by the way, blood bank want to know if we need the three pints for Maria Pereira.'

'What group is she?'

'A negative.'

'Oh, yes, I recall. Wasn't there an antibody, Idaho?'

Trudie nodded. 'That's right. Your state!'

'That's why I recall. Hang on to the blood it's a bit early to release it yet.'

'Sure. If we keep it, we won't need it, huh?'

'Exactly,' said Anne, smiling, 'like an umbrella.'

Trudie left and Anne turned back to her work. When the thought hit her, it was like a thunderbolt.

A-neg with Idaho!

She searched back furiously for the case notes.

Daniel O'Donaghue – O-pos.

Jennifer Pitt – O-pos.

Phil Peters – A neg. With Idaho.

Ludovico Palucci – A-neg with Idaho.

Philip Farkas – O-neg.

The two deaths so far were both blood group A-negative with an Idaho antibody.

And so was little Maria Pereira.

She sat, staring at her notes. Could that be the common link? Could that antibody be reacting somehow with the membrane and causing the lung problems – think immune reaction short of rejection Jules had said. How she hoped she was wrong, that this was coincidence, because if she was right....

Maria Pereira....

She reached for the phone. It rang a moment before she picked up the receiver.

'ICU, Dr Bell.'

'Hello, Anne. Jules here. Two things. First, your dead John Doe, the old vagrant.'

'Yes?'

'I took a section of the vein the i.v. was in. We don't always do it if we find another cause of death, but it's sometimes productive in forensic cases.'

'Yes?'

'It had traces of scoline in the wall.'

'Scoline?'

'Yes. You know, the anaesthetic agent? It went through the vein and extravasated into the vessel wall. Otherwise I'd have missed it. The only thing is, the post-mortem request doesn't mention any operative procedure.'

'There wasn't one, Jules. He was a pneumonia case.'

'Pneumonia? So why should he have had scoline?'

They were both thinking the same thing.

'Did you check the other two cases, the cardiac cases, for traces of scoline?' she asked.

'Of course. First thing I did was check the tissues. None.'

There was silence again before Anne spoke. 'I'm going to have to think this through, Jules. We're talking possible foul play here. What was the second thing?'

'That lung exudate on the two cardiac patients?'

'Yes?'

'It's definitely not nice. It's full of inflammatory cells, and has a very high surface tension. I think it could even be a barrier to oxygen transport. I'm beginning to think it could possibly have been the cause of death after all, blocking oxygen transport, practically drowning the patient.'

There was silence again.

'You still there, Anne?'

'Sure, Jules. You're laying some heavy stuff on me here. Listen, have you ever come across an antigen-antibody reaction that could produce this, especially a blood-group related reaction?'

'I can't recall. I'd have to think about that. Why?'

'Both the dead patients had the same blood group and antibodies. I'm just wondering if the membrane is reacting with the blood antibodies to produce an exudate on the membrane, and doing the same thing to the lungs.'

'Anne, that is very very interesting. You just gave me a whole lot more tests to run, you know that?'

'Tough Jules, so you're not going to sleep for a day or two.

Welcome to the club.'

'Just kidding Anne. I'll crack this, believe me. It's the most interesting piece of work I've seen for months. You may just be about to crack this case, Sherlock, with a little help from your Watson here. I'll be back to you. Keep me posted on the scoline thing.'

She put down the phone. Thank you, Jules, she thought. You're OK.

Scoline.

They rarely used scoline in the ICU, and John Doe certainly never had any.

So that made it ... murder?

She had to talk to someone. In fact, it was time she found out exactly what side of the fence Jerry Weinberg was going to come down on when push came to shove. She picked up the phone and called urology to check he was in and left the office.

James Sinclair was with Jerry Weinberg when she arrived.

They both stood up.

'Hi. Sorry to interrupt, but I really need to talk to you about things, Jerry.'

'Shall I leave?' asked Sinclair.

'I'd rather you stayed James. Your advice would be helpful too.'

'OK, sit down and tell us what's on your mind,' Weinberg said.

She told them the scoline tale. Jerry whistled softly.

'What are you suggesting Anne?'

'Jerry, this patient never had scoline as a prescription item. In his condition, it would take only a small amount of that drug to kill him within minutes. The only way the drug could have got into his body would be by contamination, or by deliberate injection. The traces of the drug were found in the wall of the vein and surrounding tissues, indicating either a badly placed i.v. or a sudden bolus injection.'

'Murder?' whispered James Sinclair.

Anne nodded, her face serious. 'It's the most likely possibility.'

'And the other two?'

'No scoline. But possibly a blood-group related antigen-antibody reaction. We're working on it. So, what do we do next?'

Jerry rubbed his chin thoughtfully. 'Well, I suggest we keep this between ourselves and Jules for now. If this gets out, along with the other problems, the Press will have a field day and when the shit hits the fan, some sticks.'

'Do we call the police in?' asked Sinclair.

Anne answered. 'Jerry, do you remember that vice cop who helped out with the Laura thing last year, and came in when Sam Brown was attacked?'

'Sure. Joe Kennedy. We met him just the other day in Mulligans. He's been moved to homicide.'

'I liked him, Jerry, he was reliable and discreet. He handled the Sam Brown case with more consideration than I thought possible from a cop. Could we call him, have him over, take his advice?'

'Good idea, Anne,' Jerry responded. He looked closely at her and added, 'and I'll have to tell David Meeson.'

She glared at him. He shrugged.

'Anne, he's the CEO for Christ's sake. If this got out and he hadn't been told....'

She relaxed. 'I understand,' she said. She stood up and made to leave. 'I'll keep in touch,' she said.

'Good,' Jerry replied, also standing and moving around his desk towards her. 'And Anne,' he said, with a hint of embarrassment, 'just remember, we're with you on this, all the way.'

They stood facing each other. She wanted to hug him, to feel some encouragement, some support, but what he had said was enough. She looked over at James Sinclair. He smiled and nodded.

'Me too Anne. You're not alone, believe me.'

'Urologists,' she said, warmly. 'They may be piss artists, but you can certainly rely on them when the going gets tough.'

She left. She felt better. Back in the ICU she called into Maria Pereira's bay. Trudie was checking her over. Her parents had gone for a coffee.

'Trudie, I want to tell you something.'

'OK.'

Anne looked at the small child on the ventilator. She wouldn't hear what they said. 'The John Doe who died, remember him?'

She nodded as she went about her work.

'He was injected with scoline by someone. He was possibly murdered.'

Trudie turned away from the child for a moment, a look of surprise on her face.

'You're not serious,' she said.

'I'm entirely serious. We're calling in a local cop we know to look into it. Trudie, can you think of anyone on this team who could do such a thing?'

'You must be joking. No one. Not here.'

'That's what I thought. Trudie, I trust you more than anyone here. We built up this unit together, we saved it from extinction. Now, someone or some people are trying to destroy us. We've got to find out who. Think about it, then let's talk and see if we can't make some sense of this thing.'

The nurse turned away from little Maria Pereira to face her boss. 'Doctor Bell,' she said, 'no one, no one is going to screw up this ICU. I am as proud of the nursing here as you are of the medicine. This is the best unit on the East Coast. I'll defend it as much as you will. We'll beat this thing. Together.'

Doctors and nurses do not usually hug on duty. They broke the tradition.

CHAPTER 16

'Murder? A patient murdered in this hospital? On this goddamn ICU?'

David Meeson leapt to his feet as Jerry Weinberg told him of their suspicions.

'It's not proven, David, but it's possible. We're looking into it. I want to bring in a friend from the Boston PD to have a quiet snoop around. We're not certain yet, and I don't think we want to make it public at this point.'

'Look Weinberg, I'm sick to death of the problems this ICU is causing us. I'm just not going to stand for it. I've stood aside for too long and let you medics fuck up. Get this cop in and bring him here to see me, then report back to me twice a day from now on with *all* the details of progress. You hear me?'

'I hear you, David.'

He turned and left. Meeson picked up the telephone.

'Get me the ICU,' he barked at his secretary.

It was fifteen minutes before Anne Bell could respond to David Meeson's order to get her ass up to his office immediately. When she walked in, she was none too pleased.

He was pacing the floor, and turned when he heard her enter. 'Ah, Dr Bell. I have just learned from the chief of surgery that there is some question of foul play being involved in one of the recent deaths in your unit. Is that correct?'

'That's one of the possibilities being looked into, yes.'

'Well I have to tell you that I am amazed and disgusted that such a thing could happen. I am suspending you, Dr Bell, from your position in this hospital until the matter is resolved.'

'Oh, don't be stupid, man,' Anne retorted, not believing what she was hearing, 'you can't do that.'

'Can't do that?' He almost screamed the words. 'Watch me, lady! You're in charge up there, and you've presided over three deaths in the past two weeks, almost scuppering the most important research project this hospital has ever had, and now I learn that one of the deaths might be murder. You're a disaster, woman. The buck stops with you, and I'm relieving you of your duties until further notice.'

'And what about the patients, Mr Meeson? Who'll look after them?'

'The chief residents can act up until I make alternative arrangements.'

'Have you discussed this with any of the other doctors? With the chief of surgery?'

'I don't need to discuss it with anyone. I'm the CEO here, and I've had enough of you medics fucking up. Get your things and go home.'

He sat down, and waited for her to leave.

Anne stood in front of him, her anger rising. She clenched and unclenched her fists as if she might punch him. Then she took two paces forward and leaned over the desk.

'Listen, you apology for a man. If you dare to suspend me from this hospital, I'll sue you out of sight for wrongful dismissal so fast your feet won't touch the ground. I'll make sure you never work in this town again. I'll have your balls, Meeson, and I'll take great pleasure in shoving them down your miserable throat.'

Meeson smiled.

'You heard that, Lindy?' he said into the intercom.

'Yes, sir,' came his secretary's reply.

'Get out, Dr Bell. See you in court.'

She turned and left. Meeson gave a long sigh of satisfaction and leaned back in his captain's chair. You just shouldn't leave things to medics, he thought to himself. They always screw up. They needed management and, from now on, he would take control of this tiresome ICU problem before the entire surgical unit got closed down. Christ, a murder, in his ICU. What the fuck next?

'Lindy,' he said, 'get Dr Weinberg and tell him I want to know as soon as this homicide cop arrives. I want to speak to him myself.'

Anne went to the ICU via urology. She walked into Jerry's office without knocking.

'Thanks, Jerry,' she said. 'I just got fired.'

He leapt to his feet, and walked round the desk to her.

'What? That's impossible. Fired?'

She looked up at his blue eyes, and handsome face, and suddenly her eyes filled up with tears.

'Fired,' she whispered, and burst into tears.

He put his arms around her and pulled her to him in a big hug. 'Anne, Anne. Come on. You can't get fired. I won't let him get away with it.'

He held her for a few moments until she got control. She sniffed loudly. 'Sorry,' she said, sheepishly. 'That was stupid.'

He grinned at her. 'Never thought I'd see it, Anne.'

She grinned back at him. 'Don't tell,' she said.

He gave her a tissue from the box on his desk, and she blew her nose.

She looked up at him. 'What should I do, Jerry? I need to be here to sort this mess out.'

'Go home, Anne. Jim and I will talk to Meeson, and also to Joe Kennedy. I'll call you and keep you posted. We'll have you back here in no time at all, I promise you.'

She nodded. 'Thanks, Jerry. I knew I could count on you.'

She left, and went back to the ICU, calling Trudie into her office to tell her the news.

'It's not possible,' responded the nurse, 'what are we meant to do without you?'

'The chief residents will have to act up. Fortunately they're experienced guys. It will put a big burden on you as chief nurse though. You'll have to watch them like hawks, and keep the clinicians involved. Bother them with any problems. Especially Gary, with little Maria. Call me at home if you want any advice.'

The nurse nodded. There was a tear in her eye.

Anne turned away from her. 'Don't, Trudie,' she said, holding her hand up. 'You'll set me off. Don't think about it. It's all a big mistake. I'll be back in no time. And I'll make Meeson pay all right. Now go on back to work, and keep in touch.'

Trudie paused for a moment, wanting to speak, then left, wiping her eye and making for Maria Pereira's bay.

Anne packed her briefcase and left.

There was a look of determination on her face.

* * *

Joe Kennedy looked for the phone. He could hear it ringing, and he knew it was on his desk somewhere. But his in-tray had overflowed with papers and documents days before, and that side of his desk was a mess. It was also where he kept the phone. He made a mental note to move it into his out-tray later. There was always more room there.

He finally located the phone and put the receiver to his ear, shuffling some of the papers into a semblance of order as he listened.

'Hi Doc,' he said. 'Did I speak too soon the other day?'

He smiled, but the smile slowly evaporated as he listened to Jerry Weinberg. 'Why sure,' he said eventually. 'I can come over and take a look. An hour?'

He put the phone down. Murder on an intensive care unit, he thought. That's a new one. But hell, any cop worth his marbles knew that murder could happen anywhere. So, if you played the game for long enough, you'd eventually get one on an ICU. He found himself looking forward to a trip back to UHSM and crossing swords with that feisty young ICU director.

Anthony Skiathos was sitting on the sofa in the corner of the office at his home in Miami. He looked troubled. His face was pale, making the blue veins on his temples stand out even more. His bald head was perspiring gently.

'Tell me again, Menos,' he said.

'She went to Boston. Stayed in the Ritz-Carlton for one night, then flew home.'

'Why should she tell me she was going to see Helen in Palm Beach, and then go to Boston? It doesn't make sense.'

They stared at each other. It didn't make sense if you didn't think it through, Menos thought. But when you do, it makes plenty of sense. He held his boss's eye, waiting for the next question. It was not long in coming.

'I mean, who the fuck does she know in Boston?'

They looked at each other again neither stating the obvious.

'She told me she was going to stay with Helen tomorrow,' Tony said. 'This time when she leaves, follow her again. I want to know where she goes, and I particularly want to know who she sees there.'

Menos nodded. 'You OK, *Capo*?'

The big man nodded. 'Just a little pain sometimes, here in my heart.' He got up to leave. 'I'm going for a rest. Remember, tomorrow. But be discreet.'

He left Menos sitting in the office. You may have saved his life, Dr Masters, thought the *consigliere*, but you are playing a dangerous game here. A very dangerous game indeed.

Jerry Weinberg walked straight through Lindy's office into Meeson's sumptuous CEO suite. He was on the telephone and looked up in surprise at the intrusion.

'I'll call you back,' he said into the mouthpiece, 'something's come up here. Hell, Weinberg, can't you knock like anyone else?'

'This is urgent. You can't fire Anne Bell. You've got to reinstate her.'

'What is this with you guys trying to tell me what I can and can't do around here? Anne Bell, as chief of intensive care, and therefore the person holding responsibility for what goes on there, has been suspended on full pay pending an investigation into recent fatalities in that unit.'

'Then unsuspend her. She's needed there. The Pereira girl needs expert help. Anne's close to finding the cause of death in the first two cardiac cases, and she may be the only one who can help find out if the old John Doe was murdered.'

'No single person is that indispensable.'

'Anne is.'

'I disagree. Look Jerry, this is a God-send for us. I know of a chief resident over in Portland my oppo there told me about. He's looking for a move to Boston. He's red hot, into managed-care, health reforms as well as being clinically brilliant. We should have him here.'

Jerry looked at him, aghast. Was he using the ICU problems to oust Anne Bell and import some management-orientated whizz kid from Portland? He could hardly believe what he was hearing.

'I'll pretend you didn't say that, David. I want Anne Bell back to work and I want it today.'

'Dream on, Jerry. She stays out.'

'Then you have my instant resignation as chief of surgery. You shouldn't have done this, David. You've got a fight on your hands now.'

He turned and stormed out. This time, David Meeson was not smiling when the door closed.

Joe Kennedy was waiting in Jerry's office when he burst in. 'Someone rattled your cage, Doc?' asked the policeman, standing up to shake hands.

'Something like that, Joe. Our CEO just fired Anne Bell.'

'What? Is she a suspect?'

'No, of course not. The man's a fool. There have been some problems down there, but none of her doing. Sit down, I'll get some coffee then I'll tell you the story.'

Twenty minutes later, Joe Kennedy knew as much about the cardiac cases and the John Doe as Jerry did.

He sat, looking down at his notes. 'Well, it does seem the first two and the last one are unconnected. What motive could anyone have to murder an old guy on an ICU? Have you known of any other cases in your time here?'

Jerry shook his head. 'People die on ICUs all the time,' he said. 'We usually know the cause. There haven't been any instances like this I can remember. But you'll need to talk to Anne. She'd know.'

Kennedy nodded. 'Why don't we go talk to your CEO. I'd like to meet him.'

They walked together to David Meeson's suite and told Lindy they needed to see him. She looked at Jerry, wondering for a moment if he was going to get violent with her boss, then knocked timidly on the door and announced them.

Meeson looked up darkly at Weinberg, then held out his hand to the policeman.

'Detective Kennedy, nice of you to come over and help.'

'My pleasure.' He flashed the tin at the administrator. 'I gather this is a bit sensitive and you'd like to keep it out of the Press if possible?'

'That's right.' He looked at Jerry. 'No need for you to stay, Dr Weinberg,' he said pointedly.

'Oh, I'd prefer Dr Weinberg to stay if you don't mind,' said the detective, with a tone of finality in his voice. The CEO didn't argue.

'Yes, it's all terrible, of course,' he continued, 'and we don't want any cover-up, but if it can be sorted out internally, then made public, when it's been solved, it would be so much more preferable than having the Press camped on the steps outside analysing every preposterous possibility. We already have enough of them out there because of the Pereira kid.'

'Oh, yeah. How's she doing?'

'Fine,' said Meeson and Weinberg in unison. 'So far,' added Weinberg.

'Well, as I told Jerry, I'll certainly look into it. Homicide is homicide, wherever it happens, and it's right up my street. I need some things though.'

'Anything,' said Meeson.

'Well, I need the names, addresses and c.v.s of all the ICU staff, and especially those who were on duty for the twenty-four hours when the John Doe bought it.'

Meeson nodded.

'I want a room in or near the ICU to conduct some interviews.'

'You've got it.'

'And I want Dr Bell reinstated.'

Meeson looked like he had been stung.

'What?'

'I want Dr Bell reinstated. She knows more about this ICU than anyone else in the hospital. She's an unlikely suspect – I gather from my initial assessments that she was home at the time the patient died. She has more motivation than anyone to try to find the perpetrator. I don't consider that there are any grounds to suspend her.'

'Excuse me, Detective, but don't go trying to over-extend your authority. I hire and fire around here.'

Joe Kennedy shrugged. 'If that's how you want it,' he said, turning and making for the door. 'Sorry I can't be more help, Dr Weinberg.'

'Where are you going?'

'I'm going back to the station to report this case in. They'll send a homicide detail down to get things moving. No doubt the *Boston Globe* boys will find out pretty soon and get down here to cover it. *USA Today* shouldn't be too far behind.'

Meeson glared at the cop, then at Jerry Weinberg, who stood there as if butter wouldn't melt in his mouth, then back at Kennedy.

'Wait,' he said eventually.

The policeman paused, his hand on the door handle. 'Yes?'

'You're telling me she's an integral part of this investigation?'

'Yes. If I found out she was responsible, you'll be the first to know. But I need her here either way.'

Meeson stood before them, sensing he was beaten.

'I'll call her,' Weinberg said. He didn't need blood on the carpet. They had got what they wanted.

They left. Once in the corridor, Weinberg gave Joe Kennedy a sidelong glance. 'Thanks, Joe,' he said. 'I owe you one.'

'Glad to help. It was true anyway – we do need her. Where to now?'

'Let's go to my office and call Anne. Then we can get her back to see you and you can co-ordinate what you want to do.'

They walked on for a short way before Jerry heard Joe mutter, 'What a prick!'

CHAPTER 17

Tito Pereira saw Anne Bell walk across the lawn near his apartment to leave the hospital grounds by the side gate. She looked upset. He was about to run after her when he saw a second figure emerge from behind the building, and follow her. He looked familiar, somehow, but he had his back to him so he could not see his face. The white suit was like you might see in Havana. He almost turned away, thinking he was imagining things, but then Anne half turned to shut the gate, and the man in the white suit stopped and bent down as if tying his shoelace. But Tito could see he was watching Anne Bell the whole time. And his shoes had no laces. He continued watching as Dr Bell left and as the man in the white suit followed her, he decided to investigate. No one should be following the woman who was helping to save his daughter. He sensed something was wrong. He left the apartment and ran down the stairs in time to see white suit closing the gate.

White suit was having a bad time. He had reached Boston and located the hospital where all the papers said Maria Pereira was having her surgery. He checked into the Holiday Inn around the corner, and spent two days casing the place. He located the operating suite, the intensive care unit, and the chidlren's ward, but a security guard had seen him loitering around and asked to see some ID. He pretended not to understand and slipped away but, the next day, the same guard had spotted him and he had had to leave quickly. The only thing he did get to see was the same doctor entering the ICU each day, the doctor whose picture in the paper had identified her as Dr Bell, the chief of intensive care.

She would know.

* * *

Anne reached the 'T' and waited for the train to Arlington, unaware of the man in the white suit close by, or anyone else for that matter. Her mind was occupied with the events of the day. The depression she had felt initially had given way to a deep and resentful anger at the way she had been treated. She decided she would call Siobhan O'Connor that evening and seek advice about the legality of her suspension, and its implications regarding charges of negligence and guilt. She got on to the crowded train and sat down wondering what she was going to do for the next few days, and how they would get on without her. Especially little Maria Pereira, with her A-neg Idaho antibody blood. She made a mental note to call Jules Wellbeloved and Gary Masters also. They had to see if there was something they could do before Maria got sick, if indeed the blood groups had anything at all to do with any of it.

Tito felt in the pocket of his jeans with a sense of panic, relaxing when he felt the subway token. It was left over from their sight-seeing trip. He felt certain now that white suit was following Anne Bell, and sensed that all was not well. He was determined to follow them, to see what was going on, but when they entered the station he thought he might have to give up the pursuit. He had no money with him. But then he felt the token. He pushed it into the slot and followed them to the platform, keeping his distance to remain unnoticed. When the train stopped, he got into the next carriage to theirs, keeping Anne in view through the small window between the carriages. When they reached Arlington, he got off the train, dawdling a little, watching Anne Bell leave, then letting white suit reach a safe distance in front of him before following them. I know this man he thought to himself. But from where? When? Who is he? And what does he want with Dr Bell?

She reached Commonwealth and turned the corner, walking into the drive and up the steps to her side-door entrance. She put the key in the lock and turned it, pushing the heavy door open. She was suddenly aware of a man in a white suit beside her.

'Hey, you....'

Before she could say any more he had pushed her into her hallway and kicked the door to, then suddenly he was behind her, his arm around her neck and she felt the sharp point of a knife at her throat.

'Where is he?' he hissed in her ear, his accent unmistakably Hispanic.

She shook her head.

'Where is he?' he repeated, tightening his grip on her, pushing the knife just a little more into the skin over her carotid artery.

'Who? What?'

'The pig, Pereira. I need to see him. We have business. Where is he staying?'

'I don't know.'

'*Señorita*, I think me and my friend here will have to help you remember,' and he moved the knife from her neck, down her cleavage over her abdomen and up under her dress until she could feel it directly over her clitoris.

'You like a little fun, yes? Me and my friend both would like a little fun with you, I think? So, where is he?'

He relaxed his hold on her throat to let her speak.

She shouted, 'Fuck off you little creep!' at the same time as she stamped on his foot. He gasped in surprise but held on to her.

Then the doorbell rang.

Anne froze, and felt his grip tighten and the knife once again reach her neck.

'Be silent.'

The bell rang again, then again, and was joined by thumping on the door. Then a voice said, 'Dr Bell, Dr Bell, I know you're there. I am not leaving until you talk with me.'

Still the doorbell went on ringing.

'Open the door, Dr Bell.'

She knew it was Tito. The fool. What on earth was he doing here? The knife went in harder. 'Who is it? Do you know this man?'

Then, as if in answer, the voice said, 'It is me, Tito Pereira.'

She felt him stiffen, then he edged her closer and closer to the door. She tried to scream *run, Tito, run* but he was squeezing her neck too tightly. She saw him reach over her shoulder to take off the latch, but before he could do anything else, the door burst open, knocking them both backwards. He flung her to the ground as Tito appeared in the hall, his outline dark against the evening sun behind him.

'So, Dr Pereira, you come to me to save me the trouble of finding you,' white suit hissed. 'How considerate. And now, you must die in the house of this doctor.' He looked down at Anne Bell, lying stunned on the hall floor.

'Mendoza,' Tito said softly.

'Ahah! You remember me.' He tossed the knife expertly from hand to hand, as if preparing it for action.

'Of course. You killed my friend, Jose Fernandez. You were coming for me.'

'You got out just in time. But when we saw the films from Krome on TV, saw you betraying your own government, your own people, it was decided you should be punished. That you should disappear here in America, and they would think you just ran out on your wife and your sick baby.'

'It was decided? *Who* decided? You and your killer friends in the SS I suppose.'

'We decided, on behalf of our government and our leader. So remember, in eternity, that betrayal of your country is treason, and treason leads to execution.'

He advanced towards Tito, the knife in his right hand now, as they circled one another, Tito desperately searching for something to arm himself with, noticing the baseball bat against the wall behind the door, but unable to get to it. White suit was swinging the knife from side to side now, backing Tito towards the opposite corner, preparing for the strike, the blade making a whistling noise as it scythed through the air. Tito waited until it made its next upstroke, then lunged for his assailant, his right hand grabbing for the knife-wielding wrist, and finding it. He reversed his body into white suit, holding the knife in front of him where he could see it, and starting to bang his assailant's wrist against his knee to loosen its grasp.

But strong as Tito was, white suit was a professional, and he was using his free hand to pummel at Tito, his kidneys, his chest, his neck, the side of his head. His fist was hard, like a piece of solid wood, and Tito found himself beginning to weaken. But still he kept hold of the knife hand, banging and banging, knowing that to stop, to let go, was to die, to waste all they had struggled for – their freedom, their future. So he refused to give in to the increasing ferocity of the blows, and the pain, until at last, he felt the grasp weaken and saw the knife fall to the floor. He kicked it with all his strength and saw it skim along the floorboards down the hall. He turned to try to face his agressor, but white suit's expert blows were more than a match for Tito's untrained punches. Finally, he felt himself pushed against the wall, where he fell to the ground. He looked up to see Mendoza reaching down to his right leg, and caught a glimpse of the black-handled stiletto in its scabbard. He pulled himself to his feet, but the knife was already out, with Mendoza's arm slowly retreating in preparation for the deadly underarm throw.

'Now, you can die like the water rat you are,' he growled.

He hesitated for only a split second, perhaps from the look on Tito's face, perhaps because he caught a glimpse of movement in his side vision.

Whatever the reason, he was too late.

The baseball bat hit his skull as if Anne Bell was going for a home run in the World Series, and the man in the white suit went down like a sack of potatoes.

Idaho potatoes even.

Tito looked at her. She stood, panting in the hallway, holding the bat ready for a second strike, then slowly realizing that it wouldn't be necessary. She raised her eyes to his, and they looked at each other, Tito bruised and bloodied, Anne stunned but ready for more if necessary, before they turned their gaze to the motionless figure on the floor between them.

'Is he dead?' Tito asked.

'I don't know,' she replied. 'I hope so.'

All her natural medical instincts to care for the sick and injured had vanished in this case. She hoped he *was* dead.

She lowered the bat, but kept it in her right hand as she advanced towards the prostrate body of the assassin. She leaned over him, and put her left index finger on his neck, feeling for the carotid pulse.

When he grabbed her wrist she screamed in sheer terror but before she could escape he had grabbed the bat and knocked her aside roughly, rising to his feet and searching for Tito, bleeding freely from his head wound but wielding the bat with the bravado of a drunk man.

'C'mon, Tito, come to Fidel's messenger,' he crooned.

He saw him then, leaning against the wall in the hallway, outlined by the evening light from the street, holding his left flank, his right hand hanging limply by his side.

'Ahhh, there you are, betrayer of the regime, enemy of the people's republic. You thought you had finished me, but you see, truth will conquer, right will vanquish, Fidel will rule forever.'

The bat was swinging from side to side, just like the knife had, but instead of a whistle, it made a swishing sound in the air. Swish! Swish!

His head continued bleeding, but still he came on, determined to finish his task.

'Stop there,' Tito said quietly.

He stopped.

'Stop here?' he asked, looking around, sounding almost puzzled by the question. 'But why?'

'Because if you take one more step I will kill you.'

Anne Bell tried to sit up, but her shoulder was aching like hell and she knew she was unable to intervene, as she watched the scene unfold.

'One more inch, I will have to kill you.'

He nodded, sarcastically. 'Oh sure. But not before I beat your brains out with this bat, and then give her the same treatment. Perhaps. After a little fun. You know, Tito? Like we did with your sister Carlita last year? Oh yes, Tito, she was a real little raver.'

He watched Tito's eyes, expecting surprise, or fear, seeing only hatred, before reality dawned on him as he watched Tito take two paces forward, saw his arm move back, recognizing the movement and thinking that's what my arm does before....

Tito's arm raced forwards and the stiletto left his hand in a perfect straight line. The man in the white suit saw it glint as it passed through the thin ray of sunshine peeping through the almost closed door before it hit his throat, severed his windpipe and passed through his pharynx into his spinal cord. He grabbed for it, and pulled with all his strength, extracting it and looking at it with glazed eyes, wondering why his breathing was no longer accomplishing anything, why every time he took a deep breath, he heard a gurgle of fluid instead of air filling his chest, why there was a weakness spreading up from his feet, through his body, down his arms until the knife seemed to weigh a ton. He looked again at it, as if seeing it for the first time, before falling to the floor and twitching then convulsing in death.

Tito stood in the hallway and watched him die. There was no pity left now. No humanity. This was the torturer of his sister, a cold-blooded assassin sent to Boston to deprive Carmen of a husband, and Maria of a father. He had almost succeeded. And had almost killed the doctor who was working so hard to save Maria. He looked over at Anne Bell. She raised herself slowly to her feet, and walked towards him, stepping around the now motionless body bleeding on to her hallway floor.

'Is he dead now?' she asked.

'Yes,' he replied.

They stood in silence for a long time before the phone rang, making them jump, reality intruding into the surreal atmosphere of the dusky hallway.

She walked slowly towards it, still watching the crumpled figure on the floor, and picked up the receiver, her eyes never once leaving the body.

'Yes?' she whispered, as if not wanting to waken the dead.

'Anne, you OK?'

She recognized Jerry Weinberg's voice.

'Sure, what is it, Jerry?'

'You're back. We fixed it with Meeson, me and Joe Kennedy. You're back at work as from now.'

She sensed him waiting for her grateful reply, but all she could manage was, 'Jerry, could you and Joe get down here as soon as you can? I've got a bit of a problem.'

She dropped the phone back on the hook without waiting for a reply, watching as Tito took the baseball bat from white suit's hand, to stand over him, waiting for any sign of resistance.

They heard the sirens but didn't relate them to their predicament until they realized they had got louder and louder before they seemed to stop right outside their door. Which they had.

Joe went in first, gun drawn, looking for trouble. Jerry followed, ready for a fight, ready for whatever it might take to help Anne Bell.

They paused taking in the scene – a man in a white suit lying bleeding, probably dead, on the floor, Anne Bell standing over him, Tito Pereira beside her, looking pretty badly beaten, a baseball bat in his hand.

Joe Kennedy checked the body while Jerry went to Anne, hugging her for the second time that day.

'You OK?' he asked.

She nodded.

'Dr Pereira?' Jerry looked over at the young Cuban.

Tito nodded, still watching the body as Joe Kennedy got up.

'He's dead, all right,' he said, looking at Tito. 'You do this sir?'

Tito nodded again.

'This is Dr Pereira, Joe,' Jerry said, 'the father of Maria Pereira.'

'You both look beat,' Joe said, reaching in his inside pocket for his notebook. 'Can you tell me briefly what happened before I call in?'

Anne nodded.

'So, this is what you call a bit of a problem, Anne?' Jerry asked, stroking her hair.

She nodded again, then gently broke free of him.

'I need a drink,' she said. 'Come into the living-room. I'll give you a statement, Joe.'

Jerry checked Tito over. He told him he had at least three broken ribs, a badly bruised kidney, and multiple contusions. He called the ER, and told them to send the paramedics, and prepare for the appropriate tests.

'Looks like we're going to need a double room for the Pereiras, hey Anne?' he said, replacing the phone and smiling at Tito.

Joe Kennedy sent for the homicide team, then Anne and Tito filled him in with the facts until the paramedics arrived. Anne saw Tito off in the ambulance.

'I'll be in later to see you,' she told him.

'No,' he protested, 'you must rest, I need you strong for Maria.'

She smiled. 'Later.'

Then she continued her interview with Joe Kennedy.

'I'll wrap it up from here,' Joe said eventually. 'I'll need another talk later, but I guess we'll be seeing each other over this other affair anyway.'

She nodded.

'You OK?' Jerry asked, 'anyone I should call?'

She shook her head. 'No one to call, Jerry. I'm just a single working-girl. But I'm OK, just a few bruises.'

'Pack a bag, then. We can go into the hospital, get you checked over, then you're coming home with me.'

'No, Jerry, truly, I'd rather be here, at home.'

'Sorry, Anne. I insist. You can't stay here tonight alone.'

'I'll call Siobhan, then, see if she'll sleep over.' She walked over to him and squeezed his arm. 'I know you're trying to help, Jerry. But I want to scrub that floor, get the smell of that person out of my life.'

Joe Kennedy broke into their conversation. 'Go with Jerry, Dr Bell,' he said gently, 'there'll be no scrubbing any floors here for a day or two. This is a crime scene, and we need to work on it, get samples, you know the routine.'

As if to emphasize his words the doorbell rang. Joe let the homicide team in and described what had happened before putting them to work, then gave Jerry and Anne a ride to the hospital, leaving them at the front entrance.

'I'll see you tomorrow Dr Bell, if you're fit for work. Otherwise … well … whenever.'

'Try tomorrow, Joe. I'll be here.'

He nodded, flashing his lop-sided grin as he watched her walk unsteadily into the hospital with Jerry supporting her, and thinking again what a great cop she would have made.

CHAPTER 18

Gary took a cab from the airport to the Doral Ocean Resort on Miami Beach. The early evening traffic was heavy, and progress was slow. When he finally arrived, he walked through the lobby to the elevator, getting in with a noisy Spanish family. They got out at 7, while he continued up to Penthouse Suite 5.

He knocked at the door. She opened it immediately, as if she'd been waiting for him.

They virtually ripped off each other's clothes, their lips never still as their passion overwhelmed them once more. They made love for almost an hour before either of them spoke. Finally, as he lay on top of her, moving slowly, he said, 'Hello.'

'Hello.'

'Do we really have the whole night together?'

She nodded. 'I have ordered dinner here in the room at nine thirty. The room is in the name of Carter. I will wait in the bathroom when it arrives.'

They continued moving together, slowly, rhythmically, never increasing the pace until eventually she gave a gasp and climaxed again, clinging on to him, holding him close. Eventually they showered, drank some of the champagne, then ate dinner together when it arrived, Kathryn tidying herself in the bathroom to be sure of avoiding identification. Her face was not unknown in some parts of Miami. Later, they slept in each other's arms. He woke at 2.30, and looked at her for a long time.

'What am I going to do with you, Kathryn Skiathos?' he whispered to himself. 'I think I'm falling in love with you.'

He was surprised when she answered, in a similar whisper, 'I *know* I am in love with you, Dr Gary Masters.'

He raised himself slightly, as she opened her eyes.

'I thought you were asleep.'

She continued to look at him, with her deep, black eyes. 'Did you mean it?' she asked, eventually.

'Yes. I can't get you out of my thoughts. I can't wait for the times we're together. I've never felt this for any woman.'

She raised her head and kissed him gently.

'Nor I for any man.'

This time the kiss was longer, and when they made love again, it was as true lovers. They both knew it.

The sun woke him. He got up trying not to disturb her and went to the bathroom. When he got back, she was sitting up, hugging her knees under the sheets.

'What time is the appointment?' she asked, as he got back into bed beside her.

'Ten, at the clinic.'

'We still have some time, then.'

He nodded, rubbing his hand gently up and down her smooth thigh.

'Did you mean what you said last night?' he asked.

'Yes.'

'I did too.'

There was silence as they let the realization sink in.

She slid down the bed, and pulled him down to her so that they lay on their sides, facing each other.

'What are we to do?' she asked.

'I don't know. I only know I love you. I need you.'

They lay in silence, until she rolled him on to his back and started to kiss him all over, whispering '*I love you*' with each kiss. He felt his erection returning and she sensed it, moving down to him and continuing to kiss him before taking him and loving him. But this time, he lifted her face gently from him, and raised her up to enter her to make love again, slowly, tenderly and it went on and on and on as they expressed their love for each other, neither knowing where it might take them, neither prepared to break the spell that was binding them together.

At 9.55, Kathryn Skiathos was by her husband's side waiting outside Geraldo Rodriguez's office. When the door opened, Geraldo himself came out to greet them, and bring them through. Tony had already had his ultrasound scan, cardiogram and blood tests, and the results were on Geraldo's desk.

Gary got up to greet them and he shook hands with Tony.

'Hello, Doctor,' the big man said, gripping his hand firmly. 'How is the man who saved my life?'

'Good, thank you.'

He nodded at Kathryn. 'Mrs Skiathos,' he said, relaxing his grip to shake hands with her, but finding his hand still in Tony Skiathos's grasp.

Tony smiled and released him, then sat down.

Geraldo and Gary sat on one side of the desk, Tony and Kathryn on the other.

'Your test results are good,' Geraldo said. 'Are you having any problems?'

The big man sat back and rubbed his chest. 'I have some occasional pains in my chest, over my heart.'

'What sort of pains?' asked Gary.

'Like a knife. It only lasts a moment or two, then it is gone.'

Gary flashed a furtive look at Kathryn, but she was sitting motionless and upright, her hands on her lap, looking straight ahead.

'Anything else?' Gary asked. 'Any shortage of breath?'

'Only if I try to do too much.'

'Fevers?'

'I sweat a lot at night.' He shrugged. 'But I always did, didn't I, Kathryn?'

She smiled at him and nodded.

Gary sat up, concerned.

'Is this happening more than usual? Do you feel particularly hot, or go hot and cold and shake?'

'Once. Three or four nights ago. I can't recall. It was nothing. Why? You are concerned about me?'

'I don't know. I want to examine you. The tests are fine, but sometimes you detect more by examination. Come into this cubicle for me and undress, would you?'

Tony the Greek stood up and walked heavily over to the examination cubicle, undressing and lying on the couch, his feet dangling over the edge. Gary checked his chest sounds, his heart sounds, his pulse, his blood pressure, and his temperature.

'Geraldo? Give me a second opinion on this would you?'

Rodriguez got up from the desk where he had been making idle conversation with Kathryn and walked into the small ante-room to examine Tony. When he finished, he said, 'I can't hear anything abnormal, Gary.'

'Good. Neither could I. Please get dressed, Mr Skiathos.'

The two surgeons walked back into the office and sat down, waiting for Tony to resume his seat as Gary wrote up the notes.

When they once again sat facing each other, Gary smiled. 'Everything looks pretty good to us, Mr Skiathos. I think Dr Rodriguez should check you over again in another month if that's convenient.'

'Yes, that will be fine. Kathryn and I will be going to Athens after that, if we have your permission?'

Gary felt he might faint such was the feeling of pain, panic and emptiness which suddenly overwhelmed him at the big man's words.

'Of course,' he said, not daring to look at Kathryn.

'I won't have to see you again, Dr Masters?'

'No, not if everything keeps going as well as this. Just keep an eye on the sweats, though. And if you get a high temperature and shortage of breath, you must contact Dr Rodriguez immediately.'

'Like pneumonia, you mean?'

'Yes, like pneumonia.' Only slightly more fatal, thought Gary.

'Well, it was good of you to see me today, Dr Masters. It's a long way to Boston.'

'No problem. I had other business down here anyway.'

The four of them stood up.

'I will be making a donation to your unit, to help you to continue your work. To you also, Dr Rodriguez. I will have my people sort something out.'

'That is very generous of you, sir,' Rodriguez said.

'Yes, indeed. Thank you,' added Gary.

Tony Skiathos gave an expansive wave of his hand, as if implying that he was in charge, on his own turf now that the medical business was over, dispensing largesse to those who deserved it, paying back favours, maybe getting favours in return.

When they left, Geraldo slapped Gary on the back.

'Nice result, Gary. And a nice bonus for us.'

'Yes. I don't like the sound of the night sweats though.'

'Gary, Gary, don't worry. He's fine. Now, what time's your plane?'

'Three thirty.'

'Good. So come and make rounds with me, then we can have lunch before you leave.'

Gary nodded. In truth, for the first time in his life, he didn't really want to leave Miami.

Menos drove them back to the apartment in silence. Once inside the house, he asked his boss if he needed anything more.

'No, Kathryn and I need to spend some time together. I'll call you if I need you.'

Kathryn looked at Menos, then back at Tony, sensing some unspoken understanding between them.

Menos left, and Tony took her hand and led her into the huge living-room.

'Sit down, Kathryn,' he said, a sharpness in his voice.

She did as he ordered.

'So,' he said, 'it seems I am not to die after all.'

'Yes. Isn't it wonderful?' she responded.

'Perhaps. But perhaps Kathryn, it would be more convenient for you if I did die.'

'What do you mean? Don't talk like this.'

'Why not? If I died, you would be alone. And very rich.'

'I don't want to be alone, and very rich.'

He turned to look down at her.

'But why, my darling, why? Think of all the shopping you could do with Helen up in West Palm Beach? You enjoy that, don't you? After all, you've stopped over there twice now in the past few weeks. The strange thing is, I haven't seen any of the things you bought. No parcels, no new dresses to show me, no jewellery.'

'I didn't fancy anything, Helen did all the buying.'

'I don't think so, my darling.'

She shifted uncomfortably on the settee.

'What do you mean?'

'I mean, you never went to see Helen. Oh, I didn't check with her. She would have lied for you. No, Menos has been suspicious for some time that something was going on. So he had you followed. To Boston. The Ritz-Carlton wasn't it?'

He started pacing up and down in front of the fireplace.

'Wasn't it?' he bellowed suddenly, making her jump.

'I don't know what ...'

'Now, who is it in Boston you wanted to see so badly? The only other time you went there was to get the good Dr Masters to agree to come and operate on me. Do you have other friends there I don't know about?'

'You don't ...'

He raised his hand.

'And then guess what? A suite at the Doral, reserved in the name of Carter ... *cherie*, the *Doral*. Couldn't you at least have chosen the Fontainbleu? And who should Menos see walking through the lobby the same evening, but Dr Gary Masters, the night before he tells me I will live forever.'

'I don't know what you're talking about, Tony. I have friends in Boston. I don't know about any suite, or Carter....' She stood up but he gave her a shove, pushing her back violently on to the sofa.

He stood, panting, glaring down at her.

'Once a whore, always a whore, hey Kathryn? You were a whore with nothing when I picked you up off the street. And now, when you have everything, you're still a whore.'

He bent over her and grabbed her face with his huge hand, pulling her up and squeezing her cheeks together, distorting her features, bringing tears of pain to her eyes before he shoved her away and turned his back on her.

'I have always been kind to you, turned a blind eye to your little peccadilloes, knowing you had certain needs I could not provide. But this. Whoring regularly in public with the man who has saved my life, and causing me a terrible problem.'

'What do you mean?' She sensed that his voice had taken on a tone of coldness, of inevitability. She had heard that voice before.

'Do you love him, Kathryn?'

'No ... I....' She looked down at her hands, then, without raising her head, she said, 'Yes.'

Quietly.

As if refusing to deny it.

'What? I didn't hear.'

'Yes,' she repeated, loudly.

'That makes it even worse,' he responded quietly.

'What?' She looked up at him now, hearing the quiet icy voice, the fatal tone.

'Because he must die of course,' he said. 'Thanks to you, my little Kathryn, I must kill a man to whom I owe my life.'

Her world shattered, as suddenly as if he had stabbed her in the heart.

'No! NO!'

She leapt to her feet, then sank to her knees before him, her arms entwining his legs. 'No, Tony, no, please don't kill him, you can't, don't kill him.'

She was crying now, realization sinking in as she saw Gary walking innocently down a Boston street, the car pulling up beside him, the two men hitting the sidewalk before it even stopped, inviting him to take a ride with them. Or the solitary figure following him home one evening, his hand already on the switchblade, as the cold steel waited impatiently to taste the muscle of Gary's heart, taste his warm blood before wasting it on the dark sidewalk until there was no more left to flow.

She looked up at him, beseeching him, begging for mercy. In return, he looked down at her, without pity.

She knew then she had only one choice.

She released him from her frantic grip, and stood up to face him, regaining her composure, standing tall and proud again beneath his huge presence, facing him, her black eyes as determined as his.

'I will finish it, Tony. But you must spare him. It is over, from now, forever.'

He continued his pitiless gaze as he contemplated her words.

'I should kill you both,' he said.

She did not flinch. She continued looking into his eyes. She knew he loved her, that he would grant her one last chance.

He knew it also. But his voice left her in no doubt that his threat was genuine.

'I will do it,' she whispered, 'I will finish it, forever.'

'So finish it.'

He left the room without looking back.

As the door shut, her composure deserted her, and she sank to the floor, weeping at first, then crying openly, hunching herself into a foetal position, the realization dawning on her that, as soon as love had found her for the first time in her life, it was about to be snatched from her, one way or another.

She lay on the floor, swaying gently, holding herself as if to keep the memory of Gary's presence with her, becoming slowly colder and colder until she slowly rose to her feet, dusted herself down, wiped her eyes and, remembering Tony's words, repeated them over and over to herself 'Finish it ... finish it ... finish it....'

She went to bed in the spare room. She was awakened from a fitful sleep some hours later by the maid.

'Come quick, madame ... quick....'

She sat up and rubbed her eyes.

'The master, the master.'

She jumped out of bed and grabbed her robe, then followed the maid to the master bedroom.

Tony Skiathos lay on his bed in a pool of sweat, gasping for breath. Menos was kneeling beside him.

'What is it?' she asked, rushing to his side.

'Nothing to concern you, Mrs Skiathos.'

'What do you mean, he is sick. He needs help. Have you called the ambulance?'

Menos looked over his shoulder at her.

'Of course,' he hissed, 'what do you expect?'

She heard the bell ring and suddenly the paramedics were in the room, working on him.

Before she knew it, the i.v. was in, the oxygen mask was on, and he was being wheeled out of the room into the night.

'Where is he going?' she asked frantically.

'Miami Cardiac Institute, ma'am,' replied one of the paramedics.

Menos took her arm.

'I'll look after it,' he said.

'He's my husband,' she retorted. 'I'll get dressed and follow you.'

'Don't bother,' the *consigliere* responded. 'He would not want it.'

She pulled herself out of his grasp.

'I said I'll be there,' she said, with a hint of her old control.

He shrugged, and left the house with his sick boss.

Ten minutes later they were going through the front doors of the Miami Cardiac Institute. As they waited for the elevator to the ICU, Tony the Greek pulled off his oxygen mask and indicated to his *consigliere* that he wanted to speak to him. Menos bent his head down to him, and he put his arm around his neck to pull him closer.

'You ... you know what to do ...?' he grunted.

'Of course.'

'If I ...?'

His breath failed him, and the paramedic replaced the oxygen mask impatiently.

Menos put his mouth to his ear.

'If you die?' he asked.

The big man nodded, his wide eyes staring at his lieutenant, his lungs gasping for oxygen.

'If you die,' whispered Menos slowly, 'then he dies.'

Tony the Greek seemed to relax suddenly, and breathe more easily. He nodded again, more slowly this time, satisfied with what he heard, as the paramedics pushed the trolley into the elevator.

And if you live, he probably dies too, thought Menos to himself as the doors shut.

CHAPTER 19

In a bizarre twist to the story of little Maria Pereira and her Cuban parents who braved the high seas to bring her to America for life-saving heart surgery, her father Dr Tito Pereira today had once more to fight for his life, this time to avoid an assassin's knife. In so doing, he became a hero, saving the life of the director of the intensive care unit where his daughter is being treated.

Gary Masters's eyes almost popped out of his head as he sat in his first class Delta seat and read the story of Tito and Anne Bell's ordeal the day before with the man in the white suit. Poor Tito, he thought. Well, at least the University Hospital of Southern Massachusetts was on the front page of *USA Today* again. David Meeson would be pleased. A humourless smile passed over his features. He finished the article and leaned back in his seat, remembering the previous day, and the consultation with Tony the Greek that morning. *Kathryn and I will be going to Athens.* He felt his stomach churn over again at the thought of not seeing her for months on end. Christ, how had he let himself fall in love after all this time? He had always promised himself he would avoid that weakness, for he saw love as just that, a weakness, an outside influence affecting judgement, decision-making, behaviour, an irrelevant distraction deviating attention from his own ambition and interest. Yet here he was, plotting how he could see her again, how he could stop her husband whisking her off to the other side of the world, wondering whether he should declare his love for her in public and take her away from him, even if it all came out and his career was compromised....

'Snack, sir?'

The stewardess's voice made him jump.

He shook his head. He wasn't hungry. 'I'll take some coffee,' he said gruffly. Her smile died, but he didn't care. Once he would have been flashing *her* the smile, asking her name, flirting. Now, it all seemed unimportant. He drank his coffee, then leaned back again in the seat, closing his eyes and dozing, feeling less certain and less in control of his life than ever before.

They touched down on time. He picked up his car from the short-stay parking lot and made for the hospital. His first stop was the ICU. He walked through the door, thinking the place seemed unusually empty before he realized that most of the staff were in the paediatric bay allotted to Maria Pereira. He walked quickly towards them, catching sight of a bruised Tito Pereira in a dressing-gown standing outside the cubicle, his arm around his wife's shoulder. He walked past them into the bay.

'What's going on?' he asked.

Trudie looked over her shoulder at him then back at the child.

'Been trying to get you all morning, Doctor. She dropped her blood pressure during the early hours and her temperature went up two hours later. Since then her oxygen sat's been falling. We're going to have to tube her.'

'Is she septic?' Gary asked, moving to the side of the bed, looking at his little patient, feeling her pulse in spite of the monitors above him showing second by second pulse, blood pressure, temperature.

'Don't think so,' the senior resident said, as he worked on the drip. 'We've sent blood cultures, count, crit, profile. I've got 2 i.vs going. Clinical exam normal, chest x-ray normal, ultrasound scans normal.'

Gary checked their work. They had done everything right.

'Well done, you guys,' he said. 'Get some plasma into her to raise the pressure, get her tubed, hold back the inotropes until we see her response and we get some results.'

'Doctor!' The voice was loud and determined.

He looked at Trudie.

She turned to face him.

'What?'

'We can't go on like this.'

'Like what?'

'Without Dr Bell. Fred here's doing a great job, but we need her experience. Especially now.'

'She's right, Dr Masters,' said the resident, 'we've done the basics, but from here on in, we need proper ICU guidance.'

'So where is she? Why isn't she here?'

'She was suspended yesterday, then there was this assault thing which Dr Pereira saved her from. He was taken from her house to ER and no one's seen her since. She's not answering her phone.'

'Suspended?' he almost shouted in disbelief. 'But why? By whom?'

'I don't know why, it's crazy. But we need her here, now!'

He looked at them, then down at the struggling Maria Pereira, about to be hooked up again to the life-support system and respirator. He wondered what difference Anne Bell would make anyway. If this was the membrane syndrome, the child was already doomed. He was about to watch his third patient die, only this time it was the tiny angel from Cuba, and the whole world was also watching. He suddenly felt exhausted. He looked again at the ICU team. They had done a good job but he could see their morale was dipping. They were showing the signs of a team without a leader, doing their best before they started to flounder, wondering where to go, what to do next.

'I hear you. Just do what I said, I'll see about Dr Bell. I've got my bleeper and my mobile. Call me anytime you want, for anything, however trivial. I'm available, OK?'

Trudie nodded and returned to her work.

Gary made to leave when she called, 'By the way, there was a call from Miami, they said it was urgent. You get it yet?'

'No, where's the number?'

'Your secretary's got it.'

'Thanks.'

Kathryn?

He almost ran to his office, ignoring Tito and Carmen as he left. His secretary was at lunch. He grabbed the wadge of messages she had left in his pigeon-hole and searched through them until he found the Miami area code.

It was Geraldo's number.

He went into his office and closed the door, then sat at his desk, grabbed the phone and dialled the number.

Geraldo's secretary answered.

'Oh, Dr Gary, thank goodness. Dr Rodriguez has been trying to reach you. Hold while I get him.'

He waited.

'Gary?'

'Geraldo, what is it?'

'Tony the Greek. He was admitted during the night, shortage of breath, chest pains. No evidence of infarct, pulmonary embolus, rejection, septicaemia. Nothing we can find, to treat. Oxygen saturation falling. He's on a respirator in intensive care. Any ideas?'

'I don't know, Geraldo. But I've seen it before. It's what killed my other two patients. We're searching for the answer but so far we just don't know. Is he holding on?'

'Yes. I told you before he was strong. He's just about stable. But only with every ICU stop pulled out. Hell, Gary, you didn't tell me you had two deaths.'

'I only had one when I operated on Tony. I got back to the other one. Now I've got another here....'

His voice cracked. Geraldo picked up on it.

'Oh no, Gary, not the little girl?'

'Yes, little ... Maria....'

His publicity stunt. His extra case to punch the numbers. His chance to get his programme on national TV.

He suddenly hated himself.

'What do I do, Gary?'

'Life support systems, Geraldo, and sit it out. If I get any ideas I'll call you. Oh, and you'd better tell Mrs Skiathos that there's not much hope.'

He put down the phone, suddenly realizing the implication of his words.

There's not much hope.

Tony Skiathos was going to die.

He felt almost elated for a moment until his calling, his training, his humanity stabbed his conscience, telling him that such thoughts made him no better than a murderer, a man who would take joy in the death of a husband to get his hands on his wife. And what of little Maria? Did she deserve this? So there were to be two more deaths. The death of the programme. The NIH would pull the plug now, for sure. Hell, he'd killed more patients than he'd cured, ploughing on, operating on anyone in spite of the warning signs, the advice from Anne Bell. Her judgement was looking pretty good right now. And Tony developing the illness in Miami meant it had nothing to do with Anne Bell and her unit at all. She was exonerated.

He laid his head on the desk, wondering how he would face Tito Pereira and his wife, how he would explain it all to the NIH, what he would say to the NBC Today team, to the country, how he would ever hold his head up again in UHSM. He had a sudden vision of Carmen and Tito Pereira and how they would feel when their daughter died. He felt a small tear form in his right eye and drip slowly down his cheek, and realized he had not cried since his mother had died twelve years before.

'Gary?'

He didn't move, he thought he'd imagined it. Was it his mother calling him now? Was he dreaming?

'Gary?'

He looked behind him, to find Anne Bell standing there.

He looked at her, and she saw the anguish in his expression, the tears in his eyes. In that moment she realized that he was down, really down, at the end of his tether, and she knew she had him. Now was the time to repay Gary Masters. Pete Dewan too, for that matter, and David Meeson – in fact, all the arrogant men who had trodden on her and tried to knock her down over the years. It would be so easy to turn the knife, get her revenge. Part of her told her to do it, insult him, berate him, put the boot in.

Revenge is sweet.

Instead, she walked slowly towards him, bent over him and put her arm round his shoulder.

'Gary, what is it?'

And he looked at her, seeing Phil Peters, Ludovico Palucci, Tony the Greek, and Maria Pereira, all dying at his hands. He saw Kathryn Skiathos telling him she loved him as he realized for the first time in his life he too was in love, hopeless love, love without hope, and he saw himself abusing Anne Bell and accusing her of killing his patients when he knew now, after the news from Miami, that she had nothing to do with it.

So he stood to face her, and let her embrace him and embraced her back because, at that moment, he saw everything as it really was, and he needed a hug from a friend more than anything else in the world.

'I'm not sure what I did to deserve that,' he said sheepishly, a few moments later.

She shrugged. 'Me neither, but you looked like you needed it.'

He took a deep breath, getting it together again.

'You look lousy,' she said. 'What is it?'

'Everything, but mainly Maria Pereira. She's sick. Like the others. They need you back in ICU,' he said. 'Who suspended you?'

'Meeson, but Jerry saw to it. I'm back.'

He looked at her carefully. 'You OK? I read the Press reports.'

'A bit bruised, but better than the other guy. Listen, we have to talk.'

'Then let's do it. But we need to get to ICU so let's talk on the way.'

They left his office and made for the unit.

'I've been working on all this with Jules Wellbeloved in pathology,' Anne said as they walked along the corridor. 'Phil Peters and Ludo Palucci both had A-negative blood groups, with the Idaho antibody. Jules ran some tests. The exudate on the lungs shows a strong antigen-antibody reaction and is impermeable to oxygen. We're guessing this is a blood-group-driven allergic reaction.'

'And Maria? A-neg, Idaho antibody?'

'You got it,' she said grimly.

He looked thoughtful, then stopped suddenly. 'Do you remember Ludovico Palucci? He was showing early signs of problems before I left for Miami, and I told you he had temporal arteritis.'

She nodded, recalling the incident, then realizing what he was about to say.

'We gave him extra steroids, not much, a small dose, to keep that under control. As I left, he was improving, and when I phoned later that evening, he was much better. Then he gradually went off again and died. The steroids could have given him a temporary remission from an allergic reaction. Christ, why didn't I see this before.'

They reached the ICU and they went to look at Maria. This time when he reached the bay, he paused to squeeze Tito Pereira's arm gently, saying, 'You OK, Doctor? I heard you had some trouble, helped our ICU Director?'

Tito stood up slowly, painfully, helped by Carmen. 'I'm fine, Dr Masters. But we are very worried about Maria.'

'We are too, Doctor. This is a serious problem. We've seen it twice before, and in both cases it was fatal. But Dr Bell has researched the problem, and we think we might have a solution.'

Carmen sighed with relief. There was some hope then?

Anne joined them. 'She's stable, but poorly. Needing eighty per cent oxygen to keep her saturation up. Gary, we need to make a decision here. Can we talk?'

'Talk here, Anne. Tito is a physician, just like us. He and Carmen have to be part of this. What do you suggest?'

'The evidence points to an immune reaction as a cause of the problem. We have to treat it as such.'

'Immunosuppressives?'

'Yes. High-dose steroids, and cyclosporin. Maybe even ATP.'

'Then do it,' Tito said without hesitation. Gary held his hand up.

'There's just one thing, Tito. We're not sure about this. It's an unproven theory. An educated hunch. If, by any chance, the cause is some sort of infection we haven't been able to identify, this treatment would make that worse, hasten her death.'

Tito looked at Carmen, putting his hands on her shoulder, and looking deep into her eyes. 'What do you think, *Chiquita?*'

She looked at Gary, and Anne Bell, then back at her husband.

'Without you, Tito, we would not be here, and Dr Bell might be dead now. Without you, Dr Masters, Maria would die soon anyway. I know nothing of these things. All I know is that I trust you all totally, and will go with your decision, whatever it may be, and whatever the outcome. Just ... just save my daughter.' She broke down, sobbing, and Tito held her tight.

'So it's your decision, Dr Masters, Dr Bell,' he said, without looking back at them, just holding Carmen.

Anne looked at Gary. 'She's your patient, you have the right.'

'Without your research, I wouldn't know what to do. I don't believe this is an infection. Give her the steroids. High doses, now!'

Anne nodded, then turned and left, yelling instructions to Trudie and the other nurses. Gary put his arms around the Pereiras' shoulders.

'Hang in there folks, there's still hope.'

He walked slowly back to his department, feeling better than he had for hours.

Thanks to Anne Bell.

How he had misjudged her.

His secretary was at her desk when he walked into his office.

'Miami called again,' she said, 'Dr Rodriguez. Wants to speak with you as soon as possible. Want me to get him?'

'No, give me a few minutes, I'll tell you when.'

He went through to his own office and shut the door, before stretching full length on the couch in the corner and closing his eyes.

Immune reaction. Blood group versus membrane equals lung exudate. He should have spotted it himself. That was the trouble with surgery. Sometimes you got so concerned with the technicalities, the stitching, the operation, that you forgot about the rest of the patient and missed the clues. He knew that if he called Rodriguez and asked what Tony's blood group was, it would confirm Anne Bell's theory. So it was time to make that call, and tell Geraldo to start Tony on cyclosporin and intravenous prednisolone to counteract the immune reaction, suppress the antibodies, halt the process that was laying down the oxygen-blocking exudate on his lungs and slowly drowning him.

Time to save his life.

Again.

So he could take Kathryn, the first and only girl Gary had ever loved, away to Greece. And out of his life.

Once more he felt the temptation to hold the call. Wait a little longer. Let nature take its course. He had given Tony the Greek his chance of life. Why should he save him once again, now? With so much at stake?

He got up and paced around the floor, knowing what he wanted to do, feeling the power he had to influence events and bend them to his will, but knowing all the time what he really must do. And would.

Eventually he sat at his desk and hit the intercom button.

'Helen, get me Geraldo Rodriguez in Miami now, would you?'

He would tell Geraldo to start the drugs, and he would face the consequences later. He could win her for himself on his own account. He had seen the intensity of her feelings for him, knew she felt as he did. Nothing could stand in their way. Nothing.

The phone rang and he picked up the receiver.

'Gary?'

'Geraldo. How is he?'

'I have bad news for you.'

Gary felt his heart pounding. 'Yes?'

'He's much worse. Struggling now. On every drug we can think of to support his breathing, keep his heart beating, on huge doses of intravenous antibiotics, but we're losing him, Gary. It's only a matter of hours.'

'Where are you, Geraldo?'

'On the unit.'

'Get his notes, tell me his blood group.'

'I don't need his notes. He's A-neg.'

'Any antibodies?'

'Only that fairly common one we see – Idaho, I think.'

Game, set and match, Gary thought.

'Start him on two hundred of intravenous hydrocortisone six-hourly, and give him a loading dose of cyclosporin.'

'Why? There's no sign of rejection. The graft's fine.'

'Do it, Geraldo. It's a blood-group mediated immune reaction laying down a pulmonary exudate and drowning him. Get that i.v. up now, before it's too late! And call me!'

He spent the next few hours pacing between his department and the ICU. By 6 p.m., there had been no change in Maria's condition, and no calls from Miami. He sat in Anne Bell's office, drinking coffee.

They sat in silence until he said, 'I owe you an apology, Anne.'

She didn't reply. He was right, and it was nice to hear him say it.

'I've got a patient in Miami, you know,' he continued, 'an aneurysm I put a membrane into some weeks ago. He was admitted last night with the same problems as the others here. I felt you were right when you told me your suspicions earlier, but the news from Miami clinched it. These illnesses had nothing to do with you. Your unit's clean as a whistle.'

She nodded. 'I always knew it, Gary. You should have trusted me. Now tell it to David Meeson, before I sue his ass.'

Trudie appeared at the door and burst in without knocking.

'Anne, come quick!'

They rushed after her to Maria's cubicle.

'Look!' Trudie pointed at the monitor. After steadily falling to a low of 81% in spite of 90% oxygen, the oxygenation graph was slowly, almost imperceptibly beginning to climb. It was now at 83%. They stared at the digital figures and the room fell silent, all eyes waiting for the next readout.

85%.

They looked at each other, every one of them suppressing a cheer, before returning to the monitor.

Waiting, waiting....

88%.

This time they did allow themselves a small cheer, Gary grabbing Anne's arm and holding it, Trudie with her arm round Carmen, almost holding her up as the realization sank in that her baby was responding to the treatment.

90%.

Gary turned to Tito and nodded slowly. Tito nodded in return.

'Thanks, Anne,' Gary said. 'I'll be in my office, or on my mobile. I'll look in later.'

He left them to carry on, and went back to the Department of Cardiac Surgery to await news from Miami.

He fell asleep at his desk, so when the phone woke him it was after 10 p.m.

'Yes?' he said, rubbing his eyes.

'Gary?'

'Geraldo. What news?'

'He's a little better. Oxygen saturation's coming up, slowly. Needing less support. It's early, but it's the first positive sign. How's the child?'

'Same as him. Showing signs.'

'Excellent. I'll call you in the morning, or before if anything happens.'

'Sure. Is ... Mrs Skiathos with him?'

'No, she's waiting at home for news. The big fellow, Menos is it? He's here. Hasn't left his side.'

'Goodnight, Geraldo. Speak to you tomorrow.'

He called in on Maria on his way to the parking lot. She was continuing to improve. He drove home slowly, his mind full of the events of the previous two days. When he got home, he poured himself a large scotch and sat watching the news, seeing nothing, thinking only of Kathryn Skiathos.

Eventually he went to bed, falling into a fitful, restless sleep, his brain full of confused, mad dreams, all of which ended with

Tony the Greek in a chariot, his arm around Kathryn struggling to free herself, as he roared with laughter and took her ever further and further away from him.

CHAPTER 20

Tony Skiathos was sitting up in bed when his wife arrived. She was dressed in a black blouse and tight black dress with black leather shoes. The gold watch on her left wrist, gold bracelet on her right wrist, and gold chain around her neck looked their best against her tanned skin. She kissed him, dutifully, on the cheek and sat down beside his bed. Menos followed her in, shook hands with his boss, and sat down beside her.

'You look better today,' she said.

He grunted, 'I feel better today. Except today is decision day. For today, the man who tried to steal my wife and who has now saved my life twice, *twice*, comes to call.'

He held up his fingers as he emphasized twice.

He had lost two days of his life. He could remember nothing since Menos made his deadly promise in the elevator. The next thing he knew, he was waking up on the ICU, the same ICU he now knew so well, to find Dr Rodriguez bending over him saying, 'Tony, Tony, can you hear me?'

He had tried to answer, but there was something in his throat making him gag, so he spat it out.

It was the laryngeal tube which had been keeping him alive for the past forty-eight hours.

'Good,' said Dr Rodriguez as a nurse stuffed a sucker into Tony's mouth and down his throat, sucking up phlegm and saliva with a squishing noise, making him gag again.

He tried to brush her away, but had difficulty moving his arms quickly enough. By the time he got his right hand up she was gone.

'Careful, Tony, the i.v. line.'

Dr Rodriguez again. 'Welcome back to the land of the living.'

He could see Menos through a blur. And Kathryn. Then Dr Rodriguez and the nurses.

'Where am I?'

'Your old room on intensive care. You had a setback. We nearly lost you.'

'I'm alive?'

'You're fine. We'll have you back to normal in no time, thanks to Dr Masters. He saved your life from a thousand miles away.'

He was too tired to concentrate at that point, but they told him later that there was some sort of immune reaction to do with his blood, attacking his lungs, but Gary Masters had detected the cause and phoned the remedy to Miami, just in time. Had he not done so, Tony would now be dead.

And so would Dr Masters, Tony had thought to himself, without much satisfaction.

'So, what are we to do, my little whore? You know, I told Menos that if I should die, Masters should die also. Lucky he saved me, huh?'

She sat still, almost wishing he *had* died, wondering what to do next. Her mind was in turmoil. In spite of everything he had given her, riches, security, confidence, she felt now as if she could give it all up for Gary Masters. She loved everything about him, adored him. No man had ever given her such love, satisfied her so much, felt so right. She knew that, for the first time in her life, she had found a man she could love forever, just for himself. She had used Tony to get out of the gutter. And he had used her to court glamour in public, to keep alive the public impression of manhood, virility, potency and power for his own reputation and purposes. And why not? They had both achieved their aims from this relationship. Until Gary came along and showed her what real love could be like.

'Don't call me a whore, Tony. If you go on like this, I will go anyway, no matter what you decide about the doctor. I will not live with you to be treated like this.'

He sat up, a black look on his face.

'You will stay with me and honour your vows, whore, or I swear, his death will be so horrible they will read about it in every paper in every land. He saved my life. So he will live. But only if you never see him again. Ever.'

'No,' she said quietly, but firmly.

'No?' he asked loudly, angry at her audacity.

'No, Tony,' she continued. 'You have told me you will kill

him if I continue seeing him, and I believe you.' She looked up at him, without emotion. 'I truly believe it. But I must see him once more, for only a few moments, in a private room. Otherwise he will follow me, pursue me. I must make the situation clear to him, make sure he drops me totally. You are giving him a chance. I must make sure he takes it.'

He was quiet for a few minutes, looking occasionally at her, then at Menos, then up at the ceiling, wondering if she was trying to trick him. Eventually he spoke.

'All right. Dr Rodriguez tells me he arrives this afternoon to check me over. You can see him here, in a room in the hospital, for a few minutes. Menos will wait outside the door. Three minutes, then he will terminate the little chat. That is my final offer. Take it or leave it.' His voice was bitter.

She nodded her agreement, then got up and left, knowing her heart was breaking, and wondering what she could do about it.

Gary sat on Delta flight 4671 wondering how many times he had made this Boston-Miami-Boston trip in the past six months. It seemed like hundreds. At least this time he knew what to expect. A patient on the road to recovery, and a woman who loved him waiting for him. Even if it was his patient's wife. He would see Tony the Greek, do his duty by him, ensure that he survived, mentally divorcing the patient from the husband, just as he had when he had made the decision to call Rodriguez and tell him the remedy. He could have let Tony die then. No one would ever have known. He could have let him die, then had his wife, perhaps with a great deal of money. Instead he had decided he would save the man, obey his calling, fulfil his obligations. After all, she loved him. She would come with him when the time came. He would take his wife from him by fair means. Not by letting him die when he could be saved.

The flight touched down on time. Geraldo Rodriguez was waiting for him at the arrivals hall.

'Gary, welcome!'

'Thanks Geraldo. You didn't have to come yourself.'

'Oh yes I did,' smiled his friend. 'After your brilliant deductions and diagnosis saved our patient, it was the least I could do.'

Gary smiled. 'It was a Boston team effort, Geraldo. Not just me. He OK?'

'He's fine, looking forward to seeing you.'

They drove out into brilliant sunshine and on to the hospital.

Geraldo led Gary to Tony Skiathos, now well enough to be in a normal room on the cardiac wing.

'Hello, Mr Skiathos,' he said, walking in with Geraldo and holding out his hand.

Tony the Greek looked at it, then looked out of the window without taking it.

'Dr Masters. I believe I have to thank you for saving my life ... again.'

Geraldo looked at Gary, puzzled by his friend's cool reception, then back at Skiathos.

'I'm happy to find you well, sir,' Gary said. 'I've seen your latest tests. It looks like we caught the complication just in time. But you may have to be on medication for a long time to ensure continued health.'

Tony looked into Gary's eyes, a long, cold look. 'From now, I'll be guided by Dr Rodriguez,' he said. 'But I thank you for saving my life ... twice. I have a gift in return. Menos?'

The *consigliere* appeared and took Gary's arm. Geraldo Rodriguez watched, puzzled, before saying, 'What exactly is going on?'

Gary looked at him, equally puzzled, suddenly feeling a little uneasy.

He left with Menos who walked him to another room a few doors down the corridor.

'Go in, Doctor,' he said. 'You have three minutes, then I come in, and you leave.' The voice carried an unmistakable threat.

Gary looked at him, sensing that things were not quite as he had expected.

He entered the room, closing the door behind him. Kathryn Skiathos was standing, waiting, dressed in black, just as she was the first night they met, the night she walked into his life at the Green Street Café.

He stood before her. 'Kathryn,' he said, moving to her, wanting to feel her in his arms.

'No!'

Her voice split the air like a whiplash and he stopped in his tracks.

She turned away from him and walked towards the window. He could see the Miami skyline behind her.

'I've been thinking,' she said, 'and I've come to the conclusion that, good as it was with you, it was a mistake.' She whirled to face him. 'I am married to a sick man. I realize now that I have to be with him, to take care of him.'

Gary stood, stunned, unable to believe what he was hearing. They were supposed to be embracing, planning their future....

'But ...?'

Her hand went up, in a classic Mediterranean gesture.

'It's over Gary.'

It's over, but don't believe it Gary, it will never be over, never....

'I love your body, we've had fun, but that's it. My real love and my real duty belong to Tony.'

I want you, Gary, want you more than anything else in the world. But if I say it, if we do anything else together, they'll kill you ... they'll kill you.

'What are you saying, Kathryn, it's over between us?'

He was stunned. Almost speechless.

Oh, Gary, my beautiful, perfect Gary, don't go to pieces on me, don't make it harder for me.

'It never started Gary. I don't love you. It's over. It's over.'

Just go, Gary, go ... please ... now ... I can't keep this up for much longer.

'But Kathryn, I ... I need you ... I love you, I love ...'

'Oh grow up, Gary. We had a bit of fun, that's all. A bit of fun. Now go on, get out. I don't want to see you again. Just get out, or I'll have to call Menos in and have you thrown out.'

Get out Gary, for God's sake. I'm trying to save your life here, you wonderful, beautiful man that I love, the only man I will ever love. Go, now and live.

Gary watched her, believing her act, feeling confused, rejected, betrayed. He couldn't understand what he was hearing, but knew he couldn't bear to listen to it any longer.

They stood, looking into each other's eyes, each other's souls, for what seemed like an eternity, before the spell was broken by the noise of the door opening. Kathryn turned from him and faced the window again, tears he must never see forming in her eyes. Menos stood in the doorway, leaning against the door jamb, his arms folded.

Gary looked at him, then back at Kathryn, trying to work it

out, beginning to understand a little, but realizing there was no point in staying. He turned and left, glaring at the *consigliere* as he passed him. Menos followed impassively, shutting the door behind him, leaving her alone.

She didn't think she would cry out loud, she seldom did. But once the first tear came, her head began to tremble, then her shoulders, then the sobs took over her whole body, as she sank to the floor, her legs crossed, her head falling on to her heaving chest as she realized that the one and only time real love had walked into her life, she had thrown it out. Rejected it.

Forever.

She sat on the floor in the dark room, loneliness enveloping her, knowing that she would never, ever again, see his face, hear his voice, taste his lips, or feel his love inside her.

Maria Pereira sat up and looked around. Her eyes were glazed, but she recognized her mother, then her father, and she smiled, in spite of the tubes, the drips, the catheter in her little bladder.

A sweet, innocent smile.

They smiled too, at Maria, at each other, then back at Maria, and they gave her the best hug they could, given the constraints of the paraphernalia to which she was connected, then stood back as the nurses continued their work.

They looked up as Anne Bell walked in with Jerry Weinberg.

'Dr Pereira, Mrs Pereira,' Jerry said, 'have you heard the news?'

'What news?' Tito asked, standing up to face them.

'The President has made a decision on Cuban immigration. For the foreseeable future, any Cuban who has made it to US land, or is held at Krome Camp, or Guantanamo Bay, will be admitted as a legal refugee under the old rules. Anyone who leaves Cuba from this day on will be deported back. But you're free, Doctor. You and your family are about to become US citizens.'

Tito looked at Carmen, and back at Jerry and Anne.

'That is wonderful news,' he said. 'For us. Not so good for our friends at home,' he added, looking down at his daughter, before saying quietly, 'but it is very good indeed for little Maria.'

As realization sank in, he suddenly looked very tired, and a tear ran down his cheek.

'Free, Carmen, free.'

She linked her arm through his and hugged him to her, supporting him.

'Is Maria safe now, Dr Bell? Is the sickness over?' she asked.

'Her tests are all excellent, her breathing is normal. I think she's going to be fine.'

'Thank God,' Carmen whispered, hugging Tito to her again, as if to remind him that it was thanks to him that they were there, safe, and free.

Anne and Jerry watched them, Anne realizing she wanted Gary to be there to share the moment. She had called his secretary who told her he was out of town, and was not expected back before the following day. She turned as Trudie put her head around the door.

'Joe Kennedy's here to see you, Dr Bell.'

'Put him in my office Trudie, we'll be right out.'

'Dr Pereira,' said Jerry, 'there are some visitors to see you, Mr and Mrs Powell from Miami. Is it OK for them to come in?'

'Of course, sir.'

'I'll send them through. And we'll sort out all the immigration formalities, don't worry yourselves about them. You did us all a big favour coming here, looking after Dr Bell when she was in trouble. When this is all over, if you decide to settle round here, we might be able to see about a job here in UHSM if you're interested.'

'Thank you,' Tito replied. It was all getting too much for him – he felt overwhelmed with kindness and good news.

Jerry noticed. 'Sit down, Doctor, take it easy. You've been through a lot,' he said quietly, moving up a chair for him to sit beside his daughter.

'Don't worry, Doctor, I'll take care of him,' Carmen said, gently pushing Tito down on to the chair.

A few moments later, Jerry returned accompanied by Mr and Mrs 'JT' Powell. Tito got up and shook hands with JT as Mrs Powell hugged Carmen and bent anxiously over Maria. Jerry left smiling. They would be all right. They had made plenty of friends in a short time. He walked into Anne Bell's office and sat down.

'So, Joe, what have you got to report?' he asked.

Joe Kennedy sat back in the chair and took a sip of his coffee. He wished all cases could be this easy. He had gone through the c.v.s of all the ICU staff, then looked in detail at those on duty when the John Doe had snuffed it. Then he had turned up at their houses, flashed his badge, and interviewed them all in turn.

All except one.

Melanie Brooks.

No one had seen her around her apartment for days. He got an entry warrant on a possible felony count, knowing the apartment would be empty. It was. The next day he called the previous hospitals she had listed on her c.v. Three of them had never heard of her. The one that did remember her recalled an unexplained, unexpected death on the ICU during the time she worked there.

'She did it, for sure,' he said. 'It's an open and shut case.'

'For Gary,' Anne whispered.

Joe Kennedy and Jerry Weinberg looked at her, puzzled.

'Who's Gary?' asked Joe.

'Our local whizz kid heart surgeon,' Jerry replied. Then, looking at Anne, he asked, 'Why Gary?'

'To protect him. Two of his patients had died. I was blaming him, pushing to have his work stopped, have him suspended.' She sighed. 'She fancied him. Thought she could get him into her bed, maybe even marry him. She'd had a couple of bad marriages, wanted a new start. Her eyes lit up every time he walked into the unit. Maybe she thought he'd be forced to leave if another of his patients died. So she killed a stranger, to take the heat off him, move it to us.' She shrugged.

Joe Kennedy nodded. 'That might be some of it. But there's often a pattern in these cases you know, and there may be one here. It seems like she did it before, at another hospital. Maybe others we don't know about. Perhaps Gary was just the catalyst.'

She nodded, thinking of Melanie, how she had rated her work, liked her, even. It didn't seem possible.

'Well, Anne, don't let it worry you too much,' Jerry said. 'You should be pretty damn pleased with yourself after the way you tracked down the cause of the heart patients' problems. It's all down to you that Maria's well now, and we all know how this hospital would have looked if she'd died.'

'I always knew you'd make a great detective, Dr Bell,' Joe said, grinning.

'Well, I thought I might have to look for an alternative career at one point Joe; nice to know I could have come to you for a job.' She looked at Jerry. 'Where is Gary anyway?'

'He's down in Miami putting your solution into practice on his patient there. He owes you, Anne. I think things are going to be different round here from now on.'

Joe Kennedy stood up. 'Got to go folks,' he said.

Jerry shook his hand. 'Thanks for everything, Joe; you're the best. Let us know if there's anything else we need to do from this end.'

'Sure, but we'll handle it from now on. We'll find Nurse Brooks, before she does another, don't you worry. And thanks for calling me in,' he added, with his lop-sided grin, 'you know we need the business, and you never disappoint us, you guys here at UHSM!'

They laughed, and he left. Jerry and Anne sat facing each other.

'Well, that's it, I guess?' Jerry said.

'Hope so,' she replied. 'It's been a hell of a Fall.'

'Sure has.' He stood up and stretched. 'I think I'm going to jack in this director's job.'

She looked surprised. 'Why?' she asked.

'I hate it, Anne. Dealing with people like David Meeson is impossible. They're on a different planet to the rest of us at the sharp end. They use medical directors as levers, to get their irrational message over in a rational form, to fool you into accepting it because it comes from one of your own. I've had enough of it. I'm not a politician, I'm a urologist.'

'You're both, Jerry. You did the job better than anyone else I can recall. But I have to say, of the two, I prefer Jerry the urologist!'

He laughed, reassured that she supported his decision.

She laughed too, thinking perhaps things were beginning to get back to normal again at UHSM.

CHAPTER 21

He sat alone at a streetside table outside the Green Street Café in Coconut Grove, just as he had the night he first met her. It was quiet, just him and four other diners. Further down the street, a bohemian-looking couple chatted on a sidewalk bench outside a craft shop, a huge Great Dane sitting between them bedecked in a baseball cap and sunglasses.

He missed Miami. It had a touch of class.

He ordered a pizza. When it came, it looked excellent, as it always was at Green Street.

He took a slice, but he wasn't hungry, and it was a struggle to eat it. He washed it down with a gulp of Bud.

He sat for a while then, waiting.

Waiting for the click of her heels on the sidewalk.

Waiting for her voice asking, 'Is it good?' as she passed.

When the café closed the waiter asked him to leave so he could take the table and chairs inside, but Gary hardly heard him. The waiter shrugged, and left him sitting alone at the single table on the sidewalk.

Alone.

Like he had always been.

Until Kathryn Skiathos walked into his life.

He sat there for a long time, remembering their meeting, almost feeling her presence through the memory, not wanting to admit she would not be coming, but not wanting to leave in case she did.

Hoping desperately that she would.

But knowing she would not.